Screams shattered the morning. Below him Beano Shippers—
that red hair—ran stumbling, looking over her shoulder like
something was after her, her trail marked by a dropped
towel, a wadded dishcloth, and ... maybe a plastic soap
dish. Her screams bounded off the canyon walls and echoed.

On top of the cliff Reuben leapt along with her, down frozen
tides of basalt, trying to see over his shoulder up the little
side canyon she'd descended. Nothing came after her, no
bobcat, no bear. She ran into the arms of the geologist, who
had come to meet her, the others in close pursuit.

"Whoa," he said, "hold on there, Red."

She burrowed her face in his plaid jacket and pointed back
the way she'd come. Something was dead back there, she
cried. . . .

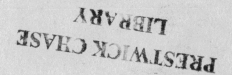

Also by Cecil Dawkins
Published by Ivy Books:

THE SANTA FE REMBRANDT

CLAY DANCERS

Cecil Dawkins

IVY BOOKS • NEW YORK

Ivy Books
Published by Ballantine Books
Copyright © 1994 by Cecil Dawkins

Library of Congress Catalog Card Number: 94-96132

ISBN 0-8041-1261-4

Manufactured in the United States of America

First Edition: November 1994

10 9 8 7 6 5 4 3 2

I want to acknowledge indebtedness to my friend the late Elizabeth Fisher, author of WOMEN'S CREATION, for some of Freya Markus's theories.

1

"Are you telling me what I think you're telling me?"

Tina smiled grimly and kept her mouth shut. She'd said all she was going to say, and that was already too much. She looked steadily past Freya Markus out the trailer window. She'd spent all afternoon out there on the dig sketching finds with Reuben. The pink and yellow ridges of the Parajito plateau fell away like the crenellated spine of a fat-backed dinosaur dipping to sniff the green snake of the valley. It was the grand panorama of her ancestral ground, and it stirred in her feelings she resisted.

Freya Markus said, "The Greeks killed messengers that brought news like this."

A sound came from one of the back rooms, a sheaf of papers sliding to the floor. The archaeologist stepped toward the hall and the site trailer rocked. "Who's back there?"

Polly Quint, the graduate student from Colorado, stuck her head sheepishly out of the records room. "Did you want something, Freya?"

Eavesdropping. Tina ducked her head and smiled. Polly Quint's ubiquitous presence clearly annoyed Freya Markus, but she controlled herself admirably. "Those files can wait till tomorrow."

Blond and freckled, flat-chested as a triathlete, Polly laid a sheaf of papers on a tray of labeled finds stored in brown paper bags and pouted past Tina out the door. How much had she overheard?

1

Freya Markus called out irritably, "Anybody else back there?"

No answer.

"If you are, you can damn well call it a day." Still no answer. "God," she said softly, "out of thirty thousand Anasazi sites on this plateau, I had to pick this one." Tina smiled. She had heard Freya tell her crew chief she could *smell* a rich site and this one reeked. It was the ruins of a large community, its buildings once three stories high, and barely touched by earlier diggers.

But something prevented her saying such things to this woman. Freya Markus made her doubt herself, betray her better judgment, and lie awake nights obsessing. She was unlike Tina's idea of Teacher. She put no distance between herself and the students; they called her Freya. She pulled no rank, required no obeisance, exacted no alms. She said what she thought, and if what she thought today contradicted what she'd thought yesterday, she would throw out a hand, "Oh well," she'd say, "learn to deal with paradox," and that was the end of it. She worked alongside the crew, got just as dirty, was just as exhausted at the end of the day. Her raucous laugh often pealed out over the mesa. But she was just as likely to withdraw, answer questions in monosyllables if at all, and bite your head off if you intruded on her intricate cerebrations.

Just now she sighed, threw her pencil down on the couch in a gesture that said, I quit, I give up.

But Tina couldn't imagine her giving up on anything. Tall, with a kind of lumbering grace, she was hard to keep up with tramping up and down the canyon road from the meadow ringed with ponderosa pine and Douglas fir where they'd pitched their tents for the summer, overlooked by cliff dwellings that time had rendered inaccessible. Her faded overalls and work shirts and high-topped work boots had set a fashion on the dig. The bandana, pulled back and knotted under her hair at the nape of her neck, hid most of her dark heavy mane. Her eyes were shards of amber and shards of green glass, the coyote color of mixed ancestry—

part Spanish or Indian, part Anglo. Her skin hinted at the old gold of melanin. Who was she? Where had she come from? In half a summer on the dig, Tina knew no more than she'd known the first day: born in Caracas, educated at Yale and Stanford, her reputation made in Central and South America. Once she had ventured to ask, "What got you into archaeology anyway?" And Freya, bent over her microscope, had answered absently, "I wanted to know what happened."

Along with several generations of her ancestors, Tina described herself as Santa Ynez Pueblo because a hundred fifty years ago her people's village, decimated by invasion and smallpox, numbering then about two dozen, had abandoned their lands and homes to be taken in by other Rio Grande pueblos, chiefly Santa Ynez because they spoke the same Tiwa dialect. But now the Tsorigi numbered almost four hundred and they wanted their land back, and the old pueblo on the mesa top. The government in Washington, which had long since incorporated it into federal lands, had hinted to the tribal elders it was on the verge of humoring them. And Tina, her loyalty divided between the tribe and the dig, had just intimated as much to Freya Markus.

The archaeologist lifted a flexed hand and nibbled at calluses at the base of her fingers. "So when is it going to happen?"

"I never said it was."

"Oh, come," she said with an impatient gesture, "I know this is Indian business."

It was true. Whenever the men wound up their long hair in *chungas*—loose knots at the back of the neck—and went to the kivas, everyone whispered *Indian business*.

"They probably haven't told *you* when it's going to happen," Freya said. "I suppose some senator up for reelection will be here. There'll be a do of some kind."

Avoiding the sea-change eyes, Tina watched Caspar Dreyfus, the crew chief from MIT, checking off implements as the students turned them in over at the old tan army tent. Sonny Concha and Horse Rios, two Pueblo boys hired for the summer to man the wheelbarrows, trundled them over and stood them on end. Some of the Earth Watch volunteers walked past on their way back to the campground.

"Oh, I see. Now I get it," Freya said irritably. "Everyone comes home for Naposunshare." She squinted at the wildlife calendar on the wall and crow's-feet appeared at her temples. "My God," she whispered, "what's today?"

Tina concentrated on the peaks across the valley, still snowcapped in July, and the thunderheads piling up where the distant highway, not visible from the mesa top, ran into the river gorge. They had piled up like that for a week now, though you only saw the rain shafts way down at the south end of the valley, bent at the knee by the wind, what the people called "the rain walking." But the summer was so dry the moisture evaporated in the lower atmosphere without ever touching the ground, and the rain walked mostly without feet.

Freya Markus let go the calendar page and grabbed her head in her big hands. "God, how I searched for this place. It must be *old*, it must be *isolated*, it must be on *public land*," chopping the air with a hand for emphasis, "because you people don't often let us go poking through the ruins of your ancestors."

You people.

"You don't want the *spirits* disturbed." A hint of irony colored the tone of her voice. She paced in a narrow circle. She raised her eyes to the ceiling in exasperation and her eyelids fluttered. In spite of herself, Tina admired the dramatics. "There's this whole do about getting all those bones back from the Smithsonian for proper burial."

"The Smithsonian," Tina said, "has over nineteen thousand Native American skeletons. And there are two million more in museums around the country. Government agencies let people onto Indian lands for all sorts of things—mining, lumbering, tourism, archaeological digs . . ." It came spilling out like a pebble had started an avalanche.

Freya Markus snorted impatiently but Tina went on. "We assumed the First Amendment protected our religious rights, but the Supreme Court let us know it does not. The Court said we have peculiar ideas about what is sacred and left to our own devices might take over the country." She laughed, then stopped herself. Who was she to protest? Her mother was Catholic and she herself nothing unless you counted as religious a certain awe of mysteries like black holes, quasars, the expanding universe.

Freya waved an impatient hand like brushing away a gnat. "Don't visit the sins of the fathers on *me*. The only guilt I accept is my personal own."

Tina felt like a child rebuked. The guilt nagging her was not much different. She'd been away for years at school, and then in Santa Fe pursuing personal goals rather than the communal goals of her people.

Now that the sun was dropping, a lizard emerged from the cool beneath a rock and froze outside the door to assess the danger. "There's still time," she said. The lizard shot away.

Behind her Freya muttered, "As soon as they get the land back, the *caciques* will run us out of here." Tina thought it was true. The priests in their blankets, watchful visages as stern as a frieze on a temple, were hostile to the dig. "But Cruz Domingue disagrees with them," Freya said with satisfaction. "He favors the dig."

Cruz Domingue was the Tsorigi headman, chief honcho, tribal governor-in-exile, and, unknown to Freya Markus, Tina's maternal uncle, her mother's older brother and, because of the matrilocal way of the people, closer to Tina than her father had been. He had maneuvered her onto the dig as artist to protect the people's interests, but she wasn't sure she was doing it. She might be compromising them instead. And all because she'd come under this woman's spell and caught her passion for digging up a past Tina had every reason to believe was her own but until now had never felt much urgency to uncover.

So maybe it was guilt that impelled her to say, "You might be happy for us. We're an endangered species."

That short bark of a laugh again. "We're *all* an endangered species." And Freya brushed past her out the door.

Oh, that's unfair. She marked one up against this woman she knew she'd come to hold to an impossible standard. Dropping down on the step outside, she sat hugging her knees, watching their leader go.

At lunch break she'd seen Cruz Domingue's new blue pickup down by the pond at the foot of the canyon. He was down there in khaki pants and shirt, just a grandfather taking his grandson fishing, but she knew he'd come to talk to her.

"They finding anything up there?" He nodded toward the mesa.

"A little. The ruin is older than they'd thought."

He shrugged. So he already knew it, probably from stories handed down. "Just old pieces of pots? Is that all?"

"No. Some tools made from elk antlers, a red effigy head carved out of something called hematite, snail-shell ornaments, copper bells, the skeleton of a macaw . . ."

He nodded. "The old ones traded our turquoise for things from the South."

The South meant Mexico. Why had he chosen her when she knew so little? When she asked him, he'd shrugged. "The people don't have all that many artists to pick from."

"Some pottery with lightning patterns. Like this." She drew in the sand with a stick. They were standing on the narrow shore of the pond, trees pressing close behind them. He didn't move his head, but she knew he watched. "Some are incised," she said, "no paint on them."

"Like pinched with the fingers?" He lifted his hand as high as his big silver and turquoise belt buckle and pinched daintily with his blunt fingertips by way of illustration. "Nothing that could be part of the stories?"

Tsorigi stories were like jigsaw puzzles with pieces missing. She shook her head. "Only rock pictures you already know about."

His expression didn't change but she knew he was disappointed. He was looking at his grandson a little way off again with his line in the water.

"Are we going to get the land back from the government?" She knew the question was impertinent. She thought he wasn't going to answer.

He called and the child ran over. Her uncle put his hand on the boy's head and with stubby fingers pulled him close to his knee. Then he said, "The people all come home for Naposunshare."

That was all, but it was enough. A surge of joy took her by surprise. Then she remembered Freya Markus and the dig. Naposunshare, the black clay dance, was soon now, very soon.

The thought must have surfaced on her face. Cruz said, "That woman, she knows what she's doing. We want to learn all we can from this digging in the old place."

"Yes."

"Twenty-three people," he said softly. "Just twenty-three people walked out of the village."

Not the old pueblo on the mesa that was like a chin jutting out of the face of the mountain. They had left there for mysterious reasons sometime in the thirteenth century. He meant the village beside the river, the one the Tsorigi had built after abandoning the mesa. And later they'd abandoned that one, too, because of so many dying—a plague of some kind, maybe smallpox brought by the invaders. Over the years that village had melted back into the adobe dirt it was built of. Now it was little more than a few sage-covered mounds, of no interest to anybody.

"They brought out the songs, some of them," Cruz said. "They brought the dances, the stories, they gave us Naposunshare. But there was many more things."

"Will they stop her?" Tina asked.

He turned away and called the boy, already back at the pond's edge with his fishing rod. The child came running. With a rough hand her uncle kneaded the small head against his knee and walked toward the pickup.

"I'll tell your mother you are all right," he said over his shoulder.

Sitting there on the step, Tina watched Freya Markus's denim jacket move away across the ancient plaza, heading probably for the kiva they'd discovered early in the dig. The semi that brought the big trailer, unable to make the final turn onto the mesa top, was backing to get more room when the dual rear wheels sank, the motor ground to a keen, and Freya Markus rushed over, vexed at yet another delay.

The driver swung down swearing out of the cab. Under the sunken wheel a maw gaped, mysterious, insatiable, growing before their eyes. A road machine from the valley finally eased the semi back onto the road. When the trailer was in place on the mesa top and the semi bobtailing it back to Albuquerque, Freya Markus set them all to work at the depression in the ground.

Caspar Dreyfus opposed the excavation, sure they'd only find another pit house. But Freya Markus pointed out that a pit house would put them into Basketmaker time, and that was centuries earlier than recorded habitation on this site.

Within a week, everybody on the screens and wheelbarrows and buckets, they uncovered what was left of a roof. There'd been a fire. The *vigas*—whole logs used as roof beams—were charred and broken, but they'd fallen in roughly their original pattern. They slanted into centuries of detritus filling the room below, but sheltered under the broken *vigas* was an eight-foot span of wall as untouched as the minute before the roof caved in.

Freya Markus was elated. Carbon 14 testing could date charred wood easier than wood that had rotted. And if that didn't work, dendrochronology would do the job once they cut out a section and sent it off to the lab. She had directed the building of an aspen pole ladder and, one by one, they all got a look inside.

"It's a miracle," breathed Freya, who, Tina suspected, didn't believe in miracles. "If the people fled the fire leaving everything behind, once we excavate to level we'll find things just as they left them."

She calculated the original diameter of the room at about thirty feet. Protected by the old *vigas*, a fragment remained of a low, slab-faced *banco*. The bench had probably circled the room. In the floor they found a hole with a raised adobe collar.

"What did I tell you?" Caspar said. "That's a fire pit."

"Why do you say fire pit?"

"Look at that." He pointed.

Busy sketching the wall figures, Tina heard Freya gasp. "It's a *metate*."

Caspar said smugly, "That grinding stone means there were women here."

"Yes." Freya bent and touched the stone. "There were women here."

"So if you're thinking this is a kiva, you're mistaken. A kiva is strictly a men's house."

"I think it's a proto kiva."

"You're talking Pueblo III and Basketmaker stuff side by side?"

"Not impossible. This room has been buried for a long time."

"Come on, Freya. Through several hundred years of Pueblo III living? Surrounded by a bustling community?" Caspar laughed.

"They wouldn't have dug a pit house this deep," Freya said.

Hands in the pockets of his baggy bicycle pants, Caspar scuffed around. "That's clearly a storage cyst." He pointed with the toe of his running shoe toward a dip in the floor. "And that suggests a pit house, a dwelling."

Tina sketched busily. Reuben had already photographed everything, using seven brackets as Freya insisted. Two of the figures were ears of corn with heads, arms, legs. One was an indeterminate color darker than the surrounding wall. The other had once been white.

When Caspar went back up the ladder, Freya stayed behind. "That hole is not a fire pit," she said, shaking her head. "It's a *sipapu*. This is transitional Basketmaker. I *feel* it. Give or take a century, that was about when the Roman Empire fell, and the Toltecs reached the valley of Mexico." She circled the narrow space, then stopped and stared at the wall paintings. "Oh, I know *too little* here." Her spiked fingers rose and took hold of her temples as she admonished herself. "You are presumptuous. You have always been. You should have stayed in Mexico."

"It's the corn mothers," Tina said softly. Everybody knew the corn mothers. "It's Blue Corn Woman and White Corn Maiden. They're the naming mothers."

Freya lowered her hands and looked at her.

"They name the baby and give it a soul, to bring it in from the dark." Under Freya's eyes her face went hot. She bent over her sketch pad. "They were with the people before the emergence."

"And they were women?"

"Of course."

"From the lower world?"

"Yes. Where the child has no identity. When they give the baby a name, it becomes, it's a person."

Freya said, "Then what's *your* name, Tina Martinez?"

Tina bit her lip. She wouldn't say it in Tiwa, but she translated. "It means Corn Tassels Dancing."

Freya smiled and dropped a hand on Tina's arm. "That's lovely."

This had happened early in the dig when Tina had only the vaguest idea what Basketmaker meant. Now she knew it was a civilization that went back as far as A.D. 500—or, as they said on the dig, almost 1500 B.P., Before Present.

Sitting on the rock the lizard had abandoned, watching Freya walk away, she felt the familiar tug but told herself no way was she going to follow. The dig was doomed, if not by the *caciques* running them out as soon as the tribe got the land back, then by whatever spirits were operating against them—first with the fire in the upper canyon, and then the infestation of snakes in the ruin. They were only baby bull snakes, but they'd looked like rattlers. Three students had come up with urgent reasons for going home.

She had been aware of Freya's growing impatience with the finds—mostly shards and quids and arrowpoints—and seen her exasperation when she tossed aside repros that came daily from the computer as if to say This isn't it. Nor this, nor this, nor this.

Why had she told Freya, anyway? What were her motives? Could have been one of two things: a servile need to please or her habitual discomfort with secrets. It was like Freya had something on her and could make her do whatever she wanted. Maybe the woman had charisma. Tina hated charisma. Anyway, she knew the archaeologist wasn't just here on a summer dig to give students on-site experience. No. She was looking for something.

So far she hadn't found it.

2

Sitting on top of the low wall of the room Shippers was excavating, Reuben swung his heels against it, squinting into the light, drawing in a pad on his knee. He was supposed to be drawing the broken pieces of old pots—shards—*in situ*, but instead he was drawing Shippers' ass aimed up at him as she bent with her trowel.

"*Merde,*" she said. "It's another of those damn rocks."

"Yeah?" Just keep her talking. He had rendered it first as peach, then as Christmas ornament, lastly as bivalve mollusc. Now he drew it as he saw it, filling out a pair of faded blue cutoffs.

"What are these damned things anyway?" She dusted off

the object with her little brush. "It's in the corner of the room again. The others were in corners, too."

"I dunno. Whadaya think?" Just keep her from turning around.

He and Dolly had quarreled. They'd split in the spring and he'd let Dolly keep his pad because she made good money waitressing and could pay the rent. What he had not told anybody was that he had set himself a limit—two years—in which to make it in Santa Fe, succeed, get a gallery, establish himself as artist in his own mind if in no more substantial locale.

And he had failed. He'd tried to paint but he'd never got the light right, nor the color. Everything he put on canvas looked like something transposed from the Hudson River School. How could you paint a landscape without *green*? He loved green in all its manifestations—from that barely perceptible hint in the sky at sundown to the darkest caves of the evergreens, from that forbidding military metallic to the tenderest lights in unfolding leaves.

He'd tried to sculpt and ended up with a macabre rubbish pile in his backyard. He'd tried ceramics and turned out exotics nobody wanted to buy. And his self-imposed penalty for failure—he was twenty-six, after all, and precious little to show for it—was a return to the Big Apple and his uncle Jake's garment plant. Camped out in the canyon, his tent rent-free and food supplied by the dig, he should have enough saved by fall for return airfare. The thought made him sick, so he thought about it as little as possible.

The work on the dig was about as exciting as watching nails rust, but this was his first experience living outdoors and that blew his mind. Until recently, his only taste of nature had been New York Harbor, the Jersey Palisades, and Jones Beach. He had grown up in the suburbs, which, he'd confided to his seatmate on the Delta flight west, was the next worst thing to the urbs.

His jovial seatmate said he worked at Los Alamos.

"What are you, a bomb salesman or something?" Creep had to be some kind of a salesman.

The man guffawed. "Naw, son, I'm a physicist. Look down there, will you."

They were circling to land. The big bird obligingly dipped a wing and offered up the landscape. "Down there," his seatmate told him, "you'll see thousands of square miles untouched by the hand of man."

As they dropped toward the crest of the Sandias, Reuben stared out the window. "So if you're so crazy about nature," he said to the happy scientist, "how come you're out here building bombs?"

Looking out at the craggy peaks rising, the bomb-maker said, "Hell, son, I get to ski."

Tina had got him the summer job. The Indian head man had insisted on her for the artwork and photography so she could keep an eye on things. Not that legally speaking they had any say in the matter, though they had been in on it from the beginning as a matter of PR. The Indians had tried to get it back from the federal government for decades because it contained their old pueblo on the mesa top and, somewhere down in the valley, their *sipapu*.

A *sipapu* was sacred in tribal tradition because it was where they entered this world from the center of the earth—climbing up tree roots, as he understood it. Taos Pueblo got back thousands of acres plus Blue Lake, which was their *sipapu*, while Nixon was in office. Tricky Dick did something right.

So Tina, dutifully hired by the archaeologist, had got Reuben taken on as her assistant because he was better at line drawings than she was and he needed the work. Freya Markus had hired him provided he also function as gopher around the dig.

Shippers straightened and stretched. "I wonder what they meant to the Anasazi." She was staring down at the black rock she'd uncovered.

"I dunno," Reuben mumbled. His pen worked deftly. The Anasazi. Nobody knew exactly who they were or where they'd come from, but the Pueblo Indians strung out in their villages along the Rio Grande claimed them as ancestors.

On digs in the Southwest in the summertime, the archaeology department at UNM gave credit hours to their own students as well as students from around the country. Beano Shippers of the faded cutoffs was one of them. She was a senior from Fort Worth.

Freya Markus—*Doctor* Freya Markus—had recently joined the UNM faculty as tenured full professor. Strange woman—he was shading with the broad edge of his drawing pencil—built on a grand scale, full of contradictions, given to bold gestures with her outsize hands. Back pages of his sketch pad were full of bits and pieces of her—a wrist, an eye, a profile.

Beano bent again to her work. "They only buried sacred objects in the corners of their rooms."

"Whadaya mean, sacred objects?" It was really an extraordinary behind.

"Oh, you know—feathers, shells, whatever they gave power to."

"What kind of power?" He was rounding off the gluteus maximus, going for the thighs.

She shrugged. "Like for growing crops, bringing rain."

"You believe that stuff?"

"Sure." She laid down her trowel and went to work again with her camel's hair brush. "Stands to reason if you give a thing power, that thing has the power you've given it."

"What if you give it power you didn't happen to have?" Just keep her going. He was almost finished.

"Well, you know, we *do* have power. It's the power of thought that brings things into being. Like Jesus said, 'Not I but your faith'?"

Right. He'd heard she was a Jesus freak. But sexy. According to rumor, definitely sexy.

"See, it's thought that creates the world we live in."

"Must be some nasty cerebrations coming down out there."

"Yeah. So to change the world, all we've got to do is change our minds." She straightened and turned. He flipped the grid down over his drawing and set about finishing the rock sketch.

They were at the eastern tip of a long promontory jutting out like the prow of a ship over the precipitous descent. The sun was falling fast. Piñon shadows stretched entreating arms toward the valley.

"It's the damndest thing how many rooms we've found these in," Shippers mused. "I'll have to check levels on the computer." She tapped her front teeth with the heel of her brush. "They'll say they have religious significance. That's what they always say about anything they can't identify." Her forehead wrinkled. "What kind of rock is it, anyway?"

She wasn't asking him—what did he know—she was thinking out loud.

It was black, elongated, with a lopsided knob at one end, the surface smooth with little pocks in it. "They look handmade," he said. One had looked like an egg, another like a miniature barbell.

Shippers snorted. With prominent apple cheeks and a forehead to match sheltering acute blue eyes set close together, it was a cartoon face on a centerfold body. She had great hair, though, dark red and hanging in a rope to the small of her back.

"Do I start looking for them or what? I'll have to ask Freya. Whatever she says, Caspar'll disagree. Graduate students." She snorted. "When they're not ass-kissers, they're snobs."

Reuben had noticed. "How come? What's it about?"

"Well, for one thing, she wrote this book on the Aztec calendar. Wrote it in plain English, and you know academia."

Actually, he didn't.

"No jargony gobbledegook, and that's absolutely *verboten*. Also, it made her famous, and they're all jealous of that." She reared back, stretching again with her hands at the small of her back, and her eyes suddenly registered his actual presence. "Will you get down off that wall! If she saw you sitting there banging your heels, she'd hold me responsible."

He stood up, towering over Shippers still down in the excavated room. It was L-shaped, with a fire pit at the center of the longer leg, the little logs beside it badly charred from ancient fires. She had wound them with waxed twine to keep them from disintegrating.

"Are we about finished? It's late," he said, "I'm hungry."

Over by the equipment tent the two Indian lads shot the breeze with a couple of students. Most of the others had already gone. The small wind that came up after sundown had kicked in. It whipped up the fine dust that coated the trailer housing the darkroom, the first aid, and the trays of shards. The trailer was parked beyond the terraces leading down to the ruin's central plaza, what Freya Markus said had been the ceremonial ground and meeting place.

Shippers sighed. "Sure, let's call it a day." She picked up her implements and moved off toward the tent, but he stood rooted. In the shadows of the amphitheater the ancient dancers, daubed and feathered, crouched to their stomp dance, bent over, knees rising, arms laced with evergreen, turtleshell rattles going. He all but heard the drums.

Then Freya Markus came striding through the piñons in her clumsy boots. Unmindful of him, she veered off toward the trail that climbed the mountain. He hastily stowed his pencil and pad in the roomy back panel of the old canvas hunting vest he'd found at the thrift and moved after her, leaping the low wall, springing rock to rock along the edge of the drop-off. But when he stopped and looked up to mark where she had gone, here came Tina, shredding a yucca leaf with her fingers, sauntering after their leader but keeping well behind.

Shit. Tina acted like she had a crush on the woman. He picked up a rock and flung it over the drop. He heard it crash through treetops and hit the ground below. Overhead a red-tailed hawk circled back to investigate. He watched it drop lower, then seeing no prey, circle on an air shaft and drift away.

He'd checked out the women the first week on the dig, but he still spent most of his free time with Tina and carried on in his head long discourses about art, music, metaphysics, philosophy, with Freya Markus. He told himself this celibate life had sharpened his senses. He could see farther, smell the woods, the stream, the sun, the meadow grass. Living outdoors, breathing unpolluted air, eating right, sleeping in intimate contact with Mother Earth, made him daydream of taking to the hills when the summer was over, living off the land, telling Uncle Jake to bug off and leave him alone.

He recrossed the mesa and descended one of the pole ladders to the ledge outside the cliff dwellings and walked along it past rooms with ceilings still black from the smoke of ancient fires.

He heard them before he saw them. "Goddammit, I tell you I'm not leaving here till . . ."

Till what? Till he got laid? It was the two campers from the upper meadow he'd dubbed the curly-headed boys. No mistaking the pungence of marijuana.

"Okay, but I'm not gunna—" That was Joe.

"Hey, Ruby," Willy interrupted.

Reuben peered in at them sitting side by side on the stone floor of one of the larger cliff rooms, their expensive hiking boots stuck out in front of them. Blond Willy was the leader, Joe the follower. They were undergraduates from the School of Mines in Socorro on their way home to Utah but in no hurry to get there.

"What're you two doing?" Probably waiting for some of the women.

Willy said, "You know why all living things lived in the sea till about five hundred million years ago?" He looked like a buttercup with his pink cheeks and pale curly hair.

"I guess I'm about to."

"There was no ozone layer then, so they needed the water to protect them from the sun. So you know what I think?" Taking a hit, offering it to Reuben, who declined. "I think when the ozone layer's gone we'll have to wade back in."

Unusual to see them sitting still. They'd outfitted their little Japanese pickup with every piece of sports equipment known to man. Joe lent his things to anybody who asked, but Willy went ballistic if anybody played with his toys. Ten times a day they raced up and down the canyon road on mountain bikes. They fly-fished the stream, they rock climbed, they shot targets with fancy modern crossbows, and for the past week or so they'd been giving the women scuba diving lessons in the pond. They made Reuben feel old.

He descended a second ladder to the bottom tier of rooms and the slope below. There was still time for a nap in his tent before supper. Once on the road, he hurried past some of the Earth Watch women. Duff, tall and spare, her dumpy friend Wembley, and long, tall Clarity, who looked like a farm woman out of photographs of the Great Depression. Clarity was a past-life regression counselor from Southern California, and each summer she revisited the scene of one of her own past lives, which was what she was doing here. She'd spent one of them in the mesa-top ruin when it was a bustling community.

"But we didn't *have* pots," Clarity was saying. "We were master basket makers. My mother, she didn't make baskets, though. She made rabbit fur blankets. She could trade those for all the baskets she wanted. Sure, we already had specialists. De Chardin says a culture advances as the people specialize. The arts and crafts get better than if every Tom, Dick, and Harry has to be jack-of-all-trades."

Duff, her hair gray and bobbed, walked faster to escape the conversation, but dumpy Wembley listened, nodding.

"You wove the webbing out of plant fibers, and then after you got enough skins . . . Oh, sure, we tanned them. I can show you where . . .

"My mother, she cut the skins in strips and wove the strips into the webbing. Her blankets were works of art. We used them for everything—winter capes, blankets, lining for cradleboards. We buried my little brother in one.

"Oh, sure, I had a little brother. He fell off the cliff and died. It was tragic. We lost a lot of children that way. My mother had made him a little fiber harness and tied it to a stob. But the dog chewed it and . . .

"Of *course* we had dogs. Ours was like a big, fluffy sort of collie. We called him . . . um . . . well, nowadays you'd say Spot."

Clarity would regress anybody who asked. Reuben himself, on a hot dry afternoon when he longed for the cool of an ocean wave, had come up with a life as a Viking. Clarity was more entertaining than the nightly seminars.

Up ahead by the pond at the mouth of the canyon, Rappaport Singleton, one of the campers, swept the shoulder of the road with his metal detector, moving toward the campground and his rusty old RV. He could tell you every find he'd ever made. One time a 1914 silver dollar. "You don't run up on one of them suckers ever' day." And he'd pat the shaft of the metal detector. Reuben had him pegged as mid to late fifties till Rap claimed seventy-two.

"Hey, Ruby." Waving, he swung the metal detector toward Reuben. The big magnet and his Brunton compass hung, as usual, from his wide leather belt.

Reuben broke into a reluctant trot and caught up. "Find anything today?"

Rap Singleton winked and patted the pocket of his denim jacket. The women walked by, Wembley eyeing them, and the old man whispered, "Shh. 'At ol' girl's so nosy she could look through a keyhole with both eyes."

Reuben laughed. "So what's in the pocket?"

"I'm not saying yet. But if it's what I think it is . . ." He threw back his big shaggy head, closed his eyes, and shouted, "Halle-fuckin-lujah!"

The Earth Watch women glanced over their shoulders.

Rap Singleton's camper was parked along the stream where the canyon narrowed, beside where a beaver had built his lodge. Reuben often walked down and sat with him after supper because in a certain mood he liked to listen to the old man talk about his travels. Sometimes Rap got out his tile rummy set and they'd play a game by the light of the Coleman lantern while moths immolated themselves.

He belonged to an organization called Loners on Wheels. He told Reuben he'd driven all the way to the Northwest Territories in that old RV. He wintered in Southern California where some shut-down air force base had been turned over to the Loners. They parked their campers on the cracked tarmac of the runways. They were organized. They elected officers. They had weekend get-togethers—cookouts, square dances. "Sometimes we team up, a bunch of us," Rap said, "and go down to the Yucatán in winter, up to Alaska in summer."

Reuben, who felt like an alien himself, found the ways of the humanoids endlessly interesting.

And sitting at the picnic table outside Rap's camper, there was always a chance he'd glimpse the beaver. It had built its lodge out of branches and tree trunks. You could see the stumps along the stream where he'd sawed them off a foot aboveground with nothing but his teeth. Mostly young aspens. The rangers said a beaver killed lots of trees building a house, but it was probably a lot fewer than people killed building theirs.

"I'm going into Santa Fe tomorrow," Rap said. "Think you could get the day off, Ruby?" Santa Fe was about an hour's drive.

"Maybe." He could take his clothes to the Laundromat. They were getting pungent. And he might stop by his pad, let Dolly know he was just fine, couldn't be better. "You running out of groceries?"

"Nope. I got plenty of rice and beans. You get all the protein you need from the combination, you know that?"

Every New Age vegetarian in Santa Fe knew that and was only too happy to tell you about it. Rap was a little New Age himself with his long hair and the gold Gypsy earring in the bulbous lobe of his left ear. It was the first thing he'd found with his metal detector. He'd had the ear pierced to accommodate it. He thought it brought him luck.

"You going in for a shave and a haircut?" This was a tease. Rap was a slob.

"Naw, I got business at the county courthouse." He patted the breast pocket again and winked.

They crossed the little stone bridge and stopped at his camper parked on the grass between the road and the stream where the canyon narrowed before flaring out into the meadow. Eyeing the humpback beaver lodge, Reuben said, "What time you want to leave?"

"I got to get up on the mesa top first for a little reconnoitering. Up there you can sight things at a distance—" he winked again "—get the big picture, know what I mean? But I'll head out for town about eight o'clock."

"If I can go I'll meet you here, but if I'm not here don't wait for me."

"Better set your alarm," Rap called after him. "This light can fool you. In a goddam canyon you got to break day with an ax."

Reuben leapt the stream and made his way among the trees on the other side. It was a trail he liked to take because hardly anybody ever did. It was cooler there and you could smell the water. But back at his tent, the nap was not to be. There was a note pinned to the edge of his tent fly with a pine needle. "I need a jerry can of water." That was Lily Jaramillo. She and her husband Pete were in charge of the kitchen *sombra*.

He glanced in his shaving mirror hanging from a rusty nail somebody had driven into a tree trunk, and stroked his beard. He kept it long enough not to look accidental, but not so long that it could curl much. He'd meant to trim it. Now he wouldn't have time. He sighed, unzipped the screen, and crawled inside. It was a small dome tent, maroon and gray, suspended from an outside frame. He'd bought it secondhand out of *The Thrifty Nickel*. He kept his clothes in it, but mostly he slept out under the stars. In the dead hours before dawn they were huge, like they'd zoomed in for a closer look while everybody slept.

He flung himself down on top of his sleeping bag in his maroon cocoon, hands clasped under his head, contemplating a day in town. Maybe he and Dolly ought to talk some more. He'd thought of a lot of grievances he'd forgotten to mention.

3

Hooper John had been dancing and he was sweaty. As he lay on his stomach looking over the edge of the rock ledge, twigs and dirt stuck to his skin and he kept absently thrusting himself up and scraping them off. With the twigs and piñon needles and dirt, off, too, came some of the symbols he'd drawn on his chest with red clay and soot and charcoal and an ocher he bought at a store in Santa Fe that sold paints to artists.

The moth-eaten breechclout left his bodily creases comfortably free. It was better than jeans, which he wore very tight, but he had to keep jerking it down and bunching it to protect his privates from the rock. The big white Stetson hat shaded his head and shoulders from the sun, not so hot now it was falling. The Stetson didn't go with the breechclout and the evergreen and crow feathers Scotch-taped to his arms, it antedated his new true identity, but he wasn't going to forswear the hat even in the service of rites that he otherwise stuck to uncompromisingly as far as he could tell from what he could get out of the old man.

A mean old bastard, but sometimes he told John things, when he wasn't playing tricks. Tricks like, when John had been living with him a short time at the village and asked what was that thing propping the door—a smooth rock with a saddle in it.

"Indian pillow," the old man said.

"For your *head*?"

"Sure. Make you strong-headed. You want to be Indian, you gotta sleep on it."

"I don't see you sleeping on it." But John tried it anyway for a few miserable nights till one of the women laughed the way they did, tee-hee, and told him it was a grinding stone for corn. A *metate*. They didn't use them anymore. They bought their grits and meal from the supermarket like everybody else.

But at other times the old man would tell him things like, "We are weak now. We have our robes. We have our blankets. The old ones, they were like the animals and didn' feel even the winter cold. They were plenty strong."

Hooper John wanted to be strong. One day he would live outdoors in winter and not feel the cold. He was already training for it.

He'd been lying there on the ledge for some time, waiting for her to appear. The binoculars, too, weren't strictly according to code, but he'd early seen that he would need them, so he'd pinched them from a camera store in the mall. He was looking down from his ledge into what he could see of the enemy camp. In shorts and jeans and T-shirts with mottos, they were dragging back from all day violating the sacred grounds of the ancestors. Here came Sonny Concha, Santa Ynez and a good guy, and Horse Rios, who was bad news. Sonny was Santa Ynez, but Horse was Tsorigi, and he gave plenty of indication that he didn't care for John, so John was watchful around him.

He hadn't a view of the whole meadow, only the lower end, because the ledge where he lay overhung a small side canyon that flowed at an angle down to the arroyo and followed it to the pond.

Early on, this redheaded girl had discovered the hot springs. Kept it to herself or they'd all have been there fouling the place. Soon she would be heading up the arroyo, looking back to check that nobody followed. Until a month ago, nobody much had ever gone to the hot springs but Hooper John. Now he didn't go there anymore, but he kept his eye on the place from up here on the ledge.

He'd been dancing behind the rock, his secret place. He found it all by himself one day chasing a rabbit. He was trying to learn how to get it right, hunting rabbit with a sling like the Pueblo men. Pretty soon now they would have the big rabbit hunt out in the sage flats this side of the river. Of course, they did it from horseback, and John had no horse he could call his own. They formed a circle maybe ten acres wide, and at the signal, a wild whoop, they whipped their ponies to a gallop and converged at a dead run in the center, and any rabbit caught in the circle would start up and run like crazy but get beaned on the head anyway by a rock in one of their slings.

You leaned low over the pony's neck, the sling whirling around, singing in your hand, picking up speed so the rabbit didn't have a chance. Maybe he could get the neighbor to lend him a pony. With that in mind he'd been doing chores for the man—bucking hay, mending fence, peeling bark with a draw knife, watering his horses.

If that didn't work, he had his eye on a horse across the river. It belonged to a Mexican farmer—Spanish, they said out here—a black and white paint pony. Easy to spot, but he could take some soot and change the pattern and make it hard to recognize. Anyway, no Mexican—Spanish—was likely to come on Pueblo land looking for his pony. The Indians wouldn't like it.

He had chased the rabbit that day till it went over the edge of the cliff. At first he thought the tomfool rabbit had killed himself rather than be killed by him. But rabbits didn't have any inborn sense of honor. That was Disneyland. He'd come up to the edge and found that, probably when the ground was wet after a rain, it had crumbled and sloped down to a shelf. The rabbit had just run down the slope and disappeared.

So John slid down to the ledge ten feet below, but the rabbit was not there. He looked over the edge again, only to find another ledge. This one was too far down for him to jump without breaking a leg. He found an aspen pole and skinnied down it like a bear. But the rabbit was not there either.

That's when he found the hole. It was in a sort of upside-down V between some rocks. He'd yanked the brush away, looking for the rabbit, and out with its roots came a hunk of earth. And there it was, a hole big enough to get his shoulders through.

It was dark inside. He could smell the rabbit, smell its fear, and he imagined it hunkered down, not far from his face, ready to spring. He shot back out of there. He didn't want to be bit by any rabbit. He could get a case of rabies that would set him foaming at the mouth.

He imagined himself weaving through the village, foaming. He imagined them falling down in awe of him, thinking he'd turned into a shaman.

When he pulled back out of the opening, more dirt came with him, and a little landslide, and the rabbit shot past him to freedom. He didn't even turn and watch it go. He sat back on his heels, amazed by what he was looking at.

It was a pretty big cave from what he could make out. The entry hole he'd accidentally opened let in enough light for him to see it had once been a dwelling cave. He'd seen pictures of them in *National Geographic*. When he was homeless and found himself in a town, in cold weather John spent his days in the public library, where it was warm and they were likely to have easy chairs tucked away in corners. And he read *National Geographic*, daydreaming what it would be like to live in whatever wonder spot caught his fancy. John read a lot at the public library. He considered himself self-educated.

He stooped and crawled inside the cave, a little in awe, a little afraid. Overhead he could see where the stone overhang of the ceiling had split off and come crashing down to cover what was once the wide cave mouth where plenty of daylight would've come in. He whistled low and breathy. It was dark, but there were figures of some kind on the walls, and rooms built out of stones, and a hollowed-out place in the floor crisscrossed like a piecrust with sticks, shreds of something still clinging to them, like bits of—maybe it was hide.

Then something mysterious happened that he couldn't describe. The hair stood up on his arms. He backed to the opening and scrambled out, gulping air. He threw the brush back over the hole to cover it, and clambered up to the shelf, then clawed up the incline to the mesa top, tearing off a fingernail, crazy to get out of there.

But the secret place drew him back with the old man's kerosene lantern. So far as he could tell, nobody had been there since the old ones carved their shapes and symbols, their message left for him alone to find all these aeons later. He'd taken this as a sign, and after lying in the cave all night, shivering in the dark and surrounded by spirits, he rose renewed in his determination to become one with the tribe. For he thought the spirits of the cave were friendly. Unlike those Jesus people howling everybody to eternal damnation, they spoke to him gently in a language he wanted to understand. He came whenever he could get away unobserved. John was observed far less than he imagined, but his was a cautious nature that demanded allegiance of all his rasher instincts. The place behind the rock was his source of power.

Old Eliseo was probably looking for him right now, expecting him home for his bowl of *posole* and a limp tortilla folded around refried pinto beans. The old man could go fuck himself. John was more and more irritated with him, perhaps because the old man was essential to his endeavors, though he told himself it was the other way around and the old man couldn't do without *him*.

Just as John had stumbled upon his secret place, the old man had stumbled upon John. So was that another sign or wasn't it? There was this bar in Albuquerque that he had frequented because the men there struck him as Real Men

from whom he might learn something if he paid attention—
cowboy-looking men in big hats and silver belt buckles, Indian men who particularly appealed to him because some of
them wore their hair long and braided with bright strips of
felt. He'd go in and sit in a corner watching, nursing all
night a single glass of draft beer slowly going flat. Then
one winter night there happened what he thought of as The
Misunderstanding. One of the cowboy-looking men smiled
at him in the men's room and said, "Hello, son. I see you
been watching me."

And John made the mistake of smiling back.

"If you'll just step outside," the cowboy-looking man
had said.

And when John, hoping to find a friend, obliged, the
man hit him first in the stomach, knocking the wind out of
him so he thought he was dying as he lay there in the falling snow, and then kicked him in the head, and it hurt so
bad he mercifully lost consciousness as, muttering "Dirty
faggot," the man turned back to the bar.

The next thing he knew, the old Indian was bending over
him in the shadows, his head and shoulders silhouetted
against the distant glare. "You gotta hangover, boy? You
drunk?"

He was one of the men in long braids, John could see
that much in the orange neon light spilling around from the
front of the bar and the fast-food places on Central Avenue.
"What you doin' out here in the snow?"

The old man had a thin cotton blanket up over his head
like an Arab, which he took off and put over John.

"Who are you?" John managed to ask.

"They call me Eliseo," the old man said. "How 'bout
you? You got a name?"

And lying there bleeding from the ear and staining the
snow, he'd answered, "My name is Hooper. John."

And the old man said, "I better take you home and fix
you up. You don't look so good, Hooper John."

Then John lost consciousness under the cotton blanket.
When he woke up he found himself on a low *banco* against

a mud wall in a dim room with a hard adobe floor and one small window high up to let out the smoke, and a corner fireplace where the old man squatted, feeding in piñon twigs and patiently blowing on the flame.

From his vantage point high up on the ledge, he saw her coming, the one he was waiting for. It was about time. He never could see her face, only that red hair. First he felt the familiar excitement, like it was hard for him to keep still. Then, like always, the sight of her made him mad. She would never want to know him or be his friend. He knew this in his bones.

She always took the shortcut up the arroyo, then had to clamber over rocks. And she always came alone. That was because, once at the hot springs, she took off all her clothes. He approved such female modesty.

She had on a loose, baggy T-shirt that came down to the ragged edges of her shorts. Over her arm she carried a towel.

She looked around to make sure she was alone, then bent and tugged the shirt off over her head while her breasts hung loose and creamy white, with big pink nipples. She unzipped her shorts and stepped out of them. She wore no underwear. She never did. Her bush was dark, not bright like her hair. He could be the only one who actually knew that, John reflected.

Then she sat in the pool up to her shoulders, with her arms stretched out along the containing rock which, he knew from experience, was hot, too, from the spring. The spring was quite a way up the steep slope and concealed by boulders. It was big enough for maybe two people to sit in it up to their shoulders. It kept itself secret, like his cave, because what water flowed out of it seeped into the ground or evaporated in the dry air or emptied in a trickle that soon lost itself in the saw grass and baby tamarisks.

He waited for her to wash her hair. It was at this point— her quiet in the pool, him quiet on the ledge—that the time took on a magical feel to it and he daydreamed, like with the *National Geographic*. The daydreams were sometimes

lewd, sometimes sweet—like, he plowed her till she split
and screamed for mercy, or like she cradled his head in her
lap and told him he would one day make something of
himself and he believed her.

She was going to do it. She slid all the way under and
he knew what would follow. Once her hair was wet, she
heaved herself out and sat on a rock and sudsed it from a
bottle she'd brought rolled up in the towel. He got his best
look at her when she sat on the rock.

Hair full of suds, she walked over to the thin stream
leaving the spring and squatted for the rinse. He figured
this was to avoid getting soapsuds in the spring. He admired such foresight. He would never have thought of that.
Afterwards, she tiptoed back up the hill, balancing over
rocks with her arms out. Maybe she was tender-footed.
He'd never had much truck with women.

She splashed back into the hot springs and wiggled. You
could tell the water felt good. He could feel it himself just
watching. She slid all the way under, then came up and
peered around a boulder and down the arroyo. Soon she
would step out on the flat rock and towel her head, then
pull the towel around her and fasten it above her breasts till
it hung just to her thighs, like a little girl's dress.

Then it would be over. She'd pull on her shorts and shirt
and tennis shoes and pick her way down the rocky slope to
the arroyo.

Watching her go, he would feel lonely and abandoned,
then mad as hops. No telling when she'd be back. She
didn't come every day, but *he* did, didn't he? And sometimes waited till almost dark and not a sign of her.

But today that's not how it happened.

Stock-still, John lay on the ledge and watched a figure
bounding rock to rock up the arroyo. He expected her to
jump up and put on her clothes. When she didn't, he almost
cried out to warn her.

But she craned her neck and lifted a lazy wave at the intruder. John couldn't believe it. She was just lying there naked.

He recognized the fellow. It was the black-haired guy, one of the ones with the big-tired bikes, who insulted the cliffs with ropes and cleats, who played around and smoked weed and didn't work at the ruin. This *chulo* climbed the last rocks and stood over her, then bent and cupped her breast in one hand.

John was shocked, outraged, betrayed. His heart beat in his ears. She reached up and sort of cupped this guy's privates in his loose blue shorts, and he straightened and took off his clothes and let himself down in the spring with her. She was *under* him. They were *doing it* in the water.

John lifted up a little off the rock and fondled himself. When he fell over on his back with his eyes closed, he was moaning, cursing, telling himself he'd been stupid to trust a woman to be any different from what he'd always been told. Sluts. Cunts. *Putas*. They were all alike. They were all whores. Well, he'd show them. He'd get rid of the whole lot down there in the meadow. He'd do the Indians a favor and get shut of them all.

4

Reuben lined up with the weary students at the kitchen *sombra* and filled his cup with coffee and his bowl with chili. He stashed one of Lily's thick flour tortillas in the chili and another one in his mouth and made his way toward the picnic tables.

Lily cooked for the outfit, and her husband Pete split the wood and built the fires and tended the generators. He also descended to the valley every few days to get the mail and replenish stores, taking along a list of the students' needs—

soap, shampoo, a bottle of wine or a six-pack to cool in the stream. Pete was bald, rotund, easygoing. Lily was angular and wired. When she was mad her eyes turned black and you didn't mess with her.

They'd parked a utility trailer up near the road with an awning stretched the length of it. They stored food in there where the bears couldn't catch the smell and pay surprise visits at night.

With the permission of the BLM, the Jaramillos had put a *latia sombra* over their outdoor kitchen and dug a long pit and thrown a heavy wire-mesh grill over it with a sheet metal griddle at one end where they cooked the hamburgers and hot dogs and vats of chili and beans and *posole*, and kept giant coffee pots warming.

The only complaint about the food was the scarcity of salads. They'd all hunted wild greens and concocted their own until Freya Markus put a stop to it because, she said, they could poison themselves. The wild hemlock, for instance, growing near the stream might look a lot like yarrow, but it was deadly.

Reuben settled on a bench next to the Earth Watch volunteer from Calgary, newly a widower, who could be counted on to smile and move over and never say a word. Freya was talking with the geologists, husband and wife, who'd showed up late that afternoon. He was tall and narrow-faced in steel-rimmed spectacles, and she was plump and motherly. Freya was talking with her hands, upset, angry, explaining—what? He had no idea.

He spent the next hour helping Lily with the scrub-up. Once finished, he hung the big pots on the outside wall of the utility trailer. One night a talented black bear woke up the campground playing them like a xylophone. It was dark by the time he looped the sleeves of his sweatshirt around his neck and went to look for Tina.

The seminar was well under way. A fire in the stone fireplace and a Coleman lantern hanging overhead lit the three-sided log lean-to at the top of the meadow. Caspar sprawled at the center of the picnic table with his disciples spread out on either side of him. Out on the grass the undergraduates sat with a pair of Indian fishermen—their hobbled horses grazed down by the stream—the husband and wife geologists, the Earth Watch people who showed up at every dig and paid good money for the privilege of doing slave labor at seven thousand feet under a pitiless sun, probably, he thought, the kind of people who used to go on Lindblad tours. And since the BLM made it a condition that the seminars had to be open to everybody, there was always a scattering of campers from the upper meadow for whom this was the only nightly entertainment. Reuben scanned the crowd but he didn't see Tina.

Freya Markus usually led the seminars, impatiently interrupting the students when they started showing off their yuppie academic expertise. "Go down the rabbit hole," she'd shout, slapping the table impatiently, "Down the rabbit hole with you!" She'd early warned them that to be an archaeologist they had to toss out the textbooks and fall down the rabbit hole through a time warp.

But tonight she'd left it to the graduate students. Down in her travel trailer by the stream, you could see her silhouetted against the closed blinds, pacing. Something was wrong. What was the matter now?

They were arguing about some fibers Pilar, one of the lowly undergraduates, had unearthed that morning in the kitchen midden. He'd photographed them, just some old gray fibers twisted together, what was the big deal? He skirted the audience, peering in the dark for Tina.

Pilar stood bunching and folding the bottom of her T-shirt over her sturdy wrists, hair dyed the color of oranges and chopped off an inch from the scalp. "I think it's a Basketmaker sandal." Her voice was small for her chunky frame.

"Nonsense," Caspar said. "The craft was used throughout the Pueblo period, long after the Basketmakers invented it." Count on Caspar to rain on the kid's parade.

"What makes you think it's Basketmaker?" That was Polly Quint.

"Well." Pilar squirmed. "Anyway I mean in Pueblo I didn't they you know start doubling the soles? I thought well anyway it's just a single sole. And that's Basketmaker, isn't it?"

One of the Earth Watch people wanted to know the Basketmaker dates, and Pilar, eyeing Reuben making his way alongside the audience, locked her fingers together and lifted her elbows and did a shy little torso twist. He winked and she smiled, and her fingers unfolded and wriggled together like a nest of chubby grubs beneath her chin. "In some areas it goes back to like you know maybe around the year 500."

Caspar sucked on his pipe. "That's 1500 B.P."

"Yeah," Pilar said, "B.P."

Polly Quint murmured helpfully for the sake of the campers, "B.P.—that's Before Present."

Pilar dropped back cross-legged on the grass next to her idol Jade from Burbank, California, who had appeared on the dig in black lizard cowboy boots, a gauzy lime-colored petal skirt, a man's green suit vest over a tank top that looked like sleeveless underwear, and a round black old lady's hat with a floppy pink flower sitting forward on her head.

Caspar sounded long-suffering. "And it's patently impossible. We know we're at Pueblo III on top of the mesa. That's the period of the Great Pueblos and it puts us somewhere between the twelfth and thirteenth centuries. These villages were rarely inhabited for more than a hundred years. Let's cut the romance, shall we."

But Duff, the Earth Watch woman, said without looking up, picking at something in her lap, "Maybe it was inhabited at different periods. That was fairly common, wasn't it?"

Reuben moved into the shadows behind the audience, hoping to spot Tina in what light overflowed the shelter.

Duff's sidekick Wembley said, "You mean they built these elaborate towns like Mesa Verde and Chaco and didn't live in them any longer than that?"

Pilar nodded and said in her small voice, "That's one of the Anasazi mysteries."

Every week a new batch of campers chimed in with the same old comments.

"I've read it was drought that drove them out."

"I heard it was the Navajos."

"Probably had to flee their enemies."

"That's one theory." Caspar's drawl implied not a very good one. "But the thick walls of the multistoried houses would have served as fortifications, and the supposedly warlike enemies would have approached on foot. The horse arrived centuries later with the Spanish."

"But at Chaco," Beano Shippers murmured, always afraid of offending Caspar, "they did seal up some of the doors and windows and make entrances through the roofs." When Freya wasn't there, the women deferred to Caspar, but he had no competition from the other male graduate students: Steve Many Hands, a Plains youth from the Midwest, was too shy, and the Mexican student, Bobby Ybarra from Guadalajara, didn't give a damn. Reuben wondered what Shippers, a lowly undergraduate, was doing up there in the shelter among the elite. Smiling, she slapped at something. In the front row the curly-headed boys were tossing pebbles at her.

All the while Clarity, the past-life counselor, sat there knitting with the look of a skeptic that said, I'd be glad to answer these questions if you care to ask.

"And the Navajos came along centuries after these ruins were abandoned," Caspar drawled. "It was the modern-day Pueblos they raided." When the graduate students were in charge, the talk always strayed.

Reuben moved up beside the Indian fishermen. He'd spotted the back of Tina's head and was trying to get her attention while the campers made their comments and the graduate students listened with patronizing patience.

"It was probably an epidemic."

"You mean to say they haven't found any burials?"

"You're actually telling us they built these beautiful

towns and after eighty years or so just walked off and left them?"

Week after week, the students got to show off to a new batch of campers.

Reuben caught the attention of the girl he'd thought was Tina. It was tiny Jade. She turned and smiled at him, mouthing *Me?* He put a finger to his lips. Where could she be? He hadn't seen her at supper either.

"Well," Caspar said, "I think the answer to that is fairly simple."

Answer to what?

Steve Many Hands pulled a long face at Reuben and mouthed, *Asshole.* Their estimates of Caspar agreed on every point.

"They had no wheels. They had no horses," Caspar said. "Though trading was widespread and there was long-distance foot travel for ceremonies, dances, things like that, on a day-to-day basis these people didn't stray far from home. In eighty years, with a population like that at Chaco Canyon, the surrounding area would be stripped of all the necessities of life—wood, game, wild edibles. The soil would be depleted, agriculture would suffer. These people didn't expect to live forever in one place."

The retired rancher from Calgary cleared his throat. "Then why such elaborate towns?"

Caspar tapped out his dottle on the leg of the picnic table. "Well, clearly they were a peaceful people who valued cooperation. So what do you think happened in such a culture to the natural aggression of the male?"

Pilar giggled and Polly Quint rebuked her with a look, whereupon Jade audibly muttered, "Cocksucker."

"A lot of it," Caspar said, "got channeled into all this elaborate building—the beautiful stonework, the soaring towers . . ."

Pilar fell back giggling on the grass.

Reuben walked the sidelines, peering at faces. Willy, the blond curly-head, taking his reel apart on a canvas rag and oiling it in the light from the shelter, asked, "How come they built those wide straight roads at Chaco? You hear all kinds of things—like ceremonial parade-ways, human sacrifices."

Clarity's needles clicked impatiently. She'd had a life at Chaco, too.

Caspar said, "We build straight roads ourselves wherever possible, why shouldn't they?" Good old Caspar.

Somebody said, "But Anasazi is a Navajo word."

Clarity's head bent to the click of her needles. Madame La Farge. Reuben's own mother knitted without ever looking down.

"We don't know what these people called themselves," Polly said. "When the Navajos came—centuries after these ruins were abandoned—they called the vanished builders the Anasazi.

"It just means 'the old ones,' " Polly Quint added helpfully.

"Actually," Steve Many Hands muttered, "it means 'the enemy ancestors.' "

Polly said, "Tell us about your find, Margaret." Beano's real name was Margaret. She began taking the black rocks out of their labeled paper bags and putting them on the picnic table. So that's why she was up there in the shelter. Reuben glanced at them—he'd sketched and photographed them from every possible angle. He circled the back of the shelter and surveyed the audience from the other side while Beano talked.

Bess Cochran of the husband-wife geologist team stepped up into the shelter. "They could be tektites." She picked one up.

"It's some kind of natural glass," Jim Cochran said. He held one of the rocks to the lantern light. "This is volcanic country. But I never saw any volcanic glass like this in the Bandelier formation."

Caspar said, "Could have come from anywhere. These people were magpies."

Bess Cochran touched the rocks one at a time. "This one

looks like an egg. And look at these, a teardrop and a club. Where you find one tektite, you're likely to find others."

"What are tektites?" a camper asked.

Bess Cochran said, "Nobody knows. They're very mysterious."

The widowed rancher from Calgary said softly, "They've often been given special significance by aboriginal peoples. And they're valued by mystics, clairvoyants, healers of all kinds."

Beano Shippers nervously stowed them back in their labeled bags. "Anybody wants a look, see me up here later."

"We can take them to the lab and have them checked out for you," Jim Cochran said, but Beano looked uncertain. Reuben leaned into the shelter and asked her if she'd seen Tina. Beano shook her head.

"Hiking around this morning," a camper said, "we saw a petroglyph with the body of a man and the head of a bird. What does a thing like that mean?"

"A petroglyph can mean anything," Polly Quint said.

Jade patted the grass beside her, and Reuben squatted on his heels. "Have you seen Tina?" She shook her head.

"It could just be an expression of the artist's imagination," Duff said. "Aren't our interpretations usually our own and contemporary?"

"They're just ancient graffiti," Caspar drawled. Depend on Caspar.

The campers were gathering their children to return to the upper meadow. One of the Indian fishermen shifted and cleared his throat. "It might be Pelawi. We call him Bird Boy." He looked down at a twig in his fingers as if shy of the sudden attention. "The raven was Pelawi's . . ." He searched for a word.

"His animal? His totem?" Polly Quint prodded helpfully.

"Some kind of a thing like that. The story goes, one day he went out hunting and he scared up a wild turkey and took a shot at it." He drew a phantom arrow from a phantom quiver over his shoulder and let fly.

"But he didn' hit the turkey. The turkey, it got away. But

he hit a raven on the limb of a piñon tree. The wounded raven said, We take you with us now. So Pelawi turned into the bird, and the bird turned into Pelawi and went home to his mother. But he still had his beak. The beak on his face told the mother this was no longer her son, but she didn' let on."

Everybody waited, including Reuben, but, as often happened in Indian stories, that was the end of it. The storyteller shrugged. "Just an old story."

The fishermen rose. "We left her some trout on a string by the trailer," one of them said to Reuben. "Tell her."

Meaning Freya Markus. He watched them pick up their gear and head for their horses. Thunder rumbled in the mountains, but it had rumbled every night for a week. Rain would be welcome, but the sky was full of stars. The seminar was breaking up.

Rap Singleton emerged chuckling from the dark and asked which one was the geologist. He clapped Jim Cochran on the shoulder and said something. His words were slurred. Sometimes he had a nip down in his camper.

Jade passed, smiling at Reuben but gabbing to Pilar. "It was like you know major but I had to deal with it ... So okay, but his parents were rich and I saw he had an attitude so I just ... Was that brilliant or what?" Her mobile lower lip dipped in the middle and the words squirted out the sides.

He sidled off to where the campers crowded around photographs pinned to the shelter walls, then, trapped, he had to stay and answer questions. A camper in a baseball cap stuck full of flies asked him what kind of camera he used.

"A Linhof four-by-five."

"What's that—Swedish?"

Reuben nodded.

"How'd you get—"

"It's got a tiltable lens."

"Prevents distortion, right?" The fly fisherman rocked back and forth, self-satisfied. "Did you know the Greeks made their pillars thicker at the top to avoid the optical illusion that they grew smaller as they rose?"

"No kidding," Reuben said without enthusiasm, sliding away in the dark. He wanted some coffee before it was all gone. He got two Styrofoam cups from Lily and went looking in the dark for Tina, but he ended up drinking both of them alone down by the stream. They might interfere with his sleep, but the coffee was hot and the night was turning cold. He rapped on the travel trailer wall and told Freya Markus about the string of fish.

The seminar dispersed. The lanterns in the lean-to went out, leaving only the dying glow in the stone fireplace. The meadow was dotted with campfires. Voices called to each other. Somebody laughed. A guitar practiced a classical phrase over and over.

He crushed the paper cups and stuffed them in his pocket and crossed the stream to make his way on the footpath back to his tent. On one side, the colonized meadow. On the other it was wild—just aspens, fir, and the rocky mountainside. When bears visited at night, this was where they came from. Away from the stream the woods were full of night sounds—tree frogs, crickets. He looked up through branches dark against the sky. The stars were lowering for the night. Out here they seemed retractable. They reminded him of the crystal chandeliers at the Met, descending as the act ended, then rising slowly as the lights dimmed and the music began. He hummed the falling first notes of Musetta's waltz, singing softly, *"Quan-do men vo,"* and tried following the ensuing complications up and down the scale, *"quando men vo soleh-heht-ta ..."* He was never sure he'd got it right, but how he loved Puccini, Verdi. He'd remained transfixed in standing room only last summer at the Santa Fe Opera to hear *La Bohème*.

Where the trail turned and the mountain abutted the stream, he saw up ahead at the foot of a fir a pair of white Levi's spread-eagle on the ground. One white knee rose up and propped itself.

"Have a hit, friend." Bobby Ybarra from Guadalajara.

Reuben shook his head. "What're you doing out here all by yourself?" Probably getting smashed on cannabis.

"I'm looking for UFOs," Bobby said.

"You think they're out there?"

"Quien sabe?" The graduate student from Mexico took a long drag and the tip flared in the dark.

"You missed the seminar," Reuben said.

"Seminar shit, man. I worked last summer for a contract archaeologist out of Albuquerque. They're the ones make the pesos, not these academic nerds."

He sucked again and held it up, and Reuben absently reached down and took a hit, then choked. "Christ, what is this stuff?"

"Prime Colombian, man. You think I'd be here if I didn't need the fucking union card? But damn if I'll sit up there with those assholes. My ego's not involved. Last summer I made forty-five greens a day just for living expenses. Slept in my truck and salted it away. Go down maybe fifteen, twenty centimeters, it was easy, man. Plenty drinking and fornicating, too. I'm taking off tomorrow. Told Markus I'm feeling a touch of giardia."

Reuben had heard that giardia lambia came back from Asia in the seventies with returning Vietnamese vets. It went from the privies into the ground water and from there into the streams. Drink from them, you got soft shit and low energy and symptoms of the Mexican amoeba. He had to boil all the drinking water in a garbage can Pete had set in the ground over a burner connected to a propane tank.

"I'm gonna sleep late and go into the mountains with those two yuppie sports," Bobby said. "They got some Indian ponies coming up from the pueblo about noon. You wanna come?"

"I'm going into Santa Fe if she'll let me."

"I see you're getting it on with the Indian chick."

"We're friends, come on."

"Yeah, I hear you."

"Can the crap, Bobby. Have you seen her tonight?" He was beginning to worry.

"Don't I wish."

Reuben stepped over the Mexican student and walked on down the trail. Bobby called after him. "You think the little green men have peckers?"

"Yeah," Reuben said. "Little green ones." About the size of yours.

5

Up ahead through the trees his dome tent glowed from inside. Tina. She'd been here all the time. He could have skipped the seminar. Closer, he saw her silhouette through the nylon wall. She was bent over hugging her knees. He jumped the stream and crawled through the zipper door and knelt in front of her.

Under their giant shadows she turned up worried eyes and looked at him. She looked about sixteen. High cheekbones, widow's peak in sync with the small pointed chin, hair draped along her cheeks and caught back in a loose bun, eyes wide, soft startled-looking mouth. He was seeing her as he hadn't seen her before: unknown, exotic, another race.

"What're you up to, kid?" he asked gruffly. "You hiding out or something?"

"I can't stand this, Reuben. No matter what I do, I'm betraying somebody."

"Come on, stop jerking yourself around."

"I feel like a slimy double agent."

"You warn her about the approaching troops?"

She nodded. "What am I doing here?" The question rose

in a plaintive wail. In the lantern light her skin was as
smooth and perfect as a nectarine.

"Ever think of quitting and going home?"

"I don't know where that is anymore."

"You can tell Uncle Cruz to go fuck himself." Bite your
tongue. Why the crudity? He'd been brought up close to
immigrant grandparents and to some of the courtesy of the
old country.

"Yeah, sure." Her dark brows dipped together like swallow wings.

"Okay," he said, "I get it. You ought not be telling these
things to an Anglo, right? So if you can't tell an Anglo, go
tell an Indian."

"Don't start in on me, Reuben, okay?"

"What are you supposed to do, hold it in? If you can't
piss it or puke it, it'll poison you, kid." He couldn't seem
to stop himself.

She turned up a puzzled face. "I'm sorry. I shouldn't
keep dumping on you." She bent to the tent flap.

"Hey wait, kid." He caught her. His voice went thick and
guttural. "What're friends for?"

She muttered into his shoulder, "I'm a Christmas enchilada."

"What could be better?" A Christmas enchilada was half
red chili, half green. "Go get your sleeping bag. We'll
throw them on the grass and look at the sky." Looking at
the sky out here was better than a shrink. It was so big it
cooled you out and assured you nothing on this minor star
at the outer edge of a perfectly ordinary galaxy was worth
stewing over.

"No. They'd think we're lovers."

She'd said the same thing when he wanted her to pitch
her tent next to his. "So what? Sounds like a good idea. I
bet I'm better at it than Pedro."

"Pablo."

The Mexican she'd fallen for last year. "Him. I'm younger and better-looking."

She laughed and gave him a sisterly shove and ducked out the door with her lantern.

It was much later, after midnight, when he heard the owl. He had moved his sleeping bag back up the hill because the coffee plus the sound of the stream was keeping him awake. He didn't know one owl from another, but this one was close. He sat up and looked around. It hooted again.

He slid out of the sleeping bag and sat on top of it to pull on his Nikes. His socks were lost in the lower reaches of the bag where he'd sloughed them off once his feet got warm. Even in the middle of summer, cold nights in the canyon he slept in his socks and sweats.

He stood up and blew on his hands, and his breath rose ghostly before him. Moonlight blanketed the meadow like snow, and everywhere there were shadows.

It had long been his theory that the landscape of life confronted him as a series of plateaus and escarpments. The plateaus were travelers' rests, welcome terrain for the weary. But for intrepid travelers like he felt himself to be, they were dim-lit waiting rooms alongside tracks to the beckoning distance.

The escarpments, on the other hand, gleaming in the light of moon or noon, spoke to him and informed his dreams.

These rises and rests of consciousness alternated at unpredictable intervals. One rise had been the flight from New York to New Mexico, the leap of consciousness a taste of the astringent air of freedom.

This summer presented another leap, one so ineffable he felt no urge to define it. It partook of an enlargement of the senses, a kind of opening to the size and shape of things heretofore unknown—the beaver felling trees to build his submariner domicile, the butterfly that one day fell in love with him and followed him up and down the stream, lighting on his shoulder, on his knee when he ate his lunch propped against a ponderosa and engulfed in its butterscotch airs, on a dollop of peanut butter on his fingertip, and on his hair, sniffing at his essence, a frustrated lover held in abeyance by forces inimical to union.

The owl called again. Then he saw it, gliding between the trees lining the pale canyon road, its wingspread unbelievable. Maybe a great horned owl. Without stopping to tie his laces, he started running.

When he lost sight of it and stood still listening, the owl called again, daring him to follow. The moon would soon drop behind the mountain but the night was still bright. Everything stood out etched—rocks, brush, a stick that looked so much like a snake he leapt out of its way.

He emerged by the pond at the foot of the canyon. He hadn't heard the owl for several minutes. He stood in the middle of the track, soaking up night and silence. A fish jumped in the pond, a liquid sound. A high wind groaned in the tops of the firs. It's gone, he told himself, you've lost it.

For no better reason than the panorama of moonlight on snowy peaks across the valley, he lifted one unlaced Nike above the other and climbed the scree toward the cliff dwellings. Halfway up he heard a soft, mysterious, slow *pat-pat*, like somebody beating muffled time.

Then he saw it again, the owl, now dipping low down the arroyo that was once upon a time a creek bed, maybe when the Anasazi occupied the rock rooms in the cliff and the old pueblo on the mesa top. The owl drifted over the low piñons on a current of air too faint for him to feel.

He stumbled downhill a little way but stopped when the owl disappeared around a bend where the arroyo paralleled the road. Then as he stood watching, it reappeared, spread wide and black over the road itself. He stood transfixed, watching till it vanished behind a ragged row of cottonwoods. Once he thought he glimpsed it again, still moving behind the trees, so he waited.

Then—he couldn't believe it—as he stood there peering at the cottonwoods lining the road, the owl reversed itself, turned back, and moved up the arroyo toward him.

He fell back and sat down hard. She-ut. He laughed soundlessly with a hand over his eyes. It had to be the cannabis. He thought he'd seen the owl turn into Bird Boy,

Pelawi, naked, hair flowing out behind him on a wake of air, running back up the tributary canyon to disappear among the tamarisks.

6

He was whizzing along past all the cars, going someplace on his ten-speed, though he hadn't had a ten-speed for ten years. It felt like flying. Something screamed at him. He looked over his shoulder and the bike started weaving.

He frowned and lifted an arm to shut out the light and pulled himself back into the dream like a turtle into its shell.

"What in God's name are you doing here!"

He pulled himself deeper under the army blanket he'd found on a shelf here last night. The broken blind moved in the wind and threw a dull, slatted daylight across his face. Then Freya Markus entered the frame and he sat up wide-awake, wanting to comb his hair, brush his teeth, wash his face. Behind her, the sawhorse tables with trays of shards.

"How did you get in here?"

He ran his hand over his hair. "I found a window cracked open." Somebody, he hoped not Tina, would be on the carpet for that.

"So you just broke in! What were you doing on the mesa anyway?"

He cleared his throat. In a minute he might retrieve his self-possession, but for now he could only mutter, "I followed an owl, but the moon went down and I couldn't see to get back, so . . . Did you just hear somebody scream?"

But that was in the dream, wasn't it? He'd been skimming along on his ten-speed and heard it and looked back and . . .

No, it almost woke him up. It was real and he'd incorporated it in the dream. "Sort of a long, drawn-out cry?"

She looked at him with disgust. It must have been in the dream or she'd have heard it, too. He shifted uncomfortably. It was that gray time between dawn and sunup. Birds twittered companionably outside. Did she always get up this early? The woman was a dynamo.

She fiddled with the kettle, turned on one of the stove burners, threw something in the sink that clattered. "It was probably a screech owl."

"Yeah," he said quickly. "Are they big? I mean, like a ten-foot wingspread?"

The smile made her a lot less formidable. She had the strangest eyes, pale flakes of green and amber, not eyes you'd expect to see in that face. "Screech owls are not much bigger than pigeons. They look furry till you get up close. It's the way their feathers fit. They're appealing creatures."

She probably knew a lot about birds and stuff.

She was dumping instant coffee into her cup. Up in the meadow Lily brewed the real thing.

"The owl I saw was incredible." He started to spread his arms but caught himself and stuck them in his armpits. "When I lost him, the moon had gone down and I couldn't see my way back up the canyon, so I just slept here." The night had turned dark and spooky after the owl's transformation, and the trailer, with its bathroom and light switches and couches, seemed like a return to normal.

She was frowning. "See anything around the dig?" She was looking at him hard.

He hesitated. The naked runner hadn't been anywhere near the dig.

"No." He shook his head.

She looked uneasily out the trailer door. "It must have been some animal, a bobcat maybe."

He heard the cry again as it had sounded in his sleep. "Yeah, maybe a bobcat." What did he know from bobcat? Maybe they sounded peculiarly human.

She looked up the mesa toward the mountain and he bent quickly and pulled on his shoes.

"You came here in the middle of the night after an *owl*?"

He felt accused, like he was hiding something. Pelawi.

"To some Northwest tribes an owl is an omen," she said.

"What kind of omen?"

"You better go get your breakfast."

What about you? We could walk up the road together. He cleared his throat. "What about you?"

"I'll grab something later." She moved toward the back room that was strictly off limits and the big computer nobody else knew how to work. He felt dismissed.

He ought to leave, but he hesitated. "I was wondering, all right if I go into Santa Fe this morning? We need to change the propane tanks." The two generators—one on the mesa top, one in the *sombra*—slurped up the gas.

She nodded absently. "Too bad you'll miss the geologists."

He stood up, elated. "Yeah, too bad."

Back in the meadow he hung his dank sleeping bag on a line, drank two cups of Lily's coffee, and had a bowl of *atole* awash with butter. He wanted to cop some of Lily's hot water—he hated washing his face in the stream—but Lily, black hair wild around her face, was in no mood to be crossed. Sometimes she and Pete got along and sometimes they didn't. Whenever they didn't, Pete silently vanished, but Lily let go in every direction: somebody'd been stealing her apples, somebody'd made off with a box of sugar, somebody'd tried to break in the trailer door, she had a good mind to throw up her hands and walk out.

So he washed in the ice-cold stream, put on clean jeans and T-shirt, grabbed his windbreaker, and walked down to Rap's camper.

No sign of life. He knocked on the door. "Rap?"

No answer.

He tried the door. Locked. He stepped up on a hubcap and peered in a window. The bed was unmade. A Styrofoam cup half-full of coffee sat on the table alongside some papers weighted down with a rock.

He stepped down and from habit glanced at the beaver's lodge. Nothing stirring there either.

"Rap?" he called. "Rap!"

Some mornings the canyon was filled with cloud and you could barely make out the ghosts of trees, but the morning was clear. He walked to the middle of the road and looked up and down. A few laggards hurried toward the dig.

Rap had said something about getting up early and climbing to the mesa top. Maybe he got interested in the geologist's talk and thought it might help him strike it rich with his metal detector. Reuben looked at his waterproof Timex and headed down the road.

"A million years ago all this was volcanic devastation, just ash and steaming mud flows and downed trees like matchsticks littering the landscape. Glaciers hung on the sides of the mountains.

"Twenty-five million years ago, it was mountain ranges and gravel plains. And over by Galisteo a forest of trees with trunks six feet across, a hundred forty feet high. Now they're petrified wood.

"A hundred million years ago, it was rain forest, strange little lizardlike creatures scurrying over its floor, dinosaurs devouring treetops and ferns and leaves, and small animals, the first mammals, roaming the dry land, pestered by newcomers, the insects."

"Louder, Jim." It was Freya Markus.

"If you keep going back, say another hundred and fifty million years, it's an antediluvian sea."

Narrow face under the striped cap chapped from the morning razor, blue eyes behind wire-rimmed glasses, in the same plaid quilted jackshirt he'd worn at the seminar, the geologist rocked on his heels on a tuff block near the rim. "A little mood music from *Fantasia*, somebody." He chuckled.

In the cool of the morning they huddled together in the amphitheater of the ruin's old plaza, hands up the sleeves of their sweatshirts for warmth, faces turned out to the landscape of snowcapped blue mountains and yellow plains. Just about everybody was there—students, volunteers, Tina, who waved to him, some of the campers from the upper canyon getting a little education on their vacation, the Indian lad, Horse, sitting off a way, glowering—everybody but Bobby Ybarra and the curly-headed boys and Rap Singleton.

The geologist settled the locomotive engineer's cap back on his head and turned up his collar against the morning breeze. "The top of the mesa we're standing on is basalt. It's what you see flowing down the sides of the volcano in Hawaii, covering houses, highways, towns. As lavas go, it's relatively safe because it doesn't often explode. In other words, we're standing on a hardened volcanic flow." He smiled again. Bit of a ham.

The students looked down at the mesa top underfoot as if they hadn't seen it every day all summer long.

"Basalt represents a quieter phase in an eruption. It's more fluid than lighter-colored flows." Voice thin in the open air. "You can walk on a cooling basalt crust while the red-hot lava runs like a sluggish river underneath. If you're careful not to fall in." Chuckle chuckle. He enjoyed lecturing. Probably a teacher.

"Basalt is a good building stone. San Francisco streets used to be paved with blocks of it. Ocean floors are covered with it because it rises from deep volcanic trenches and spreads out. Then what happens? The ocean widens as it rises. All that water has to go somewhere." He smiled, and the students smiled back. His wife smiled, too, off there with Freya Markus beside the kiva they were excavating. She really must like the guy.

So if Rap wasn't at the lecture, where the hell was he? Reuben himself was always on time. Waiting drove him up a wall. He climbed to the highest point on the promontory to get a better view of the road below. Maybe he should go back to the RV. Rap might give up and go off and leave him.

"The longest mountain range in the world—over forty thousand miles—is on the ocean floor."

The geologist's wife cleared her throat.

"Yeah, I know." He winked at the students. "I'm getting off the subject." He raised his voice. "It's a chain that forms the mid-Atlantic ridge, winding around the world, and it's all basalt. It breaks the surface in a few places. Iceland's one of the peaks." He smiled over at his wife like he'd gotten away with something. Watching the interplay, Jade nudged Pilar and said something out of the side of her mouth.

"You take the best-preserved petroglyphs in New Mexico are in basalt. It's a lot easier to carve them in tuff—you can do it with a stick—but they erode. The reason you can't excavate very deep here on the mesa top is because it's basalt. That could be why the Anasazi moved up from the cliff rooms in the first place. They'd have a floor paved by nature, that held the sun's heat in winter and never churned into mud when it rained or snowed. Over there—" he pointed "—and there, in those declivities they could catch rainwater. If you wanted to, you could wash your hair with yucca root soap without going down to the stream, heh heh.

"This kiva you've uncovered, they dug it in a spot where the basalt thinned. Probably broke through one day when somebody was pounding on a rock, breaking off chips to make a stone ax, something like that. They broke through the basalt and dug up blocks of it to use over there." He pointed.

They all turned to look at the base of what Freya Markus thought had been a tower at one corner of the ruin. She thought it had been used as a silo. You could see the thin basalt bricks fitted together at the bottom, the work of accomplished masons.

"That might give you some idea of when the kiva was

built," he said. "When did the Anasazi build those towers?"
He looked at Freya Markus.

"Fairly late," she said, "but of course the basalt could
have been thrown aside at an earlier period. Or first used
for something else, and then later become the base of the
tower."

The geologist stuck his hands in the pockets of the
quilted shirt and grunted. "Well, anyway. Below the basalt
they came upon tuff, the same tuff layer they'd dug the cliff
rooms out of, and they dug down in it for their kiva. Actually sculpted it. The walls are solid tuff, ideal for petroglyphs and paintings."

"Good Lord," said one of the campers, "dug out of solid
rock."

Clarity, wrapped up in a paisley shawl, murmured, "It
wasn't all *that* hard."

The students nudged each other, but the geologist smiled
at Clarity. "I see some of you know your geology. That's
right, it wasn't hard. Tuff's soft enough to carve. All it is
is consolidated volcanic ash. The rooms in the cliffside
weren't hard to dig out with stone axes, or even old
used-up scrapers." And he added for the sake of the campers, "Scrapers are chips of flint or obsidian, used to scrape
flesh off hides.

"But another good thing about tuff—though it's soft,
once it's exposed to the air it hardens. So once they'd dug
out their rooms they could expect them to last, and as you
can see, they were right. The kiva should have been fairly
easy to excavate."

Jade asked, "What do you make of that, you know, band
sort of running around the wall about two-thirds of the way
up from the floor?"

The geologist walked over to the ladder and let himself
down and looked inside. "I dunno," he said. "Whadaya
think?" He looked at Freya.

She hesitated as if making up her mind. "I think this kiva
started out as a pit house. First they dug down a couple of

feet in the tuff. The band you see probably marks the depth of the original floor."

The graduate students looked at Caspar, who smiled derisively.

But Clarity said, "That's exactly what happened."

Freya ignored her while the students nudged one another.

"And below the ring the wall's a bit concave," Freya went on. "They enlarged the room that way—about six inches all the way around—by digging a little farther into the tuff."

Clarity was nodding.

Caspar Dreyfus muttered loud enough for everybody to hear, "Whoever dug out the kiva probably came along centuries later."

"We'll find that out, won't we," Freya said sharply.

Maybe when they got the results of the carbon dating? These exchanges often left Reuben in the dark.

One crew had been excavating the kiva all summer, bringing up buckets of detritus and filling wheelbarrows to take to the screens. Undergraduates worked the screens all day, throwing shovelfuls at the mesh, pawing over anything too big to go through. And all day long Freya Markus kept going to the screens for an impatient look at the trays.

Jim Cochran walked back to the group. "If you think this kiva's something, in Anatolia there's a whole underground city carved down into tuff. Some of the buildings are seven stories deep. Now just follow me and we'll go down and get a view of the cliff face."

He went over the side by way of the long pole ladder, and one by one the students disappeared feet-first after him, Jade stepping daintily after Steve Many Hands, never losing a beat: "Oh, now I remember what it was . . . And oh wow, I said, chill out . . . And he goes . . ."

The little group of Earth Watch people avoided the ladders and set off down the trail that hairpinned back on itself—Duff and Wembley, the retired rancher from Calgary, who walked with a slight limp, followed by Clarity with more lives than a cat. They gathered again on the slope below, where the rooms in the cliff face were visible for a hundred yards and then hidden by a curve in the mesa.

The geologist stepped up on another stone block that had broken off from the cliff face and tumbled down. "Okay, now look up there where the basalt gives way to tuff." His body swiveled to follow his pointing finger. "As you can see, the tuff's all worn and vuggy."

By some acoustical freak Reuben on the mesa top heard every word. He looked at his Timex again. It was getting late. You could feel the sun.

" 'Vug' can mean several things, but in this case it means holes in the cliff eroded by wind and rain. The people enlarged some of them into rooms. They just improved on what nature had started. You'll find a lot of the smaller holes have been claimed by squatters—owls, mice, rats, maybe even a fox. 'Vug' comes from the Cornish word *vooga*. It means underground chamber or cavity." Now he was all business, treating the students to his erudition.

Reuben let himself down to sit on the edge of the cliff, feet dangling over the drop. This stuff was sort of interesting. He'd always just taken rocks for granted.

"A lot of the buildings in ancient Rome, including the Forum, were built out of blocks of tuff covered with marble veneer."

The geologist's wife cleared her throat.

Her better half chuckled. "Okay, so I'm off the subject again." He turned back to the cliff and pointed. "Up there under the basalt layer, where you see the top tier of rooms, the tuff is maybe twenty feet thick. In some places around here it's a hundred."

Pilar looked up and saw Reuben and waved. He waved back.

"When you have a chance, look at it up close. You'll see it has bubbly fragments of pumice in it. And here and there hard shards of volcanic glass, and even a few volcanic bombs."

The geologist waited. He wasn't disappointed. Pilar, twisting her fists in the bottom of a T-shirt with a hot-air balloon on the front of it, obligingly raised her small voice. "What's a volcanic bomb?"

"I thought you'd never ask. They're globs of molten lava thrown up by the volcano that hardened as they spun through the air. The people who lived here could dig them out of the tuff and use them as building stones, *metates*, baseballs . . ."

Everybody laughed, even Reuben sitting on the edge of the cliff. It was a great morning and he had a day in town to look forward to. Better get on back up the canyon to the RV. But still he sat there warmed by the sun, listening.

"Under a microscope volcanic ash looks like jacks, the kind you played with as kids."

The students looked blank. They'd never played jacks as kids.

Somebody was coming, crashing through the rabbit brush down the arroyo where Pelawi had disappeared. Reuben scrambled upright expecting to see Rap Singleton.

"That layer of rock under the tuff, the dark gray ledge that sticks out—the Anasazi used it as a sidewalk running along the cliff face in front of their rooms. That layer spewed out of the volcano as a white-hot avalanche known as a rain of fire. Any living thing in its path—trees, plants, animals—was instantly immolated."

The geologist's words faded behind Reuben as he leapt from rock to rock up the rise of the mesa in the direction of the sound, which came from the arroyo below. It was either a person or a large animal, maybe a cow or a bear, crashing through the scrub, but each time he stopped and tried to see, the landscape below was an innocent mix of piñon and juniper and sandy earth.

He ran farther along the cliff top, then held up short at the cliff edge, panting, looking down. Then screams shattered the morning. Below him Beano Shippers—that red hair—ran stumbling, looking over her shoulder like something was after her, her trail marked by a dropped towel, a

wadded washcloth, and . . . maybe a plastic soap dish. Her
screams bounced off the canyon walls and echoed.

On top of the cliff Reuben leapt along with her, down
frozen tides of basalt, trying to see over his shoulder up the
little side canyon she'd descended. Nothing came after her,
no bobcat, no bear. She ran into the arms of the geologist,
who had come to meet her, the others in close pursuit.

"Whoa," he said, "hold on there, Red."

She burrowed her face in his plaid jackshirt and pointed
back the way she'd come. Something was dead back there,
she cried.

Sick at heart, Reuben looked back up the little tributary
canyon. She had to be talking about his owl.

7

"So, okay, let's go over it again. What were you doing
up there, son?"

"Like I told you, I was looking for him." Over at the
sombra Lily and Pete were serving coffee, but Reuben
hadn't even had lunch.

"He was giving you a ride into town, right?"

He nodded. "We were supposed to leave at eight, but he
didn't show." Where was Tina? He felt abandoned. Why
didn't somebody bring him a taco or something?

"He tell you what he was doing up on the mesa?"

The federal marshal had gray hair—clipped so close, he
looked like he'd been streamlined for wind resistance—
high cheekbones, vinegar-colored eyes, and several slick,
roundish scars on his face, one that made his nose thinner
than nature ever intended. Skin cancers, removed, Reuben

guessed. Too many years in this high-country sun. "He mentioned from the mesa top you could get the big picture."

They were sitting across from each other at the redwood table in the shelter.

"What was he looking for?"

"How would I know? He had this metal detector. He was always sweeping the ground with this metal detector."

"But he didn't have it with him this morning."

Reuben shrugged. Rap must have got carried away and stepped too close to the edge of the cliff. Why did he feel angry at the old man? Because he'd stood him up? That was totally unreasonable.

"You were up there but you didn't look down and see the body in the arroyo?"

"I didn't get back that far." The way his voice climbed, he sounded like he was defending himself against some unjust accusation. Christ, what *was* this anyway?

There she was, down by the stream with a paper plate on her lap and a cup on a rock beside her. He waved, trying to get her attention.

"And you didn't hear anything?" The marshal got up and walked to the front of the shelter and looked around—trying, Reuben thought, to see who he'd waved at. The marshal's name was Tom Hurleigh and he had on brown cord knickers, probably the kind that laced over his calves underneath the high lace-up boots so scratched and scarred they looked like World War One cavalry surplus. But the soles were clearly new, you could see that from the yellow edges. The marshal's feet were incredibly long, like maybe narrow size fourteens.

"I *told* you," Reuben said. "I heard Shippers. Of course, I didn't know then it was Shippers. I heard *something* and it turned out later to be Shippers." Why did he feel he had to be incredibly clear about everything?

The marshal had been questioning them one by one for a couple of hours now. This was Reuben's second time around. Freya Markus had called the BLM office in Santa

Fe on the field telephone and luckily found the marshal in. He'd come right out in his Ford four-by spattered with mud hard and dry. Took him less than an hour.

Tina glanced up at the shelter. Reuben waved. "Save me some food!"

Tina stood up mouthing, *What?* The marshal looked at him. "Food!" He pointed to his open mouth, and she nodded, Oh.

"And some coffee!" he yelled. He smiled at the marshal. "We'll ask her to bring you some, too. Sir," he added when the marshal didn't smile back.

And all that time Rap's body had lain there with the sun getting hotter.

After the marshal squatted beside it for some time, and went through the pockets, and swiveled on the balls of his feet to look up at the cliff, he called his office on his vehicle's radio. It was another hour before the ambulance got there and picked up the body to take to the medical examiner's office in Albuquerque. By then the day had become a scorcher.

"You'd been friendly with the victim?"

"Yeah, sort of." Victim of what? Either the marshal liked official jargon or he suspected foul play. But that was silly. Everybody liked Rap. Maybe he meant as in accident victim. The marshal was looking at him. He felt singled out. He squirmed on the picnic table bench, aware of people in the meadow going about their business but glancing up now and then at the shelter.

Rap had fallen over the cliff back up the little tributary canyon where, it turned out, at the very start of the dig Shippers had discovered a hot spring and kept it to herself, holding out on all of them. Christ, he'd love to bathe right now in a hot spring. He was exhausted by the whole thing. He saw the body again, head at an awful angle, skull crushed, one eye open and somehow accusing, the other popped out on his cheek by the fall.

He shuddered like he was cold, but he wasn't. If anything, he felt like he was running a fever. "You might say he was my closest neighbor," he said. "His camper was just around the bend in the stream from my tent. Some nights I'd go down and shoot the breeze with him." And watching Tina join the line at the *sombra*, he told about the tile rummy and the Loners on Wheels.

"He ever find anything with the metal detector?"

"Yeah, I guess. He told me some things. One time a 1914 silver dollar down in Florida, and some antique barbed wire up in Montana."

"I mean anything around here."

"I think he found something yesterday."

"You think?"

"I asked him if he'd had any luck, and he patted his pocket and winked, very secretive."

"What'd he have on?"

"The jacket he always wore."

"One we found him in?"

"Yeah." Again he saw Rap lying there at the foot of the cliff, the gold earring glinting in the sun.

"Nothing in his pockets except a half-empty pack of Marlboros and some kitchen matches," the marshal said, then avoided Reuben's eyes like maybe he shouldn't have told him that. He tipped down the toe of his long thin boot over the edge of the shelter's concrete floor and slid it along, absentmindedly. The flannel shirt was buttoned all the way to his throat. You'd think he'd be getting warm.

"I guess he took it out of his pocket, whatever it was," Reuben said. "Must be in his camper."

"Ever been in his camper?"

Reuben nodded. "Sometimes he'd make coffee." Awful coffee, too. He glanced toward Tina.

Up the road came an Indian guy bareback on a horse with a spotted rump, leading three saddled ponies. Shirtless, in jeans and a cowboy hat, he came slowly up the rising road, looking around, taking in the meadow, long black hair loose down his back.

Rap was—had been—a screwup, no doubt about it. Murray, Reuben's father, had been a loser, too, always at the races, always shooting you some bull about how he was going to make it big. Well, he never did, did he or maybe his kid could have gone to art school without working his tail off at night jobs he hated, where he had to take shit from any bastard willing to dish it out. And then outed himself on the Long Island Expressway, carelessness and a couple of beers, nobody's fault but his own, and left them to the charity of his uncle Jake, who thought art school was for "fairies." Jake's word, not Reuben's. Reuben's best friend from the neighborhood was gay. Jake had himself a field day out of that one.

"Okay," Tom Hurleigh said. "When I've finished here we'll go down and have a look."

"At the camper?"

The marshal nodded.

Reuben felt a strong reluctance. "I was only inside a couple of times. You'll never find anything in there. It's a royal mess. Rap was a slob." Christ, what is this all about? Didn't Rap just get careless and fall off the cliff? And why keep at *him*? He wasn't the only one up on the mesa at dawn, which was roughly fixed as the time of death. Had the marshal grilled Freya Markus? He remembered the scream he'd heard. But that may have been in his dream.

"See anybody else up there that early?" The marshal rocked on the balls of his long feet with his hands in his brown cord pockets.

But before Reuben, thinking of Bird Boy and Freya Markus, could decide how to answer, a ruckus broke out up by the picnic tables, and the marshal swung around to see what was going on. Reuben slid to the end of the bench and looked. Just the curly-headed twosome wrestling in the middle of a ring of students cheering them on. Reuben sighed. If they weren't competing on their mountain bikes or in diving contests, it was over one of the women.

Steve Many Hands waded in and broke it up. And the Indian lollygagged up the road toward them bareback, the other horses bunched up behind him, taking his time, surveying the meadow, watching everything.

In canvas shorts too big for her and a T-shirt cut off below her breasts, disclosing her tan midriff, Tina came toward them barefoot across the grass. The marshal watched with approval. In one hand she carried a paper plate sagging under the weight of a burrito smothered in green chili, and in the other a Styrofoam cup of coffee.

On an expansive impulse fueled by the thought of food, Reuben said, "You remember I told you about the owl?"

The marshal nodded.

So watching the Indian approach with the horses, Reuben told him about the moonlight runner. He was frowning, concentrating, trying to see again the pale road threading through the trees, and the figure running. "And he seemed to be naked. But I could have been mistaken. The moonlight was throwing shadows."

"Is that a fact."

It wasn't a question. Reuben looked up. He'd been about to launch into the tale of Pelawi. But the whisky-colored eyes were appraising him closely, and he knew he'd made a mistake to mention the naked runner in the moonlight, something he hadn't mentioned earlier. He felt himself shrink about a foot.

Tina walked up smiling, but now the burrito looked like a soggy mess congealing in green sauce. He'd lost his appetite. Christ, why couldn't he keep his mouth shut?

8

A scout in disguise, John entered the enemy camp. Shirtless, in jeans and moccasins, he tipped his big white Stetson over his face and viewed the meadow from the shadow of its brim. The thrill he felt shortened his breath. This close to them he wanted to giggle. With the binoculars, he'd seen their lips moving, like on television with the sound off. It was strange to hear their voices.

At the least hint of danger, the hair on his arms always stood up like the hackles on a dog and he could feel it. He felt it now, rising of its own accord and moving in the air coming down the chute of the canyon. The Appaloosa wanted to trot, but he held it in. At the sight of strangers, the horses behind him bunched and snorted, trying to come alongside. He slapped the halter ropes against their cheeks. They were restless and out of humor. Below in the sun John had made them gallop. Now in the cool of the canyon, perversely he made them walk. It didn't make horse sense and they knew it.

In training or not, John wished he'd put on his shirt. He felt exposed. His jeans slid on the pony's lathered sides. He rode bareback like a proper Indian, and his moccasins hung toe-down toward the road.

All here. Up ahead, the federal marshal's four-by. He'd seen it sometimes from afar when on his own he'd monitored alien traffic on this land. They didn't know it, but he did little favors like that for the Indians. It was whispered that soon once again all this would be Indian land.

He slumped on the pony's back. Its muscles moved pleasantly under his thighs. The brim of the Stetson hid his face. His heart beat time to the pony's rhythm. Fear ran pleasantly over him like wind on water. He'd all his life sought danger—shoplifting as a kid, or dodging truck traffic to get to the other side of a highway where he had no reason to want to be, leaping over voids, snatching some old lady's purse that he knew held nothing but pennies and running off with it.

He waited to be noticed, questioned. He was ready for them: he was delivering the neighbor's horses to some guys named William and Joe camping in the upper canyon. But nobody looked at him or spoke.

He felt smug. It was like hiding in sight of everybody.

Then suddenly he felt an existential alarm. Sometimes when nobody noticed his existence, it was like he was invisible. If nobody saw him maybe he wasn't there. Rocking in rhythm to his pony's quickened gait, he studied the kitchen *sombra* where they were eating, talking, unaware he even existed.

He knew them all—Big Tit talking with her hands—not that she had big tits, he couldn't tell, but she was boss lady, and by nature he took against bosses on sight—Flower Girl with her mouth always working, Pumpkin Face with hair that matched, looked like it'd been cut with a machete, and up there in the shelter with the marshal the one looked like pictures of that bastard Coronado. He'd hated The Beard on sight, the way he moved, the way he sat there all sprawled out at the picnic table so cocksure of himself, it made John want to puke. He spit aside in the road. He could tell the marshal a thing or two if he wanted to. He didn't want to.

The giggle came again, this time out loud, and his pony swiveled its ears to listen. He knew you better watch out when a pony swiveled its ears like that. It could be a sign he'd buck. The neighbor's horses on halter ropes crowded up behind him, and sure enough the Appaloosa struck out with both hind legs and clipped one of them on the chin and it jerked its head up and screamed, nearly lifting John off the spotted back. He yelled, "Ho there!" showing off, and yanked the horses' heads down with the halter ropes.

Now they were looking. The whole meadow, it seemed like, turned and looked at him. He felt wildly gratified. He wanted to laugh but kept his composure. As far as they were concerned, he was already the Indian he wanted to be. He could tell by the way they looked at him, some looking right through him like they did all Indians, others admiring, envying him bareback on a horse, at one with nature—long hair, moccasins. He grinned.

For a number of years now—half of his life if you cared to count—he'd identified with the richly colored races. He'd been Italian, Greek, and Jew, Mexican, black. This present experiment was the last of a series originally designed to turn the tables on Isaiah Hoop. But those days of tent shows and revivals were behind him, though sometimes in John's sleep Isaiah still ranted in the torchlight about the Jews and blacks taking over God's noble white race, which was clearly meant to rule and get all the perks.

Curled up like a cur, trying to sleep on a ragged quilt underneath the altar, which was nothing more than a kitchen table with a sheet tacked around it to make it look substantial, John had very young decided he must be one of those Isaiah Hoop despised. But according to Isaiah they would soon be running things, right? And if they were running things, they'd also be running Isaiah Hoop.

Later, in white robes and white wing tips too big for him, as child evangelist he'd ranted a little himself, really got into it, women rolling on the ground, touching the hem of his garment, speaking in tongues. When he outgrew that role, Isaiah put him to parking cars in the stubble fields where he raised his revival tent outside dinky southern towns.

One good thing, John always turned a rich color in the summer sun. Old Eliseo didn't mind him baking on the flat pueblo roof so long as he wore a little something. He'd lie up there behind the fire wall and turn himself like barbecue on a spit. What worried him was, under his jock shorts his skin was as smooth and white as a slug. So what if nobody knew it? *He* knew it. So on the ledge outside of his secret place, he'd set himself to remedy that. Screw Eliseo. He'd strip and turn himself black all over. He had the certain feeling that when that happened he would be complete.

There she was, up ahead, sun glancing off all that dark red hair shot with gold. She was crossing the road with a roll of toilet paper in her hand, heading for the privy. His heart leapt in his breast, but he quieted it. *Puta*. Whore. It was all he could do to breathe. Prod his pony to a gallop, he could scoop her up and make off with her like Zorro. And then he would either rub her out or climb on top of her, he wasn't sure which.

Isaiah Hoop whispered scornfully in his ear: You're just

like a dog chasing a car. If you caught it you wouldn't know what to do with it.

Shut your mouth, John told him. He watched from under his hat brim till the redhead went inside.

Pumpkin Face with the chopped-off hair dyed the color of orange Nehi came up and walked alongside his pony, stroking its neck. "What's his name?" she asked.

He didn't know his name. "Chico," he said.

"Little boy," she murmured. "That's sweet."

Sweet, shit. But he smiled. You never know when you might could use somebody.

"Where you going with the horses?" She was keeping up with his pony.

He looked at the shelter up ahead, and the federal marshal looked absently back down the road at him. John tipped the brim of his Stetson hat lower over his face. He threw a look toward the privy.

"I'm taking them up the canyon," he said. "Some campers want to play horsey."

"What's your name?" she said. "I'm Pilar."

"Yeah?" He looked down at her. "You like horses?"

"I sure do."

Chunky little thing in dirty shorts. "I'm John." He smiled and showed his teeth. Through no fault of his own, John had nice teeth. "Maybe we'll go for a ride sometime," he added.

Her face lit up. "Are you from the pueblo?"

He felt like laughing. She thought he was Indian already. "Sure," he said. "I live down there."

"Okay. I'll go with you sometime."

Maybe you will, he thought.

Up ahead in the shelter, the marshal turned away and said something to Blue Beard. Red Hair came out of the privy. John put his heel to the spotted pony's ribs. The horses broke into an eager trot.

But before he could reach her and get a good look, she swung off across the grass toward the stream at the foot of the meadow. Somebody waved to her. He thought they called her Jippers. What kind of a name was that?

9

Standing at the edge of the shelter with his thumbs in his belt loops, Tom Hurleigh looked out across the meadow at a hawk circling treetops on the mountainside. The body was already stiff when he got there. So what did that mean about the time of death? Around dawn was just a guess. Federal marshals didn't have much traffic with bodies anymore. Time was, they had plenty, back when they made sixty cents a day chasing desperadoes all over the dry lands of the West.

It was clear somebody wanted these people out of here. Until now, whoever it was hadn't wanted it bad enough to cause any real harm. The fire in the upper canyon had been set all right, but on an island of dead trees in the middle of a marsh. It couldn't have gone anywhere without the help of a high wind. It was just a scare tactic—though fires in canyons could be dangerous, they could trap people, no way out.

And the snakes. They could have bred naturally in the ruin, but he doubted it. And if somebody had really meant harm, the snakes would have been rattlers, not just baby bull snakes that looked like rattlers. Could've been a prank—some of the fellows on the dig scaring the women for the hell of it.

Harmless fire, harmless snakes. But this was a different can of worms.

He'd phoned in the prelim report, interviewed the archaeology people. Should he get some help out here to set up some roadblocks and seal off the canyon? Some of the sheriff's men? Or maybe Tito, Lieutenant Gonzales of the Santa Fe police? He'd worked with Gonzales before.

But nothing said you had to come in by way of the road. Hell, you could come in over the mountain, or over the backside of the mesa, up from Indian Land. Or you could sneak in the front way, off the road and through the sage at night. And of course the guilty party could have vamoosed before the marshal even got to the canyon.

But if he sealed off the road, at least there'd be no campers coming in. The upper meadow had emptied out this morning before the body was discovered. The only campers left were the two kids on their way home from the college in Socorro. He had opened the registration box to get the other campers' names and addresses, and the state police would follow up, watching for license plates on RVs and pickups, trying home addresses. But if you came to the canyon planning to commit a murder, why would you put your name in the registration box? Still, it could have been unpremeditated.

He'd examined the body and the ground around it and the places where it had crushed chemiso in its fall. All he'd found was the red cover of a little spiral notebook maybe three inches wide by five inches high. No sign of the notebook itself. Maybe it had nothing to do with the body. One of the students could have dropped it. He'd put it in a Ziploc bag from his lunch box—there might be fingerprints. Not that it was likely to match any they had on file, but maybe it'd match the corpse's.

Andrew Rappaport Singleton—the name on the camper's California vehicle registration. What did anybody know of the old man? A loner who belonged to a group by the same name, a man who traveled year-round from one end of the continent to another, passing the time with a metal detector and dreaming of striking it rich, a stranger to everybody in the canyon until a week or ten days ago. He couldn't think why anybody would want to kill him.

His mind kept veering to Freya Markus. Tall woman. Pretty. No, not pretty. The marshal hadn't an extensive vocabulary for describing women's looks. He tried *handsome*, but that didn't seem right for a female. Okay, good-looking, if you liked the type. His own wife had been a little thing in flowered aprons and he'd doted on her. Freya Markus was the one in charge, but he'd made the mistake of thinking it was the guy in glasses, who turned out to be a visiting geologist.

The marshal sighed and his mouth ruffled out like a baby's blowing bubbles. So she no doubt had him down as a male chauvinist pig. Pig, maybe—he'd lived alone going on five years now. But chauvinist? He didn't think so. She'd been waiting impatiently when he and the geologist got back from a walkabout, inspecting the site. He'd got her to post a couple of students and see that nobody went near it. He hated the idea of dealing with a body. His business was boundary laws, rights, government litigation.

He'd spent hours now questioning.

The Earth Watch people:

He had difficulty suspecting women of violent acts, so when they were concerned, to guard against his own inclinations he forced himself to consider them first. Two had arrived together from New England. Both in their sixties. Shared one of those small Winnebagos. The short one—Wormley? Wombley? Wembley. Right. And the tall one—Duff, they called her. They'd been heard by the space case Clarity Higgins arguing just before sunup about what to have for breakfast, and their stories matched hers. He'd questioned them separately, and both had mentioned the argument. They'd settled on waffles—with syrup, Wembley added. This was their third Earth Watch *adventure*—they'd both called it that—the first two to Central America, where they'd heard of Freya Markus. It was those tales that brought them to New Mexico. And they had not been disappointed. *Fascinating* woman. And so *approachable*.

He hadn't found that to be the case. She struck him as of two minds—one dealing easily with whatever was going on, the other, far more concentrated, engaged in its own pursuits.

Clarity Higgins. Always up at dawn because, she said, that was the best time for meditation as the earth vibrations were right. Slept in the camper on back of her truck. Gave anybody who asked a "past life" reading around her campfire. She'd heard running footsteps on the road sometime in the night. That would have been this fellow Reuben— chasing an owl, he said. She swore she'd not actually seen anything stirring until Pete Jaramillo started the breakfast fires.

The Canadian, Carmack McIntyre. Retired rancher. Very standoffish. Little to do with anybody, though people seemed to like him. Grieving the death of his wife, they said. That would be a good story if you had reason to want to be left to yourself. The marshal knew all about grieving the death of a wife. How did a rancher retire? What happened to the ranch? Did it go to sons? Had he sold it? What was his interest in this particular archaeological dig? Claimed he'd picked it at random—anything to get away from where he'd lived all his life. Very closemouthed. Answered questions in monosyllables: yes, no. This was his first Earth Watch venture, whereas the others had punished themselves this way before.

The students all seemed to be legit. He'd have them checked out. When they signed up for the summer dig, none of them had any way of knowing exactly where in the Southwest the dig would be. So their reasons for being here seemed strictly for credits toward graduation or an advanced degree.

The Jaramillos had lived in Española all their lives, fought and made up, fought and made up. Otherwise their reputations were good.

The artists. Tina Martinez had been recommended by the Tsorigi because she was part of the tribe. Though she lived in Santa Fe, she was frequently at the pueblo to visit her mother. She had apparently joined the dig team reluctantly.

Reuben Rubin. Was somebody being funny? The marshal

sounded the name in his head. Roobin-Roobin. And grunted. Reuben Rubin had been urged upon Freya Markus by Tina Martinez. He was the only one up on the mesa last night, the only one who had any kind of relationship with Rap Singleton, the only one to have been inside the old man's camper. What was he doing on the mesa last night? Owls? Naked runners in the moonlight? The marshal grunted again.

What kind of a name was that anyway? Roobin-Roobin, I been thinking . . . A nursery-rhyme name. The marshal didn't trust boys with beards.

He was tempted to write the whole thing off as an accident except there were things that didn't figure. One of them, what he'd found on the mesa top. He'd spent an hour poking around up there waiting for the ambulance to come out from Santa Fe. Another was what the geologist had told him. "The old man had a big unpolished diamond in a leather pouch. He showed it to me last night, wanting verification. Several people saw it. I asked him where he'd found it, but you know how those fellows are."

What fellows? But Tom Hurleigh had kept his mouth shut. You could find out a lot that way. Some people had to fill up a silence.

"Tight as clams when it comes to their finds," the geologist said. "A diamond in the rough just looks like tumbled glass. Scarred, opaque. But this was a diamond all right, pretty good-size one, too." The geologist shook his head. "Poor fellow." He smiled. "He'd heard diamonds are so hard you can't break them. He was thinking of testing it with a hammer when he decided to show it to me. I told him he'd've destroyed it if he had. They're hard all right, but they break. How else could we facet them?"

"Said he found it around here? Yesterday?"

"That's what he said."

That he'd found something matched the artist's story.

"Thought he'd found a diamond mine or something?"

The geologist chuckled. "Could have thought that, but it must have been brought in from somewhere else. This isn't diamond country. Far from it. There are diamonds in Arkansas, California. But the Anasazi picked up all kinds of trinkets in trade."

"Can you find a diamond with a metal detector?"

"Nope."

"What was he looking for this morning on top of the mesa?"

The geologist shook his head. "Damn if I know."

What the marshal had found on top of the cliff, all along the edge, were prints that clearly matched Rappaport Singleton's worn western boots. And places where he'd squatted on his heels, looking over the drop and smoking. There were plenty of cigarette butts and discarded kitchen matches. And other tracks that matched this Reuben fellow's Nikes, but he hadn't been able to trace those as far back as the fall site, though that meant nothing because the trail back there was mostly rock.

But it was what he'd seen at the fall site at the edge of the cliff that raised the most questions: along with Rap Singleton's boot prints, a hurried swipe in the sand like somebody had dragged a piñon branch to wipe out marks of some kind, and overlapping that, these peculiar prints, almost like bare feet, but smoother, muffled, deformed-looking, only the big toe clear, the others merged and rounded like a soft hoof. At first he'd thought some kind of an animal. But this animal appeared to walk upright.

He hadn't known what they were until he stood there in the shelter watching the Indian kid ride bareback up the canyon with the horses. Absently watching him approach, turning over what the artist had said, it didn't strike the marshal right away but registered like an afterimage.

Goddam son of a bitch, it was moccasins. They were the prints of moccasins. If the Indians were involved, this poor bastard of a federal marshal was looking at real trouble.

10

"What makes you think it's a tektite?" Jim Cochran asked.

"Oh, come on," his wife said. "I lectured about them in my 300 course, I took students through the museum."

Reuben sat quietly at the picnic table outside Rap's camper while the two geologists argued about one of the black rocks, passing it back and forth. They were waiting for the marshal.

"I'm sure there's a less romantic solution."

His wife said, "How can you be so exasperating?"

"It's just some kind of natural glass."

"Well, aren't tektites natural glass? That's why Darwin thought they were volcanic—because they *look* like volcanic *bomba*."

Freya's Cherokee pulled off on the shoulder of the road and she got out with her hands full of paper sacks. She opened them one by one and dumped more of the rocks on the table. "We've found seven so far," she said.

Bess Cochran picked one up. "This one looks like an egg. And look at these. A club and a teardrop. They're usually found in strewn fields, and they're often given some kind of special significance. They put you in touch with the gods, or they reconcile energies, things like that."

"Or remove your warts," her husband scoffed.

When the women ignored him, it looked to Reuben like the geologist fell into a pout.

"Are you saying the Anasazi picked them up and attributed some value to them we don't know about?" Freya asked.

Bess Cochran nodded. "All we have to do is locate the strewn field and we'll find some more."

"Sure," Jim Cochran said scornfully. "And I guess a depression, too. And if you don't find it, you'll say that's because it's long since filled in."

His wife snapped, "That's logical, isn't it?"

"Circular, right?" Her husband laughed.

"Usually." His wife sounded defensive. "But maybe elliptical."

It was subtle but it was definitely a squabble. The fights in Reuben's family had been over things like who didn't wash the ring out of the bathtub. But as the argument went on, he decided it wasn't really about the rocks. Just like the students, these two university professors were competing for Freya's approval. He studied Freya Markus. She wasn't seductive. She seemed to regard everybody in about the same way. And she was unaware of the effect she had. It's true she looked you dead in the eye when she talked to you, and she had a great laugh. But was that an explanation?

"I haven't a clue what you two are talking about," she said.

Neither did Reuben. Where was the marshal anyway? He eased up off the bench and slid a hand under a bun. He'd sat on some pine resin and his jeans were stuck to the bench.

Bess Cochran turned to Freya. "What do you know about asteroids?"

Freya shrugged. "Nowadays you hear it'd be a disaster if a big one struck the earth."

"Yeah," Jim Cochran said. "Especially if it hit the ocean. If it hits cold water, it'll throw up a steam cloud and we'd have nuclear winter." He chuckled, shaking his head. "The stuff they come up with."

But Bess Cochran was nodding. "Just such a nuclear winter may have been what killed the dinosaurs."

Jim Cochran muttered, "Aw hell, Bess."

"Well, why not?" his wife demanded.

"Because actually they died of mass epidemics when the tectonic plates rammed together and exposed all of them to alien bacteria."

"Just another theory." His wife turned away from him with an exasperated look. She prodded Freya's arm. "Okay, I'll give you a quick rundown. Meteors. Asteroids. They're the same except asteroids are called meteors when they impact Earth. They come from outer space. They were born with the solar system and remain unchanged to this day. They fall through space at about twenty-five miles per *second*, collecting nose cones of ionized air that swell and burn brilliantly. They're the shooting stars you see at night. They're thought to come from the asteroid belt, which is why they're called asteroids, obviously. The asteroid belt formed between Mars and Jupiter about the same time as Earth. It's a hundred seventy-five million miles broad and fifty million miles thick." She looked at Reuben as if pleased with her mini lecture, and he felt he ought to respond.

"Wow," he murmured.

Satisfied, she turned to Freya. "Know anything about Bode's Law?"

"Should I?"

Jim Cochran chuckled, shaking his head, but his wife ignored him. "A German astronomer named Bode," she said, "came up with a formula for the distances of the planets from the sun. At that time only six planets were known— Mercury, Venus, Earth, Mars, Jupiter, Saturn," counting them off on her fingers. "But when Herschel discovered Uranus, according to Bode's Law it was right where it was supposed to be."

"Heavens," Freya Markus said, as if she, too, thought she had to say something.

Bess Cochran pounced on that. "Right! But according to Bode's formula, there would have been one more planet still. It should have been between Mars and Jupiter. So if

Bode was right, what happened to it? Apparently a catastrophe exploded the missing planet into billions of fragments."

"Voilà!" Jim Cochran threw up his hands. "The asteroid belt." Clearly ridiculing both Bode's Law and his wife.

"Fascinating," Freya muttered, looking from one geologist to the other, bemused, Reuben thought, by the interaction.

Jim Cochran said as if speaking to children, "Another theory is that the matter that formed the other planets coagulated into asteroids between Mars and Jupiter because Jupiter was so big, its gravitational pull kept them from forming into a planet."

His wife ignored his patronizing tone and bent over the table to Freya as if physically blocking off her husband. "According to that theory, the asteroid belt is a stillborn planet," she said, taking over her husband's idea, too. "The iron tools they've found in Stone Age sites were made from fragments of asteroids," she added.

"Iron meteorites probably come from the cores of asteroids exposed by impact," Jim Cochran said, getting back into the discussion any way he could since opting out of it hadn't worked. Reuben wanted to laugh. "They can travel out there hundreds of millions of years," Cochran said soberly, "before hitting the earth."

Bored, Reuben was watching the beaver lodge again.

Freya Markus weighed the rock in her hand. "Then am I holding in my hand part of the missing planet?"

"No," Bess Cochran said. "That's not an asteroid. I think it's a tektite."

"So we're back to the tektites. Okay, I give up. What's a tektite, an asteroid fragment?"

"That's a common view," Bess Cochran said, "but they're not similar to any known asteroid."

"Or to any Earth rock either," her husband put in.

"So what the devil are these things?" Freya was sounding impatient. Reuben's attention returned.

Bess Cochran said, "I think—along with a lot of other people—" she glanced at Jim Cochran "—that tektites are pieces of earth rock blown sky-high by a meteor impact and melted together with meteorite fragments." She sat back and dropped her hands to her lap. "They're sculpted into these odd shapes as they spin cooling through the air."

Freya Markus looked bewildered. "Does finding them in the ruin mean an asteroid struck somewhere around here?"

Bess Cochran nodded. "But that would make it a meteor, wouldn't it."

"And the Anasazi collected the tektites resulting from the impact?"

Jim Cochran shrugged as if washing his hands of the matter.

"One or two, they might have traded for," Bess Cochran said. "But here we've got—" she counted rapidly "—seven already, and there'll probably be more."

Cochran tossed one of the little rocks in the air and caught it. "The old guy could have found *that* with his metal detector. There's enough nickel and iron in it."

Freya reached out and took it away from him.

The retired rancher from Calgary stepped around the side of Rap's camper. Surprised, they all turned and looked at him. "Asteroids are precious sources of knowledge," he said, his face flushed as if he were angry.

Jim Cochran laughed like something was funny. "What are you, a closet geologist or something?"

The man from Calgary smiled, a small man, always clean and polite. "I was an undergraduate in earth sciences, but I had to go home and run the ranch. I've tried to keep up." He scratched a raw red rash on the back of his right hand, moving toward them with his slightly rolling gait. "Carmack McIntyre," he said. He put out his left hand and Bess Cochran shook it. The Canadian shook Jim Cochran's hand, too. It looked like an afterthought. Freya Markus was slipping the black rocks back in the paper bags.

"But only a very small percentage of them could conceivably come from the asteroid belt," the Canadian said.

"How do you figure that?" Jim Cochran asked.

Carmack McIntyre ignored him. "The conclusion is inescapable that most come from elsewhere, and are misnamed 'asteroids.' "

"Well, now," Jim Cochran said, watching his wife. She was smiling at the little man and tucking a strand of hair back behind her ear. "What're we talking about here? Some mysterious something going on in the sky?"

The rancher didn't look at him. "They're more valuable than you know," he said softly to Bess Cochran. His hair was a sandy gray. His eyes looked watery, like he was about to cry, but they always looked that way.

Here, Reuben thought, was another interesting interplay. Clearly the little guy and the geologist's wife *liked* each other.

Freya's eyebrows shot up. "Are they?"

"We know how valuable they are," Jim Cochran said. "Meteor pirates break them up and sell the pieces for a lot of money."

"Who to?" Freya asked, gathering up her paper bags.

Jim Cochran said, "Scientists want them, museums want them, collectors . . . These New Age folks want them for all kinds of nonsense."

"Healing," Bess said, "or psychic predictions, astrological forecasts . . ."

Jim Cochran laughed. "They can cure your cold, scare away ghosts, remove your warts and bunions . . ."

"They have the power to tell us things we've never imagined," Carmack McIntyre said softly, his eyes still on the geologist's wife. "They ought to be left in the earth till technology advances enough to unlock their secrets."

Bess Cochran looked at him with tender pity. "You may be right," she said softly, like saying, "There, there" to an upset child.

Calmer, he said with an air of mystery, "Why do you think they travel in clusters?"

Jim Cochran scoffed. "They don't. If you see a bunch of them traveling together across the sky, it's because a big one broke up."

McIntyre ignored him. "And why do they always like to land in deserts?"

"They don't *like* to land anywhere," Jim Cochran said. "When they land in deserts you can *see* them. Land in a forest, they're pretty much lost."

"What do *you* think?" McIntyre asked Bess Cochran.

She said soothingly, reluctantly, "I think Jim's right."

The retired rancher flushed and looked down, scratching his rash.

The sound of a motor neared. They all looked up the road. The marshal's four-by rounded the bend and pulled off on the grass. Tom Hurleigh got out and approached, rifling through a bunch of keys. Freya Markus gathered up her rocks and headed for her Cherokee.

Bent over Rap's door lock, which was giving him trouble, out of the corner of his eye the marshal watched her go. He'd had it all fixed up what he would say to her. Miss Markus—Freya—I thought maybe the two of us ... sit down over coffee and go over this thing ... value your perspective. Something like that. Then he could make it seem businesslike, maybe ask more about where she'd been at the time of ...

No, that wouldn't do because then she'd think ...

But the Cherokee pulled away in a cloud of dust, the key turned, and the marshal stepped inside. The camper was a mess, bed hadn't been made, half-filled coffee cup on the table. A little desk, hinged to the wall and standing on two legs, was ringed with coffee stains and littered with papers and catalogues. A deck of cards was laid out for solitaire. And weighted down by a rock, a windowed envelope that appeared to be a bank statement. Finding the diamond in this mess would be unlikely.

He beckoned to Reuben, and Reuben reluctantly, taking his time, shoved past Jim Cochran and the retired rancher and climbed in the door.

"Okay," Tom Hurleigh said, "take a good look. See anything out of the ordinary?"

Reuben shrugged. He'd avoided thinking much about

Rap, but standing there under the low ceiling, surrounded by the old man's things, it came bearing down on him—how Rap had been enjoying life, traveling around, being a Loner and doing the two-step with the ladies at their winter dances. Seventy-two but looked ten years younger. Full of life, lots of mileage left in him.

The dark wood paneling drew the space in on you. It was claustrophobic. Suddenly he wanted out of there. But he planted his feet and shook his head to clear it. It was the least he could do for Rap. "The times I was in here it was pretty much a mess." Reuben himself had always been fastidious and kept his space in order. His mother bragged about him to her friends.

"Take your time," the marshal said. "Look around. Is that where he usually kept his metal detector?" The handle stuck out of the space over the cab probably intended for a kid's bed. Whatever he was doing on top of the mesa that early morning, he hadn't been sweeping the ground with it.

"I guess so," Reuben said. "Yeah." He walked over and touched it. "And that's his magnet. He carried it stuck in his belt." It hung from a nail on the wall.

"So if his detector detected anything small and metal, like a coin, the magnet would find it for him," the geologist said with his foot propped up on the step and his head stuck in the door.

"Yeah," Reuben said. "He always had it with him, that and his compass."

Tom Hurleigh went through the drawers one at a time, rifling through socks and underwear and kitchen utensils. He got down on his knees and went over the floor with his hands, lifted the mattress off the bunk and looked under it, stepped up on the windowsill and went through the bunk over the cab. He removed the stove burners and looked under them, went through the pots and pans, and lastly opened the door to the minimal bath.

Unexpectedly, it was neat. Obviously Rap had used it as a closet. A pair of sneakers and a pair of winter boots stood side by side on the shower floor, and from a bungee cord strung from the showerhead to a screw head in the opposite wall hung three jackets—a nylon windbreaker, a down parka, and a natty tweed sport coat, orange and green. And still clothespinned to the bungee cord, where Rap had rinsed them out and hung them up to dry, a pair of roomy boxer shorts with the elastic about to go.

Those empty boxer shorts got to Reuben and he looked away while the marshal went through the jacket pockets. All he found was a pouch half-full of stale tobacco, and a wadded handkerchief. Sighing, he lifted the lid of the toilet and found what was left of a ten-pound sack of dog kibbles. "What the hell's this?"

"He had a dog," Reuben said. "He told me. It died of old age last winter."

The marshal rummaged through the bag of kibbles and came up empty. He straightened and sighed. He picked up the bank statement from under the paperweight on the desk. He read the California address, then turned it over, grunting, pointing to the back. "This mean anything to you?"

He handed it to Jim Cochran, who frowned over it, shaking his head. "Just some letters."

Outside the door Reuben watched Carmack McIntyre quietly fade back into the trees.

"Maybe the diamond pouch dropped out of his pocket when he fell," Bess Cochran said.

The marshal nodded. "We'll have to search."

Needle in a haystack, Reuben thought.

"Let me see that." Bess Cochran took the envelope out of her husband's hand. Frowning, she read "NWNWSESEC. Add a few slashes and some periods and commas," she said, "these could be coordinates of some kind. Look." She showed her mate. "Here he's drawn a square, as if he meant to write in the degrees and angles."

The marshal took back the envelope and squinted down at it. "Coordinates?"

Bess Cochran shrugged. "A map of some kind, located by lines and numbers."

Reuben tried to see over the marshal's shoulder. Something was ringing a bell, something Rap had said. He almost had it when he heard a splash outside. He leapt to the window. The dive had sent shock waves striking the grassy bank.

The marshal said, "Just a beaver," and turned to Jim Cochran. "I guess there's no diamond here for you to identify, but I'd appreciate it if you'd describe exactly what we're looking for." He put the envelope back on the desk, and the paperweight on top of it.

Jim Cochran shrugged. "Looks like tumbled glass, whitish, opaque. It was about twice the size of a pencil eraser. But I doubt if it was all that valuable."

While Tom Hurleigh stared thoughtfully at the geologist, Reuben, watching, read the marshal's mind: maybe not, but not everybody would know that, and if a diamond that size is missing—and it looks like it is—that could be motive enough for murder.

11

A dig comes to be like a small town. Tina was trying to catch up on her journal before lunch. She liked keeping some record of her days, but lately the journal had been neglected. *Cliques form. Affairs start. Envies are born. Jealousies surface.*

She looked up from her favorite perch on top of a large granite outcropping where she could not only survey the road in both directions but also keep an eye on the Saturday bustle down in the meadow—clothes washing, horseshoe throwing, groupies gossiping in the sun. Down by the stream, Beano Shippers and her following were planning their Sunday service, always an ecumenical amalgam of Methodist Sunday school, New Age prayer circle, Indian sweat with *pahos* passed hand to hand, and Girl Scout campfire with candles floating down the stream on bits of bark. Reassured that she wasn't missing anything, she bent over her pad again. *And rumors are rife. Somebody's coming. Everybody knows it. We've known it for days, no telling how.*

But *when* was a foregone conclusion that morning when Pete Jaramillo returned from the valley with coolers of steaks and corn in the husk and vine-ripened tomatoes. There was going to be a feast, and it would be today because so much food couldn't languish long in the inadequate refrigeration system. Also, it was Saturday, and weekends were likely times for visitors. They were all keeping watch, casting frequent eyes on the road. But when a vehicle ground around the bend it was usually just another truck camper lumbering toward a campsite in the upper meadow. But nothing discouraged them. They all knew someone was coming.

A good thing, too, she thought. It would help put the accident behind them, and the gloom it had cast over the dig. No one had known Rap Singleton well, so they couldn't exactly grieve. But the incident had left them numbed. The federal marshal had located a cousin, but he hadn't yet arrived to pick up Rap's camper which sat there beside the road to remind them on their way to and from the mesa. The marshal muttered about having it towed to the valley, but nothing had come of that.

Reuben's got a crush on our leader, she wrote. *People respond strongly to authority figures, some fawning and kissing ass, others behaving like rebellious adolescents.*

So which am I? she wondered. Frowning, she put down her pen and started brushing her hair. Earlier she'd heated water and washed it.

Footsteps skidded down the slope and Willy fell panting beside her.

She smiled. "Where's Joe?"

"We're not Siamese twins," Willy said. "We're not physically linked, you know."

"No fooling?"

His hand nudged her ankle. "D'you know how viruses enter living cells?"

She moved her foot. "I haven't the faintest."

"They're shaped like tadpoles, see, with a head and a tail, and this tail is strongly attracted to the cell. So it attaches itself and dissolves the cell wall and invades, and new life is born. Remind you of anything?"

"So what're you saying, Willy? You're ambitious to be a virus?"

"No, look, it's a beauty-and-beast scenario. I mean like, the beast just wants to be human, the virus just wants to be alive." He ducked his head to look up at her. His eyes were China blue, and his hair the color of a baby chick.

"Just think," he said, "same patterns throughout nature, repeating and repeating. Mysterious, huh?"

He dropped his hand on her ankle and she shoved it off. "Chill out, Willy."

"Look down there." He nudged her arm, pointing to where a huge rock face had long ago broken away, leaving a hidden alley between itself and the cliff it had once been part of. In the hidden alley, a couple were making out. She looked quickly away without identifying them. Willy laughed. "I've staked out that spot for future reference."

"Hey, Willy!"

It was Joe down in the meadow waving. Willy sighed. "Joe promised Pilar we'd help her make the potato salad. I peel, Joe chops."

"What a couple of cons."

"Come on, we work for our feed."

He leapt to his feet and, in his many-pocketed hiking shorts and expensive hiking boots, which also had little pockets on the side, loped off down the slope toward the kitchen *sombra*.

She picked up her brush. And brushing her hair dry on the high rock outcropping, she was the first to see the Jaguar. Its silver coat dulled by the dust of the canyon, it snuck purring around a rock shoulder below on the road and crept low to the ground toward her.

Her brush stopped midair.

Its windows were tinted, you couldn't see inside. It slowed and stopped in the road below her with its engine running, then inched forward, turning, nosing down the meadow track as if searching out its prey by means of some autonomic electronic sensing system, a self-propelled robot without driver or passengers. Then, swerving slowly, it set its course toward the travel trailer down by the stream.

Reuben watched it cross the meadow. He'd been lying idly on the grass when Jade and Pilar found him. He'd made the mistake of asking, "What's a tektite?"

"It's a stingy technologist," Pilar said.

"Ha ha," Jade said. "Try, it's a football cheer—Go *Tech*, Hold *Tight*!"

He was watching Bobby Ybarra and Steve Many Hands argue. They'd made a spear from a tent post with a tent stake attached to the end with duct tape, and an atlatl from an aspen sapling stripped of bark and grooved with a hunting knife.

They'd already had a go at throwing the unwieldy spear. Bobby Ybarra had managed maybe twenty yards, with Steve Many Hands—the tall, good-looking Plains Indian youth with a ponytail—showing off for the women watching from the shelter, going him some better. They were grabbing the makeshift atlatl out of each other's hands and posturing with it, disagreeing about how it worked.

"You fit the spear into the groove, see, like this," said Bobby Ybarra, in electric blue shorts and orange muscle shirt and flip-flops. "It gets its power the same as a slingshot." He raised the atlatl over his head, flexing his muscles, and slung it forward. The spear dropped off and plopped end over end on the ground.

Steve Many Hands fell back on the ground laughing, and Pilar cried, "Yeah, right! Way to go, Bobby!"

"Nah," said Caspar Dreyfus, coming up and trying to get hold of the atlatl but unable to take it away from Bobby.

The women watching from the shelter giggled, and Bobby Ybarra said over his shoulder, "Quiet, please. You're witnessing a groundbreaking experiment."

Steve Many Hands sprang up and grabbed the contraption, fitting the spear into the groove. He drew back the atlatl and let fly. The spear arced downfield like a thirty-yard pass and fell gracefully to stick up in the grass. The women in the shelter clapped.

Carmack McIntyre walked toward them from his Volkswagen camper and picked up the spear. He smiled at the scientists. "This could be a little dangerous, boys."

Bobby Ybarra flushed and looked away at being called a boy in front of the women, but Steve Many Hands grinned sheepishly. The rancher handed him the atlatl and they stood there talking while Caspar walked off the distance, calling out yardage. The atlatl had gone easily twice as far as Bobby's spear throw.

"Cheese, the damn thing works," Steve Many Hands said to the rancher.

The man from Calgary nodded. "It was a big advance over the spear. They used it for centuries before coming up with the bow and arrow."

"Imagine hunting bison with that thing, or even with bows and arrows," Steve said. "Those guys had balls."

The rancher said, "It took some courage, but mostly it depended on the cooperation of a group of hunters."

"It was a team sport," Caspar drawled.

Reuben watched the Jaguar roll to a halt down at the travel trailer. The driver's door opened and a man got out and opened the rear door. A figure emerged—small, hunched, dressed all in black in garments as shapeless as a toga. Judging from the size, it had to be a woman.

The trailer door opened and Freya Markus exclaimed, put out her arms, and descended to embrace the visitor. They hugged and kissed and Freya guided her guest inside.

As if this were the cue he'd been waiting for, Pete Jaramillo began throwing steaks on the grill over the cooking trench. You could see the smoke rise, though you couldn't hear the hiss.

"Who was that?"

Reuben looked up. Tina stood beside him, black hair loose and hanging below her waist.

He shrugged. "Must be a personage."

She knelt and drew her hair forward over her shoulder and began braiding it. He wanted to touch it, see what it felt like. Bobby Ybarra was watching, smiling. Reuben met the Mexican student's eyes and, smirking, Bobby looked away.

Polly Quint dropped on the grass. "It's the maharani. Caspar's seen her lots of times." She leaned back on her hands with her long skinny legs out in front of her.

Caspar, his straggly whiskers newly trimmed, stood over them lighting his ubiquitous pipe. Only the thought of shaving daily in cold water had kept Reuben from getting rid of his own beard when Caspar showed up with his.

"The *who*?" Tina asked.

"No wonder we're having steaks for supper," Caspar said, his drawl tinged with irony. "She was with the Leakeys in Africa. Then she broke with them and sided with Johanson."

Reuben wondered what he was talking about, but he was damned if he'd ask.

"She's a paleoanthropologist," Caspar went on. "Born in Finland, went to England, then to India. Retired now, but she taught for a while at Columbia. An honorary chair."

"Little gnome of a thing." Tina doubled a rubber band on her fingers and popped it in place around the end of her braid.

"Look who's talking," Reuben said fondly. She threw him a look.

You could smell the steaks. The corn in its husks and rolled in foil had been steaming for a while. Soon the cottonwood drum would beat a summons and everybody would drift toward the *sombra*.

"Why 'the maharani'?" Tina wanted to know.

Caspar grunted. "She was the first woman to work at Mohenjo-Daro—" he struck another match to his pipe, which always seemed to be going out "—the oldest known city on the face of the earth."

"Is it in India?" Jade asked.

"Where else? They say she became the mistress of the Maharaja of Hyderabad to get that perk."

"Worth it," Polly Quint murmured. "But isn't she a bit old?"

"That was years ago."

Tina said disparagingly, "Women are always accused of things like that when they accomplish something."

"There are more stories about her than about Margaret Mead," Caspar said.

Tina asked, "Are there a lot of stories about Margaret Mead?"

"Of course." He shrugged. "Didn't she go up the river with one husband and come back down with Bateson?"

"That's not a story," Polly Quint said. "That's the truth."

Caspar Dreyfus drew on his pipe and chuckled a smug little know-it-all chuckle that grated on Reuben's nerves.

Laughter rang out from the travel trailer, and a little later what might have been an argument. Reuben's first thought was for the steaks. He liked his rare and hoped the dinner wouldn't be delayed. The whole meadow quieted down, everybody trying to look as if they weren't straining to hear— Caspar lighting yet another match, Polly Quint examining a scratch on her ankle, Jade gazing into her palm as if trying to read the lines, Tina tickling her cheek absently with the little brush at the end of her braid.

". . . not as I do, right?" Freya's voice carried. The maharani's was a soft low warble, foreign, coaxing, patient, like luring a cat off an electric pole.

Freya broke in, "But *she may be here*."

She. Tina filed that away. The maharani's voice warbled.

"I *have* no pet theories," Freya said.

The maharani laughed.

"Okay, you can laugh. But don't forget, I'm a scientist first. One day I'll find the . . ."

It sounded like *keyhole*. She was searching for a keyhole? Anyway, Tina thought, I was right. I've got it from the horse's mouth. The woman's looking for something.

Freya's hoarse bellow of a laugh rang out, the maharani's low rumble, calming, conciliatory, joining in. Then Pete's cottonwood drum throbbed over the meadow, calling them to dinner. Weighed against curiosity, the steaks won out. They swept over the meadow toward the kitchen *sombra* like lemmings to their destiny.

12

Which was swift in coming. The steaks were done to a turn. Reuben ate his own and Polly Quint's. Polly was a vegetarian. The corn was sweet, the tomatoes ripened by the sun, the tub of potato salad delicious. But a half hour after the meal, they were making for the privies or retching outside their tents. Nobody escaped. Not even Polly Quint, which ruled out the steaks. Throats burned, headaches raged, stomachs ached. Pilar had a convulsion and Steve Many Hands passed out.

Freya Markus phoned the hospital in the valley on her field telephone, pausing in the conversation to double up and heave, and paramedics invaded the canyon with lights flashing and sirens blaring. A young resident administered first aid to everybody. Pilar and Steve were loaded into the ambulance. The maharani was too ill to be moved. Tina, spared the worst of the plague, was assigned to care for her. The geologists, just back after the meal from a weekend in Albuquerque at the university, looked for Beano Shippers and told her, "We found out about your rocks." But Beano just put a towel to her mouth and peered at them miserably. So the Cochrans became instant nurses, as did Sonny Concha and Horse Rios. The Indian boys had been lucky. They'd had their lunch at the pueblo.

The marshal was back the next morning asking questions. Lily and Pete shook their heads. Nobody had tampered with the food. Pete trimmed and cooked the steaks. Lily took care of the vegetables. The tomatoes were simply washed and sliced. The corn was cooked in the husk.

What did everybody drink?

Gallons of iced tea. Lily made it herself. Some was still in the refrigerated trailer, and Lily knew there was nothing wrong with it. She had been thirsty after her bout with the sickness, and she'd drunk several glasses. It had made her feel better.

Had the kitchen been left unsupervised?

No. Lily was always there. Pete, too. And even the students who helped. Students were scheduled to help with meals Saturday and Sunday noon.

Which students? Where were they?

The girl was that one called Pilar. She was plenty sick. And those young campers from the upper canyon had helped in exchange for a meal. Pete had gone up to their campsite and found Willy rolling in agony in their pop-up camper, and Joe outside with his face in the stream. Pete pulled him out and kept him from drowning. But he was unconscious. They'd taken him to Santa Fe with the other two in the ambulance.

The marshal took samples from the gallon jar of mayonnaise. The onions were all gone, but they were just onions. Lily had used them in enchiladas on Friday. She had boiled the eggs herself, and Joe had scooped them from their shells to add to the potato salad.

Now the marshal wanted to know more about the fire in

the upper canyon and the plague of serpents. "The Indian boys who rounded up the snakes," he said to Freya Markus, who was slowly recovering, "they just happened to be on the premises that day?"

"No. They work for me. I hired them for the summer."

They were talking in low voices inside Freya Markus's trailer, Tina lying on the couch and the maharani sleeping in the small bedroom at back with the door closed.

The marshal wanted to speak with the boys, and Freya went to find them. The marshal talked with them outside under the trees, their voices muted by the voice of the stream.

Across the trailer room on the built-in table, its pages ruffling in the breeze through the open windows, lay a spiral notebook, the pages covered with a big, bold scrawl Tina recognized. She averted her eyes.

But the notebook just lay there, out in the open, for anyone to see. As she watched, the wind blew the curtains and ruffled the pages. She could clearly see that every page had a running head. A date? Was it a record of some kind?

I will not touch it, she told herself, I will not look.

Outside, Sonny Concha and Horse Rios answered the marshal's questions, denying, shaking their heads. The marshal's voice droned. Then one of the boys'. The wind turned the pages without assistance from her till the notebook lay open at the last entry. The opposite page was blank. The date at the head was only one day past.

The door banged open against the wall. Freya Markus's eyes took in the room, Tina, the open journal. While outside the window the marshal watched the Indian boys walk away up the meadow, she reached out and closed the notebook.

Tina bit her lip. She looked out the trailer window where Cruz drove across the grass in his new blue pickup and stopped beside the stream. He waited in the cab with the door open and the heel of his boot resting on the ground outside.

Inside the trailer Freya said, "Well, have you satisfied your curiosity?"

Tina sucked in her cheeks, watching the marshal walk over to her uncle's truck. "The boys say they don't know anything about the snakes," he said to Cruz, "except that they caught eighteen in the ruin and released them down by the river."

Tina watched the men outside the window while Freya Markus watched her. "Anything else you want to know, just ask me," she said.

Tina couldn't look at her.

"Please, I'm sorry. I didn't . . ."

Outside, the marshal pulled a scrap of paper out of his pocket and held it for Cruz to read. "Ever hear of this fellow?"

Freya sighed. "How is Solveig?"

Tina turned back from the window. The notebook was no longer on the table but under Freya's arm. "She's still sleeping," she murmured.

Tina watched her go through the Pullman kitchen and the door to the bedroom at back. Outside, Cruz frowned down at the scrap of paper and shook his head. "I never heard of nobody with a name like that. How come you're asking?"

"We found a fingerprint," the marshal said. "On the red notebook cover. We ran it through the computer and came up with this."

Grunting, Cruz got out of the truck and leaned on the wheel well, looking into the truck bed. "You think something's going on," he said.

"It looks like somebody's trying to run these folks off the dig."

Her uncle nodded.

"Whoever it is didn't mean any harm by setting the fire or planting the snakes. Those could have been pranks. But now we've got a murder on our hands."

Murder. Tina's hand rose to her throat. Low murmurs came from the back of the trailer, but she focused on the scene outside. The marshal was saying, ". . . died from the fall, but they found a head wound just over the ear, dealt with an object shaped something like brass knuckles."

Cruz nodded. "Could've hit his head on a rock when he fell."

"No such luck," the marshal said. "The forensics people say the weapon was metal."

"Stunned him and shoved him over—is that what you're saying?"

The marshal nodded. "But there was a struggle. They found a little dried blood under a fingernail."

"That give you anything?"

"If we had a suspect we could try to match it up. Meanwhile, I'm asking myself, who wants these people out of here? And frankly, Cruz, the answer bothers me."

Her uncle looked into the pickup bed, the marshal into the stream. Finally the marshal squatted on his heels, picked up a stick, and doodled in the dirt. "We've known each other a long time, Cruz."

The voices behind her in the trailer rose, arguing, but Tina was intent on the scene outside. The marshal waited for Cruz to say something. Cruz, however, didn't. The marshal, squatting on the ground, was at an obvious disadvantage with Cruz towering over him, waiting, giving nothing. It was a subtle power struggle. The one going on behind her in the trailer sounded not subtle at all.

"So, okay," the marshal finally said, "I'll give it to you straight." He started to rise, had pushed himself halfway up, when Cruz suddenly squatted on his heels beside him. The marshal hesitated, then let himself back down. Tina smiled. It was Indian-Anglo stuff, though maybe the marshal didn't know it. He glanced up at the trailer and she drew back from the window. She was turning into a spy, all right. Listening at windows, reading other people's journals. The voices behind her quieted.

"What I mean to say . . ." the marshal said.

"You're askin' who wants these diggers out of here," her uncle said.

"I know you people don't want them digging in these ruins," the marshal said.

There it was again: *you people*.

Cruz turned slowly and looked at the marshal.

"Am I right?" the marshal asked.

Cruz shrugged.

"So, okay, tell me who else would want them gone from here."

Cruz shook his head.

"Dammit, Cruz, help me out a little."

At the marshal's tone, Cruz raised his eyebrows. Tina wanted to laugh.

"Goddammit, I've got a murder on my hands," the marshal said.

Cruz said, "Maybe some boys start a fire and let loose some baby snakes. I don't know nothin' about that."

The marshal's hands hung limp and empty between his knees. "Okay," he said finally, "Maybe I oughtn't be telling you this, but at the fall site up on top of the cliff I found the prints of moccasins."

Cruz raised his eyebrows, pursed his lips, and slowly nodded. "So," he said, "that tells us somethin', don't it."

"Yeah." The marshal looked relieved.

"It tells us somebody's tryin' to frame the Indians."

The marshal looked shocked. "What the hell do you mean?"

"You can't hardly find no Indians wearing moccasins anymore," her uncle said. "All of 'em wear these Reebok shoes."

Tina stifled a laugh against her fist.

The marshal's mouth pursed and clammed up. Finally he said, like slamming his ace down on the table, "Okay, Cruz, I'll give it to you straight. This business could hold up the land transfer."

After a minute Cruz said, "What do you mean, Tom?"

"I'm saying," the marshal said, "you Tsorigi have no tribal police, no trained personnel of any kind, and Santa Ynez has no jurisdiction here. The land may have to stay

in federal hands till this thing is solved." He said it triumphantly, What do you think of that?

They eyed each other. Cruz rose and stood over the marshal with his fingers cupped toward his palms like they
were itching to make fists. "I talked to the senator yesterday," he said. "Funny he didn' say nothing about that."

The marshal, squatting there, didn't look up at him or
say anything. Somebody was bluffing. The marshal? Did he
think Cruz was shielding a tribe member and this would
flush him out?

Her uncle squinted up at the meadow and nodded. "That
makes it pretty clear then, dudn' it." Tina could tell he was
very angry, though probably no Anglo would be able to
read that in his face.

"What do you mean?" The marshal spoke softly, as if
maybe he'd rather not know.

"It means somebody don't want us to get our land back."

"Aw, come on, Cruz, what're you talking about?"

"Fires, snakes, now this killing . . . It looks to this Indian
like somebody's found a way to keep the land transfer from
happening."

The marshal's head came up. Cruz's head wagged sadly.
"And everybody coming in for the rabbit hunt and the cel-
ebration. They gunna be awful disappointed."

The marshal stood up. "Dammit, Cruz, now I don't want
any trouble."

Her uncle walked over to his truck, got in, and turned the
key in the ignition. And the marshal groaned and grabbed
the back of his neck and stood there watching the new blue
pickup waddle over ruts back up the rise to the road.

Freya tiptoed out of the back room, the notebook no
longer under her arm, and Tina moved away from the window. "How is she?"

Freya shook her head. "Tell me about Naposunshare."

"The black clay dance? It's the only dance that's our
own and no other tribe's."

"The Tsorigi?"

"Yes."

"Why *black* clay?"

Tina shrugged. "I'm not sure anybody knows."

Freya nodded. "That figures," she said thoughtfully. "Not many people know why they trim evergreens at Christmas either, or paint eggs at Easter. Both practices go back to pre-Christian times."

Tina said, "The dance means a lot to the people. There's not much left that's purely ours. So much has been lost."

Freya frowned down at the big hands clasping and unclasping in her lap. "Could black clay be interpreted to mean black *rock*?"

Wanting desperately to be helpful after the business of the journal, Tina could only shake her head. "I've always just heard black clay dance."

"Sit down." The archaeologist patted the couch beside her, but Tina took her seat on the edge of a chair and waited. Freya's brows dipped to a point over her nose. "I've seen you watching me. I know you're wondering what I'm doing here."

Tina lowered her eyes.

"Look, I'm not some pot pirate. I'm not looking for treasures to steal from the tribe, if that's what you're thinking."

Tina looked hopefully up. Freya Markus was leaning toward her, arms resting lightly on knees spread apart and moving side to side as if unable to keep still. The archaeologist's eyes were fixed on her as if she were weighing whether, with Tina's divided loyalties, she could be trusted. "Oh, it's a buried treasure, I grant." She laughed. "And buried very deep in unrecorded time, but it's nothing like gold, or valuable pots, or a cache of turquoise. What I'm looking for is—"

A knock at the door and Reuben stuck his head in. "Ready?" he asked, looking from Freya to Tina and back again, eyes full of questions.

Freya scowled. "Just a minute."

Reuben, reluctantly Tina thought, closed the door. Freya's hand fell on her knee. "Stay with her," she said.

For a moment Tina couldn't think what she was talking about. "See if she needs anything when she wakes up."

Oh, the maharani. "Where are you going?"

But Freya had already grabbed her gray hooded sweat-shirt and ducked out the trailer door where Reuben was waiting. Tina watched them get into Freya's Cherokee and head off up the meadow toward the road, where they were joined by some of the graduate students and Earth Watch people, who piled in on top of each other.

Before settling down with her book, Tina crept in for a look at the old woman and found her propped up among the pillows, looking out the window, hugging to her chest a silver flask with the cap off. She smiled at Tina. "The trees are so peaceful."

Tina looked out at the trees.

"Who are you, dear?"

Tina said her name and that she was in charge of the photography and sketching on the dig.

"I envy you," the maharani said. "All that wealth of years before you to squander as you please." She sighed and her breast rose and fell. "Mine are almost spent. How is it we laugh and talk and buy and sell and drink wine and make love, and all the time we are dying?" She turned her head on the pillow and looked out the window, then sipped from the flask and stoppered it with a kind of finality and set it back on the little table. She patted the bed. "Sit down, child." She studied Tina. "Are you Indian?"

Sidling onto the foot of the bed, Tina nodded.

"You're going to be an archaeologist? No, I think not. You haven't the patience, have you? No, I would take you for a dancer."

Tina opened her mouth to deny, but the old woman reached out and took her hand. "Here, let me see about you. I'll read your palm." Her voice was low and guttural. She spoke with some difficulty. She turned Tina's hand palm-up and passed her fingers lightly over it. "We'll see what we can see." She did look like an old gypsy woman with her braids wound round her head and her sharp eyes. "You are not sure about all this digging, are you?"

Startled, Tina fidgeted. The old woman laughed, disclosing gold in her back teeth. "I am teasing you, child. Excuse an old harridan." She squeezed Tina's hand and grew serious. "You like my Freya, don't you. But I must tell you she is on the wrong course. She has always been intractable."

Attempting to sit up against the pillows, the old woman was taken by a coughing fit while Tina sat by helpless and alarmed. She picked up the glass of water on the bedside table and offered it, but the maharani swept it away, heaving up each breath as if it might be her last. When it was over, her face was flushed. "Forgive me," she said, her voice little more than a whisper. "It is my lung." She indicated her chest with a limp flap of her fingers. Then she closed her eyes and waved Tina out of the room.

Outside there was a commotion. Bobby Ybarra skidded to a stop on one of the mountain bikes, excited, gesticulating, pointing down-canyon. The marshal rose from where he'd been sitting on a rock beside the stream. He stood up and took his pipe out of his mouth. He listened, then hurried to his vehicle with Bobby running after him, abandoning the mountain bike.

Even before he'd cut off his motor beside Rap Singleton's camper, Tom Hurleigh could see the broken window, glass fragments scattered on the grass like heavy dew. He bent over his keys and hunted, opened the door, and drew back the dingy curtains to let in light. There was a single footprint on the desk. The shoe had been wet. Now the footprint of the lugged sole was etched in dried mud. It looked like a middle-size jogging shoe. Could belong to a male or a female. Whoever it was had come through the stream.

"Can I do anything?" Bobby asked.

"Just stay outside."

Some of the students stopped on the road to see what was going on. The marshal concentrated. He ought to be able to tell what was missing. His eye circled slowly. Metal detector, magnet, cooking pots . . . He opened the door to the bathroom. Everything okay in there. He went through pockets, through drawers, making a thorough search. He was baffled. Nothing seemed to be missing.

Then he remembered the envelope with the mysterious markings. He swung around to the desk. Damn. Sure enough, it was gone. Why the devil hadn't he taken it with him? Maybe he was getting too old for this job.

Then he saw it on the floor underneath the desk, splashed with coffee from the old man's last cup, which a large fragment of glass, or perhaps a foot coming in through the shattered window, had overturned. The cup lay on its side, its contents spilled.

Relieved, he stooped and picked up the envelope and put it in his pocket. He took another look around. As far as he could see, nothing was missing. So what had they been looking for? Whatever it was, they hadn't found it. Maybe somebody had surprised the thief and he'd had no chance to search. If that was it, maybe he'd be back.

13

Reuben wondered what they'd been talking about, Freya and Tina. He caught himself resenting Tina's easy access to the archaeologist just because she was female. He still felt queasy from the poisoning, but Freya Markus wanted the hot spring recorded, and what Freya wanted, Freya got.

"Perfect!" she cried.

He watched her kneeling there on a rock at the spring's edge, scooping up a handful of the whitish clay from the bottom, clasping it in her fist till it adhered in a ball. She held it up, showing it triumphantly. "This is it—their clay quarry. I've looked everywhere, and here it was all the time. Look at this."

She'd been furious at Beano Shippers for concealing the spring. She'd almost sent her home. But Beano had begged and pleaded and sworn on her Bible, and finally, on probation, been allowed to stay.

"We'll have no trouble at all matching this to the Anasazi shards. It's the right color, the right percentage of mica."

Surreptitiously Reuben raised his camera and got a couple of shots. The smile, the pallor, the dark smudges under her eyes from the food poisoning, made him feel protective. So when he caught sight of sunlight glinting off metal halfway up the canyon wall, his impulse was to thrust her behind him.

Instead he bent over the camera and said softly, "Don't look now but we're being watched."

"What do you mean? Where?" Alarmed, she looked around.

"Don't do that!"

"How do you know?"

"A reflection. Could be a gun. Just back off and head down the arroyo. Wave to me as you go."

Caspar's scowl said, Who do you think you are? But the Earth Watch widower from Calgary put a hand under Freya's elbow and started back down the rock-strewn path.

"Go on!" Reuben hissed, fiddling with the camera, not looking up.

Steve Many Hands hung back. "What're you going to do?"

"I don't know. Go on, get out of here."

"What about you?"

"I'm right behind you."

"Don't do anything foolish."

"Get out of here, man. Go!"

Head bent over the camera, he watched them move

away. He could swing the camera up toward the spot where he'd seen the reflection, then hit the telephoto lens to bring him in. Get a picture, whoever he was.

But meanwhile he might be as dead as Rap Singleton.

So instead he set the camera down on a rock behind the spring. Slowly, casually, he stripped to his jocks and let himself into the pool and laid his head back and closed his eyes. After a moment he slit them open upon a sky full of mare's tails. Then with his head back that way, he was able to scan the canyon wall.

There it was again, near the top. Not steady. It kept flickering. Something was moving up there.

In spite of the warmth of the sun and the hot spring, he felt a chill on his shoulders lying there with his face offered up, a perfect target. He wouldn't even hear the bullet. Fear weakened his bowels, already weak from the poison. He would never make a soldier. But he zeroed in on the spot. Somebody was on a ledge up there.

In ages past, boulders had fallen off the face of the cliff and piled up at the bottom. He might be able to climb up there, but he didn't think he could do it without being seen.

The flashes stopped. For several minutes he didn't see the glint of sun off whatever it was. He stood up and stretched. He yawned and scratched his armpits as lustily as an orangutan. Then he stepped out of the spring and took off his jocks—a good touch, he thought. Nobody would think he suspected their presence if he stood there buck naked, wringing them out. He'd never felt so exposed. He bent and pulled them back on, then taking his time, drew on his cutoffs and sneakers. Fiddling with his fly, he walked off under the overhang as if to take a leak, leaving T-shirt and camera behind. Once he was under the overhang, nobody on that high ledge could see him without leaning over and bending double, a risky business.

He made his way leaping boulder to boulder, finally pulling himself up toehold by toehold. At first the going was easy. He was exhilarated. He was rock climbing! He saw himself from down below, fearless, scaling the cliff. Then he stopped, panting to get his breath, and looked down. Chee-zuss.

He'd never been fond of heights. The going was much slower now. He pulled himself up another tier of the basalt outcropping to what looked like an animal path. It looked like the top layer of the birthday cake had slid in the oven, leaving a thin, lopsided ledge. It was like scaling the layers of a gigantic cake. His fingers were raw, his wrists ached. He groaned. What do you think you're doing? Think you're John Wayne? Think again. Look what you've got yourself into, fathead.

He fell against the cliff face and caught his breath. He'd come up against a narrow shoulder like a glob of vanilla icing that had run down, blocking the path. He couldn't go any farther. At first he was relieved. He'd given it his best shot, hadn't he? If he couldn't go any farther, that wasn't the same as quitting, was it? Then he made the mistake of looking down again and, terrified by the drop, grabbed at some rabbit brush. He closed his eyes to get hold of himself, then hugging the shoulder, tried inching a toe around.

He couldn't believe he'd made it. He lay with his chest against the slanted cliff, panting, smiling, seeing himself from below as part of a frieze on a cornice. He looked down again.

Oh God. He closed his eyes and tried to swallow, but his mouth was as dry as a husk.

The path ran a little way farther, then ended where the ledge petered out beneath the face of the cliff. This really was as far as he could go. He took a careful step back so he could look up and see what chance he had of climbing out, and what stared down at him caught him squarely in the solar plexus. His chin dropped. He gulped a lungful of dry desert air that rasped in his throat.

The ledge he was standing on hid the cliff face from below. What he saw now could only be seen from this precarious perch or from the opposite canyon wall, thin as a blade, fit only for nesting cliff swallows.

As high as a person could reach, the rock face was covered with petroglyphs. The life, the energy, sprang out at him and he fell back and inadvertently sat down, breathing *Jesus, Jesus*. He felt like a neophyte in the workshop of artists of some book of life. Harsh outsize forms, dynamic shapes owing no more debt to perspective than the Egyptians: fleeing bison, running figures brandishing spears overhead, zigzags of serpents, some with horns like giant snails, four-pointed stars, some with faces, trailing sprays like fireworks at a prehistoric state fair, pinwheels, tall figures shaped like ears of corn, small, cavorting animals—dogs or wolves—everything in motion, the whole dominated by one huge figure.

The eyes stared out lordly as some potentate surveying the doings of his minions. The figure was squatting—in a deluge, it looked like, lots of little drops of rain etched falling all around. He frowned and moved up closer. The figure's shanks and feet and toes pointed sideways, and two protuberances underneath . . .

"Huh," he said out loud. The figure seemed to be shitting a two-pronged turd. It must be some kind of symbolic thing.

Turning, he saw what the face looked out at. A V-shaped notch reaching halfway down the opposite canyon wall framed a far, green mountain meadow full of grazing cattle. The shadow of the notch fell diagonally across the face that he knew, in some way impossible to define, was female.

His gaze slid off the giant figure and snagged upon what seemed at first negligible—a small, primitive stick man. He frowned, his mind scanning, computing, trying to recall something to its visual screen.

Christ, talk about synchronicity. He knew about synchronicity from Jung's foreword to Richard Wilhelm's translation of the I Ching, to which he was devoted. Twenty-four hours ago what he was looking at would just have been another primitive stick figure scratched in rock.

In his excitement, he leaned back, and frantically caught himself. The heel of his hand met solid rock, but the fingers closed on empty space. Warily he turned. He'd caught the edge of the cliff. Christ. He skidded forward. He had to get out of here, tell Freya Markus what he'd discovered.

But he couldn't even *look* down, much less face the perils of that descent. And he couldn't stay where he was.

That left just one alternative. He looked up. He stood up and stepped back as close to the edge as he dared and peered up at the cliff. The climb would be the shortest way out, but if he fell, he'd fall back to this ledge. With a broken leg, he'd really be trapped, no way to get down, no way for anybody to get him out. He thought of the humiliation, of Freya Markus.

Calm down. Don't panic. *Think.*

The cliff face was not smooth. It grew bulges like the trunk of a diseased tree, and around the bulges were natural indentations. Above the layer with the petroglyphs, the rock was lighter, sand-colored, full of holes. Vuggy. It was a layer of vuggy tuff. Easy, Jim Cochran said, to dig into. If he could just get up there.

He cast around on the ledge and found a dark, wedge-shaped chip, maybe flint, with a point on it and a few serrations along its edges. The summer had made its mark; he suspected it might be a worked piece.

But to get to the tuff layer he had somehow to scale the basalt layer that held the petroglyphs. The cliff was not quite perpendicular. It slanted slightly back. He backed off and leapt and got his arm around one of the bulges and, straining, pulled himself up a foot or two off the ledge. He groped frantically for a fingerhold, but he couldn't hang on. He dropped back onto the ledge, sucking in more dry air, and moved away from the precipitous drop to hug the warm cliff face and get his breath.

He tried again, choosing a different bulge, and this time managed to get his arm more firmly around it. Cheek against rock, groping with his free hand, he found a finger hole. Hanging there he rested, catching his breath. Empty space yawned behind him. Gravity pulled at him. He was afraid to breathe because each breath expanded his chest against the cliff and thrust him backward. But his arms were trembling. He scratched his cheek turning to look up.

Why hadn't he mapped out the cliff face before he started, planned the climb so he'd know which way he was going, where to find the holes? He couldn't hang on much longer. He had to move up or fall back. This time he'd made it higher up the cliff. Falling back, he might miss the ledge and plunge. He heard his dying scream, like one he had heard before.

There was no wind and the sun beat down. He was sweating hard. It was getting into his eyes and he had no free hand to wipe it off. He cursed and rolled his forehead against the rock face. It helped a little. His stomach clutched in a cramp. He strained to look up.

A long oval-shaped hole about ten inches above his head looked deep enough. He hugged the bulge with his arm and raised himself a few inches. He tried folding himself over the bulge. The rock dug into him, but he took a deep breath and let go, running his hand desperately over the cliff as high as he could reach.

He made it. His fingers closed around the smooth lower lip of the oval-shaped hole. He thought it was big enough for both hands. He felt around for a foothold and discovered one of the shallow indentations in the basalt layer. Basalt is hard, Jim Cochran had said. Maybe it would bear his weight.

He dug in and thrust, and let go the bulge. Now he hung from both hands in the oval-shaped hole. His arms strained. He pulled himself up and got his toe on top of the bulge. He crouched there, panting, heart beating in his throat, guts cramping again. He held his breath and tightened his ass till the cramp subsided. Then he lay sweating against the tuff layer, the soft layer the Anasazi had dug into for their rooms.

Holding on with one hand, he fished the flint out of his pocket. What he needed was another foothold, not too high. He started digging. It wasn't as easy as the geologist made out. Cochran said the surface hardened when exposed. If he could just chip the surface away.

He chipped out a shallow foothold. He thrust the rock into the pocket of his cutoffs. Then, pulling himself up with his hands in the oval-shaped hole, his toe found the chipped indentation. And reaching again, feeling over the cliff face with his fingers, he found another hole, smaller, and pulled himself up. With better purchase, he chipped the toeholds deeper to keep them from crumbling under his weight. He was taking his time now, resting his wrist, sighting his route, licking drops of sweat that fell off his brow. Moving this way, finding fingerholds, chipping toeholds, he moved slowly upward.

Then a catastrophe. He'd thrust his digging rock in the back pocket of his cutoffs where it would be easier to fish out with his fingers, forgetting the hole in that pocket till he heard his rock hit the ledge below and fly off into space. He heard it hit a treetop in the arroyo. It took a long time falling.

Now you've done it. He closed his eyes and breathed a prayer he'd learned at his mother's knee.

But the natural holes were closer together now, bigger, deeper, as if the cliff were more badly eroded near the top where the wind got to it. He was grateful for that wind. It was cooler now that he was higher up. He tried longer reaches. His muscles ached and his arms trembled, but he pulled himself up. Don't look down, he told himself. See how close you are. Up there's the mesa top.

With his chest scraped and bleeding and his nails torn, he heaved himself over the cliff edge, fell on his face, and lay gasping. He breathed slowly, discovering the depth of his lungs. He'd done something he would never have tried before. It was the influence of Freya Markus, to whom nothing was impossible. It was this summer. Maybe it was the beaver.

He remembered what he was doing up here. He got to his knees and looked around. Here the piñons grew back from the edge. He crawled over and peered down to orient himself to the hot spring. Climbing, he'd taken a diagonal route. There it was, down in the arroyo, maybe a hundred feet to his left, with the cluster of tamarisks below it. And he was looking diagonally down upon the ledge he thought the flashes had come from.

Whoever had been there was probably long gone. He thought of being watched in his hazardous climb. A rock tossed from that higher ledge could have sent him flying.

He walked down the crest till he stood above the ledge. The edge of the cliff had crumbled down to it, maybe ten feet below. He turned and scanned the low piñon woods behind him. Only a couple of crows watched from the top of a tree. No one in sight. He climbed carefully down the slope to the ledge below and looked over the edge to find the spring, and found himself looking down at another ledge. Someone had leaned a log against the cliff at an easy angle. But whoever had been down there was gone. The ledge was empty.

He had climbed back to the top and started down the trail toward the dig when he heard the sound: low panting, muttering. He stopped and listened. Footsteps. No, someone nearby was dancing. And singing. Softly, hardly more than a whisper. Hi-ye-yi. Yo-ho-ho-ho. Hi-ye-yi. Singing like you heard on the Indian program on the radio. But no drum. And the eeriest thing—it seemed to be coming from below the edge of the cliff.

But he'd just been down there and there was nothing, no one. This mesa was full of tricks. Owls turning into people. Bird Boy running naked at midnight. Now he was hearing voices.

He waited, but the singing had stopped. Now there was only the conversing of the crows in the top of the piñon tree.

He dismissed it as an aberration resulting from stress, or maybe the picture wall had worked on him till he heard the old ones singing. He walked again toward the trail head. Then a low humming rose behind him. Somebody was coming. He spun around and froze as a figure rose up over the edge of the cliff.

They looked at each other. Time passed. Reuben crouched, cold in the sun with his knuckles on the ground like a lineman waiting for the play, his muscles aching, his chest bleeding from the rough edges of the cliff face.

The outlandish figure stood poised in surprise on the edge of the cliff, dark chest streaked with ocher and charcoal, naked but for breechclout and moccasins. The face had rectangular eyes and the smooth awful snout of a missing nose. It was frightful, like some kind of space being. Big knobby ears stuck out on either side of a head bald and lumpish and earth brown except for a green-looking beard. Around the neck, against the hairless chest, dangled strings of turquoise and feathers: some kind of fetish or charm—it was a *paho*—and something else fleetingly familiar. But Reuben's mind wasn't functioning. All he could do was stare.

They froze there speechless, motionless, watched by the chuckling crows. Then arms out, crouched, the figure moved toward him.

Reuben moved, too, and the apparition, almost upon him, leapt aside. They dodged back and forth, Reuben trying to let the apparition pass but inadvertently blocking his way. Then the figure lowered its head and charged, butting him in the middle. Reaching, grabbing, trying to ward him off, Reuben went down.

Doubled over, clutching his ribs, spitting up on the ground where close under his face an outsize ant trundled something bigger than itself over a hummock of sand, he saw with horror that the brown, lumpish head had collapsed and come off limp and weightless in his hands as the headless assailant leaped over him to run off in the scrub.

14

John flopped panting onto his own *banco* across from the old man's in the room lit by the corner fireplace and the single high window. A knot in a *viga* looked down at him like an eye. It was always watching—when he woke up in the morning and the last thing at night when the fire burned down.

The old man had the fire going all the time now. Though it was summer, he was always cold. Place stank of smoke and cooking grease. The old man got off his bed to do the cooking. Hooper John wouldn't touch it. Leave that to old men and the women.

Outside, some boys were playing stickball, shouting and laughing. He could hear their running feet. In front of the house next door, Joaquin underneath a pickup banged at a rusty muffler.

"What you doing all got up like that?" the old man asked.

John had thought he·was asleep. "Leave me alone. I ain't done nothing."

"You wanna turn people off, dressing up that way? Where you been all this time?"

"Nowhere. Nonna your business." John's heart was still pounding in his throat. He closed his eyes and counted his breaths, trying to quiet them.

"Lettum see you like that, they not gunna like it."

"I been running, if you have to know."

"Runnin', runnin'. What you runnin' from, Hooper John?"

"Leave me alone, old man."

The old man's chuckle turned into a coughing fit. He was lying there across the room all wrapped up in blankets. The cough heaved his chest up off the *banco*. When it subsided he said, "Leave you alone. That's what I ought to've done, left you alone. You'd be up in the clouds with all 'um little white angels flittin' around. Singing. I understand they always singing."

"Hush up, old man."

"Now it's hush up. Most times it's talk talk talk, tell me this, tell me that, what's so-an'-so mean? How you say this? What's the word for somethin' else? Now it's hush up, old man. John wants to meditate, is that it?"

The old man coughed again. John hated that cough. It brought fear to his heart. As the old man weakened, it seemed as if *he* weakened, too. The old man could just die on him and leave him unfinished. An incomplete Indian.

John reached for the little leather case strung on the thong around his neck. He unfastened the snap and pulled out his secret prize. It was heavy in his hand, and the weight was satisfying, proving its value, that it was not a piece of junk.

What was it? Sometimes he wished he knew, but at other times he valued the mystery. At first he'd only tried to make out the writing on its back, on a panel fastened with tiny little bolts, with a bunch of numbers in columns. D. W. Brunton, it said. And Wm Ainsworth & Sons, Denver, Colo.

He undid the copper clasp. It had taken him some time to figure out that it opened at all, for the clasp was stiff, and, once pulled away, John hadn't for a time discovered that it served as a handle. But finally, carefully, he pulled on it, and grudgingly the back opened.

He'd been on the ledge the day that happened, when it opened and looked back at him with its one big eye. Some kind of a mirror, heavily encased, with a line up and down the middle, and another tiny mirror embedded at the bottom sort of pinkish and oval-shaped. You could look in the big mirror and see yourself, or you could turn it out when the sun was right and flash it around like a spook light on the opposite canyon wall. He'd been doing that when he realized there were people down at the spring. He'd gone back into his cave. Then when he'd thought the coast was clear and come on out, he'd discovered it wasn't.

His breast stopped heaving. He was breathing quieter now. He held on tight to the metal box. The thing opened on a hinge. The top part was this mirror, but the bottom was a round box with a wobbling needle, and a black thing like an arrow. He felt this small, weighty metal box held some secret that, if he could only decipher it, would tell him the truth of things. John treasured it and, though it was heavy, he wore it on a thong under his shirt where he could fondle it in times of stress and be reassured.

He reached into the niche in the wall over his head and took down the little red notebook minus its back cover. If only he could read it, maybe it would tell him something he ought to know. The pages were covered with numbers. It seemed to him that every important thing in life was hidden from him in just such hieroglyphics. And then on the final page that one word fiercely underlined: Diamonds. He looked at it and mouthed it softly, and it was like he could see them glittering in the dark in the heart of the earth.

He decided to hold a conversation with his friend, and to that end took three deep breaths and closed his eyes. He had not talked with his friend for some time. Instead, he had talked with the old man. But he'd begun to doubt the old man's ability—even his willingness—to go on living. This made John feel sorry for himself. "I'll be all right in the morning," the old man said last night, but he wasn't, was he? Look at him.

Hooper John said to his friend, He can be sick like this for a day, sometimes two, and then be fine again. Sometimes I think he's dying he's so old. But then he gets up chipper and mean as ever.

The old man was a tease, and being teased threw John into a rage. Then the old man would put up both hands and go, "Tsk tsk tsk. Control yourself. A brave don't waste himself on foolishness."

Then John would ask him a question like, "Today I saw this on a rock." And he'd sit on the stoop and draw in the sand with a stick. "What does it mean?" Sometimes the old man knew and would tell him. Sometimes he knew but wouldn't tell him. Sometimes he didn't know.

If John brought beer from the store on the highway, the old man might open up. He'd draw in the sand—"Look here, see this? This is the horned serpent. And this—" chuckling as he drew "—this is Kokopilli." The humpback flute player, humpback maybe because he'd once been a cricket, or maybe because of a dozen other reasons. This much John knew: Kokopilli had powers about which the old man grew sly.

Today the old man was sick. When he's sick, he's mean, John told his friend. What should I do?

And his friend said in a bass voice that resounded through marble halls: Be calm. Be still and stay at home awhile. Be friendly with the women and they'll bring you things to eat like they always do when the old man's sick.

Just lying there listening made John feel better.

But what'll I do? What if they find me and take me back? What if they lock me up? What if they come around asking questions? What'll I say? What'll I tell them? What'll they do to me?

Inside his breast he was quivering. The malevolent eye in the *viga* looked down at him. He reached up and took down his ring of keys from the peg driven into the adobe wall and fingered them like beads. It made him feel better, though they were keys to nothing, maybe to a truck the old man claimed once to have owned, maybe to the padlock, now missing, that the old man once kept on the door of his storage shed out back, and some miscellaneous other keys about which John had no knowledge whatsoever.

His friend said, Just take it easy, hush now. Stay home for a while and live in the eye of your mind. Look down at the spring. She's washing her hair.

John closed his eyes and watched her. He grew so heavy on his bed he could sink through the floor. The sounds outside were friendly, and he knew he was going to sleep.

I'm going to sleep, he told his friend apologetically.

Goooood, gooood. The calm voice drew it out, deep and kind down those hallowed halls. His friend spoke to him like he was a little kid, but that was because his friend was so old. John imagined him with white hair, dressed in robes like the old man's blankets, only whiter. And his friend knew everything, he could see into your heart. Even seeing John's heart, the friend loved him like a son, and that was something, wasn't it?

15

Reuben spread the mask out on the floor so they could get a good look at it.

"Hold still, will you?" Tina was leaning over him, dabbing hydrogen peroxide on his scratches with a cotton swab.

"Here's what he looked like." The masked figure took rapid shape under his pen.

Tina leaned down and touched the mask. "It's so soft and old, you think it'll crumble."

The maharani chuckled, a low warbling sound like the sound of the stream outside. "An extraordinary find, young man." She lay on the built-in couch with a blanket over her. "But where did this apparition come from? How did he fly up the side of the cliff?"

Reuben saw him rise up the cliff face again and stand there with his arms out as if for balance. He frowned, trying to see what dangled there around his neck. A *paho* and something else. "I haven't a clue," he said, turning to look at the old woman. "But he was real. He butted me like a bull."

"Powerfully built, then." The maharani's face was small and round, her eyes lively and blue. Her lips protruded and she seemed to chew her words. Her white hair wrapped her head in thick braids.

He shook his head. "No. He just caught me off guard."

"And he wore only a breechclout? Was there anything original about the garment?"

Reuben frowned. "It was skin of some kind. Dark and ragged. Parts of it—like maybe some neck or leg pelt—hung down so the bottom, the hem, was irregular. It was longer than the ones you see around here at the Indian dances."

Tina said, "Pueblo breechclouts are usually worked deerskin, white and soft."

"And these moccasins he was wearing?" The maharani wasn't looking at him, she was looking at the low trailer ceiling as if trying to get the picture.

"Soft leather," Reuben said. "No hard soles. Maybe even some holes in them."

"Homemade mocs," Tina said. "Not Kaibab or anything."

The marshal knocked at the trailer door and stepped in, stooping a little under the low ceiling. "That's it, huh?" He indicated the mask with a finger of the hand hitched in his belt. Today he had on light tan cords with the nap worn off the top of the thighs. He squatted on his heels and looked at the mask.

Tina said, "It's a ceremonial mask of some kind."

The marshal looked from the mask to Reuben, and Reuben was glad he had it to show for his strange encounter. Owl turning Pelawi, naked runner in the moonlight, a masked figure flying up a cliff face? He knew the marshal doubted him.

"I've never seen anything like it around here," Tina said.

Reuben said, "I have."

The marshal looked at him, so he told again about being at the hot spring, seeing the reflection off metal high up the cliff, and climbing the fallen boulders. No way he could describe the energy coming off that picture wall. "This mask is like the face of one of the figures in the petroglyphs," he said. "The same green beard."

Nobody said anything.

The door banged open against the wall, then slammed behind Freya Markus. They looked up, startled. Her eyes alighted on Tina. "From the mesa you can see them coming. Pickups crawling toward the canyon like a line of ants. Can somebody tell me what's happening?" Her eyes were wild.

Tina looked away. She had dreaded this moment. "It's Naposunshare," she said. "They're coming from all over. It's starting."

"And horses!" Freya said. "Strings of horses!"

"The rabbit hunt," Tina murmured. "It's before the dances."

But Freya Markus was no longer listening. She gasped and fell to her knees beside Tom Hurleigh. "Good Lord," she said, reaching out toward the mask staring up at them from eyeless sockets. Her hand hovered over it, not touching. "Where did this come from?"

"It looks like a mudhead," Tina said, "except for the green chin. And mudheads are Hopi. It doesn't make sense. There are no Hopis here. Though actually . . ."

"What?"

"Some of the stories have it that when our people came down from north of here, some settled on the mesa, but others went to Hopiland."

The maharani rose up on an elbow. "So these people might share something with the Hopi," she said. "If they came from the same stock. The eyeholes are rectangular. Is that true of the Hopi mudheads?"

Tina shook her head. "I don't think so."

Freya looked up impatiently. "Where did it come from?"

Reuben said, "After you left the spring . . ." and he told it all again, how he'd climbed the cliff face and come upon the hidden picture rock.

The marshal looked from the mask to Reuben. "Why would he attack you?"

"I don't know. Maybe he thought I was trying to stop him. I was just trying to get out of his way."

"Scared you, huh?" The marshal smiled. It wasn't a friendly smile.

Reuben shrugged. "When he butted me, I grabbed at him to shove him off, and the mask came away in my hand."

Tom Hurleigh stood up tall again under the low ceiling with his fingers hitched in his belt. "So you got a good look at him."

"Not really. He knocked the breath out of me and I fell on my back." He felt again the terror of that breathlessness, when his mouth yawned but his lungs wouldn't fill.

They were waiting, looking at him. And there'd been something familiar. But no, he couldn't place it. "He had long hair." He felt it whisper again over his bloody chest.

"Black hair? Straight hair?"

He nodded. "Yeah. I think so. It wasn't till I could sit up that I even knew I had this thing in my hand."

He reached out to pick it up and show the marshal the rent in the back, but Freya Markus dropped a firm hand on his wrist. "Don't touch it. It's ancient."

The marshal said, "Nobody flies up the face of cliffs."

Squatting on the floor, Reuben focused on the long, skinny boots beside him. Mask or no mask, the marshal didn't believe him. He stood up to meet Tom Hurleigh in the eye, but the marshal turned to the door. "The kids they took to the hospital . . ." he said.

Freya's head shot up. "Yes? How are they?"

"The girl's okay, and the Indian boy, Steve. I brought them back. And we know what poisoned them."

"What was it?"

"The potato salad."

"Oh, come on."

"The girl said the cook had overstocked on potatoes and told the kids to use them up, they'd begun growing vines. So they made a big tub of potato salad and decided to add the vines for a touch of green."

"So?"

"*Solanum tuberoscum,*" the marshal said. "Its toxicity level is very high. It's in the leaves and vines and it's a lot like its cousin deadly nightshade. Reaction time is less than a half hour."

Freya sat back on her heels. "Potato vines are *poison?*"

"Yep."

"Well, at least we know there was no wicked intent."

The marshal said, "Maybe."

"How's Joe?" Tina asked.

The marshal looked out the screen door. "Still unconscious. His parents are flying in from Salt Lake."

"My God," Freya said. "Is he in any danger?"

"He's had a couple of convulsions. Then he lapsed into the coma." The marshal went out, letting the screen bang behind him. Freya frowned after him.

"There's something else." Reuben had saved this till last. She'd had a lot of bad news lately—the poison, Naposunshare, now Joe. Maybe this would make up for some of it. "One of the petroglyphs up there is a figure throwing an atlatl."

She stared at him. He could see it sink in. "How do you know?" Her voice was low and expressionless, like she wasn't letting herself believe it.

He grabbed the sketch pad and went to work. "It's a stick figure, bent forward—like this—with one arm flung out in front of it and three times as long as the other one. And out in front of *that,* as if it's just let fly, is what's clearly a spear."

She picked up the drawing and studied it. He could see she was making herself stay calm. "It's important, isn't it?" he said hopefully, eager to give her something. "It means the petroglyphs are really old, doesn't it? I mean, when did the Anasazi start using bows and arrows?"

"Basketmaker II," she said softly. "But their use wasn't widespread till Basketmaker III."

"So doesn't this prove it? I mean, that people were here really early?"

Freya nodded slowly, eyeing him. "If this is truly what you've found." She all but whispered, "They would have been semisedentary—people in transition, who lived here seasonally . . ." Her dark eyes began to glow with something like triumph. She turned and looked at the maharani.

The maharani laughed a soft low chuckle, nodding, and said in her warbling voice, "If this young man is right, let it be enough, darling."

She turned to him. "How do I get up there?"

At the kitchen *sombra* they were lining up for dinner. Whatever it was, it smelled good. Reuben was suddenly very hungry.

"No way." He shook his head. But she was waiting. Christ, wasn't she ever satisfied? He shrugged. "I could maybe get back up there, take some pictures." The offer sounded lame. He was remembering his ordeal.

"No," she said, shaking her head. "I must stand on that ledge myself and see it with my own eyes. Tomorrow."

16

"I can't."

Tina rolled onto her back, her dream fading. She tried to hold on to it, but it was like trying to grab a cloud out of the sky. She slid deeper into her down sleeping bag, good to forty below. The night was cold.

"You know I can't. I'm no good at it even when I try."

The voice was coming from Freya's travel trailer. Tina's eyes opened to the dark.

"And I don't care. Teaching, I like. Students, I like. But I loathe committees and the mean little cliques and the jockeying for head, a job nobody in his right mind would ever want. It's not for me. A few days of it and I feel like taking to the jungle with a knife in my teeth."

Tina sat up in the sleeping bag and pulled it up over the back of her head like a cowl, bunching it around her in the cold while her eyes adjusted to the dark.

The maharani's voice was not clear, but Tina made out, ". . . may be different here."

"Oh, I hope, but even so."

The maharani murmured, "I'm afraid of your truculence." There was more that Tina couldn't catch.

Then Freya said, "Oh, I don't give a damn. I belong back in the field. I tell you, Solveig, no university pursues its existence for the sake of the students. No, it's to protect its own life—its politics, its jobs, its endowments, grants, its petty little world where one may forever strut before adolescents. I won't be sorry to get out."

The low accented voice rumbled, "But, darling, you've done enough for one summer. You'll push back history on this spot close to a millennium. That's no mean feat."

Freya laughed. "I could have told you as much before we'd turned over one trowelful of dirt."

The meadow outside was dark. The moon had gone down, all campfires were out. Tina shivered. It was the darkest, coldest part of night.

"You and your theories." The maharani had moved farther off again. Tina strained to hear. "I fear for you, Freya. You've not always been the empiricist I would wish, but you have always been a true field-worker. You must not lose your objectivity."

"Oh, come, there's never been any. Every so-called fact has been observed by subjective eyes, and you know it."

"Leave me my illusions." The maharani said something else Tina didn't catch.

"Yes, dear heart, I know," Freya said gently. "And I love you for it. And she may after all not be here."

"But you believe she is." Now the maharani seemed to be right beside the window, so close she might have been speaking to Tina instead of to Freya Markus. "Would you cut yourself off from your kind? End your days chasing dubious theories—like Lamarck, perhaps, and his remarkable toads?"

"That's cruel, Solveig. I left Central America because I needed that point in the evolution of culture where hunter-gatherers began to settle into permanent villages. Here, in the scale of things, that happened late."

"Well, you have always had a lively imagination, and you are obsessive."

"I suppose I am, and an outlaw of sorts."

"Shh. Don't say that."

Freya laughed. "Who do you think is listening?"

Tina slid down in her sleeping bag, ashamed.

Freya said softly, "I know in your secret heart you believe me."

"And you know I will never defend you."

"Look, it's no big deal anymore. I hate it when you act your age."

The only light in the meadow was in the trailer. The voices were clear in the chill night air. Tina unzipped the canvas over her window and let it drop.

The maharani's voice was low and gentle. Then, "Dear Solveig," Freya said, and it was as if she were right inside Tina's tent, "you took me as a fledgling and loved and nurtured me."

Their shadows on the blinds came together. They held each other. Then the maharani murmured at length and the taller shadow drew back. "All right," Freya said, "if life is a game like you say, you only get so many shots, it's over."

The maharani sounded resigned. "Well, if you must. Go ahead. Gamble with your career." The smaller shadow turned away.

Freya laughed, jostling playfully. "And what a career,

eh? For a bastard girl child from Caracas?" And then seriously, "Forgive me, dear heart. I owe you my life. I have never been so indebted to another human being. No, nor loved another as I have loved you."

Then the voices faded as they moved away from the window.

She must be her mother, Tina told herself. The light in the trailer went out. The cold of the night had entered the little tent as her body heat escaped through the open window.

It could be one of two things, she told herself. Either the maharani is her mother, or . . .

Her mother, she whispered. She must be her mother.

She unzipped the tent door and crawled out into grass drenched with dew. The palest gray light was dawning, the meadow engulfed in fog. Trees were vague traceries like in a Japanese print.

Out of the mist a figure crept toward her, barefoot, belt undone, chinos hanging loose, carrying shoes and shirt in hand.

"Hello!" came the whisper. "Look who's here."

Willy. So, he had spent the night in the meadow with one of the women—who?—and was creeping back at dawn to his camper in the upper meadow. He approached swiftly, reached out, dropping clothes and shoes, and caught her to him. Any other time she would have shoved him away. For reasons unclear to her, this time she did not. She felt his naked chest warm through her nightshirt. He kissed her thoroughly and she let him. Then she pulled back and wide-eyed looked at him.

He laughed and let her go, stooping to pick up his clothes. Then he went on his way.

She wiped her mouth. Why had she let him kiss her? Could be one of two reasons. Curiosity. Inattention.

No, it felt like she'd done it to prove herself some way.

At that unfortunate moment Reuben, arms loaded with wood for the breakfast fires, emerged from the fog and leapt the stream and stopped dead, eyes moving from Willy, walking away with his clothes in his hands, and back to her.

Oh, Christ, he'd seen it all. She opened her mouth to say something, but no words came.

He stared at her for a moment, then hefted his load and trudged with his burden up the meadow toward the kitchen *sombra*.

17

"No you don't. Give me that." Reuben grabbed the rope. At least the morning was cool. The crows were back in their tree. Maybe crows laid claim to a particular tree and roosted there or something. He filed that away.

"Wow! Get the hostility." Willy put his hands out innocently at his sides and asked the circle of watching students, "What'd I ever do to him?"

"Okay, if you're so sure it'll hold, let's see you go first."

They'd stopped Willy in his little red pickup on his way to the hospital to be with Joe, and asked to borrow his climbing gear. But Willy, possessive about his things, had hesitated briefly, then come along, unwilling to trust them with his equipment.

"What's the matter, man?" Willy said. "You don't trust me? I've done this a hundred times!" But he shrugged and put his weight on the rope, testing. It was attached to the piton jammed in a rock crevice on top of the cliff. He took up his mallet and pounded it deeper.

Reuben said, "We wouldn't want to scratch our pretty face, would we."

"Bite your tongue, man." Willy smiled his winning smile.

Out of the corner of his eye, Reuben saw Tina, arms crossed tightly against her breast, watching. She stood a little apart from the others, down by the head of the trail with Sonny and Horse, the Indian boys. Lighten up, he told himself. What are you, her big brother or something? There was a lot of sleeping around in the meadow. Everybody knew it. But why would she choose Buttercup Willy?

Over near the drop-off, Freya caught Tina's arm and asked, "What're they doing down there by the pond?"

Reuben looked down the canyon. Tents and brush arbors were going up.

"Before the BLM built the dam, that was the dance ground," Tina said.

And Horse said belligerently, "We still camp there, and hold the dances where we always did."

Freya muttered, "God, we're done for."

"Come here, Bobby," Willy yelled.

Bobby Ybarra moved up and took hold of the rope. Willy tested it again, clipped the safety to his belt by a D-shaped ring, and waving to everybody, wrapped himself in the rope, took hold, and dropped back over the edge out of sight.

Freya watched with her arms crossed and her fingers drumming on her sleeve. Bobby played out the rope, Steve standing by to help. Some of the students lay on their stomachs looking over, watching Willy rappel down the cliff face.

Steve peered over the edge and yelled, "Everything okay down there?"

"Smooth, man." Willy's voice sounded distant in the open air. "Wow, lookit the pictures! Okay, it's safe. You can haul me back up!"

Steve said, "I think we'll just leave you where you are!"

Everybody laughed.

"Come on, don't be an ass!" The rope flapped. "Pull me up, Bobby!"

Grinning, his black wing of hair falling over his forehead, Bobby Ybarra dug in and hauled. Steve Many Hands got out in front and helped.

A few minutes later Willy's head appeared. "Okay, who wants to go first?" He was undoing the harness.

"I'm the only one going over," Freya said firmly, stepping forward.

Groans and pleas came from the students, nothing, Reuben noticed, from Caspar Dreyfus, who stood off against the background of piñons, taking no part.

"Okay, ma'am," Willy said. "You're the boss. What do you know about rock climbing?"

"Precious little. But I've done this once before."

"You ought to be wearing these tin pants." He had them on over his jeans. He dropped the pants and stepped out of them. They looked a little like lederhosen, reinforced with extra leather in the crotch.

"They'll never fit," Freya said.

"Pull them over your jeans. They'll fit you fine."

"I'm going first," Reuben said to Freya. "I'll be down there to grab you."

"No need," she said, but maybe she looked a little grateful.

He grabbed the ropes. He'd never rock climbed before in his life, but if Willy could do it ... "Hey, Steve!"

"Yeah?"

"I want you to play out the ropes, okay?"

"Sure," Steve said.

"He don't trust us, Bobby," Willy said, smiling.

Reuben glanced over at Tina, but when she met his eyes he looked away and yelled, "Ready!"

And Steve said, "Ready."

Fear gripped him in its talons. He'd broken into a sweat. The rope tightened in his crotch and he wished for the tin pants. He backed over to the edge of the cliff to keep from looking down.

"I've got you," Steve said.

He nodded and tentatively lay back in the harness. It felt secure.

Bobby Ybarra grinned at him. "Even if you let go, you got that whatchacallit . . ."

"Carabiner," said Willy, the initiate.

Reuben looked down at the ring snapped to the harness. "Okay," he muttered. "Here I go."

He let out his breath, leaned into the ropes, and took a step or two down the cliff face. Then he kicked off. It was a little like holding your nose as a kid and jumping backward into the swimming pool at the Y.

The rope moved through his hands. He grabbed it and caught himself with a Nike on the cliff face.

"We got you!" Steve yelled down.

He steadied himself and pushed off again. The rope slid through his hands. He descended past footholds he had chipped on his climb up, shocked at their shallowness and his own dried bloodstains on the rock. Then his zigzag climb diverged from his plumb line fall.

The wind was fierce. Silent and possessive, it snatched at his hair, dried his sweat, and left him cold in the sun. He swayed in the ropes, banged a shoulder against the cliff and winced, then steadied himself and dug both feet into the cliff.

Steve yelled down, "You okay?"

Define *okay*.

He started down again.

When his toe touched the ledge, he grabbed the rope and hung on. It loosened—his whole support—and that terrified him. He scrambled to his feet telling himself, Don't look down, stay close to the wall, get hold of yourself, you've been here before. He looked around without looking down, but out of the corner of his eye he saw the drop into empty space.

He pressed his back into the cliff and swallowed. What are you, Batman or something? You found it, didn't you? You should have let well enough alone, let Steve come down, he's the athlete.

But the cliff was his. He owned these pictures. He wanted to give them to her.

"Okay down there?" That asshole Willy leaned over the edge. "She's ready to go when you give us back the ropes!"

He unwound himself, held on to the ropes for a minute, then let them go. "Pull 'em up!" he yelled.

From the top of the cliff he could hear Willy instructing and Freya answering. Gutsy woman. "Steve!" he yelled.

Steve hung his head over, the wind whipping his long Indian hair. "Yeah?"

"Keep your many goddam hands on that rope, will you."

"I got you!"

He watched her appear over the edge. She leaned out in the ropes and looked down at him.

He smiled up at her. "You'll be okay!"

A moment later she landed beside him. He grabbed the ropes before they went sickeningly slack, and she lapsed gratefully against him. "God, I was petrified." She clutched his forearms with her hands and steadied herself. He helped her out of the ropes. He watched her face as she turned to the cliff.

"Good Lord!"

He traced the crow's-feet at her temples and committed her profile to memory.

"It's marvelous," she said.

"Yeah."

"The bison! The spears! My God, it's moving! Everything's moving! It's enough to make you dizzy.

"What's this?" She touched a line incised in the rock— one of the four-pointed stars. Something like fireworks trailed behind it.

The wind loosened her hair and whipped it across his face. "The star's familiar enough, but not the contrail. And look! Here, too." Another star, this one with a face. She stepped back and looked at the big squatting figure doing its business. She put her finger out and touched it.

She put her finger on a stick man standing, it looked like, in the rain. "Could they have witnessed a rain of fire?" she asked herself. She turned and squinted into the sun at the opposite canyon wall, craggy and sharp. She looked back at the petroglyphs. "I wonder . . ."

"What?"

She squinted against the wind. "Look at that shadow." She pointed at the squatting figure's big, round, enigmatic face. The shadow of the V-shaped notch across the canyon fell sharply across it. "At this angle it wouldn't move much from month to month."

"What are you thinking?" he asked. It seemed like an intimate question.

She grabbed his arm, and all he was aware of was her fingers gripping him. "I'm not sure, Reuben . . ."

It was the first time she'd called him by his name.

". . . but it could be a calendar. The spot where that sharp angle of shadow falls on the face could tell the time to plant, the time to harvest, or mark an equinox."

He reached out and took her hand and drew her back from the edge and closer to the tiny stick figure that was his own discovery. "Look."

She looked and after a moment gasped. "Oh good Lord. Oh, shit, it is. It's an atlatl." She fell back against him. "You're right! They were here!"

He held his breath and slid his hands under her elbows. He smelled her hair in his face—fresh, clean, full of sun.

"What's going on down there, you two?" It was Steve Many Hands.

Reuben looked up. Tina, too, was peering down at them.

"Have you got your camera?" Freya asked.

"Yeah, the little one." He took it from the pocket on the front of his sweatshirt and shoved back the lens cover. "I can't get much distance. I can't get the whole thing in one frame."

"Get some close-ups."

"Yeah, okay."

Sighting, he moved back as close to the edge as he dared, and felt her hand grab the top of his jeans. "Careful!" Her fingers curled over the top of the jeans against his skin and she held on.

He felt an embarrassing stir below her fingers, but luckily a sudden glimpse of the drop cooled him out. He looked quickly back at the cliff and, raising the camera, snapped shots of the whole thing in sequence, overlapping so the seams would be clear. Then he punched the zoom and tried focusing individual glyphs. He got the squatting figure, the face, the stick man throwing the atlatl, the bison, the stars trailing tails, the stars with faces, the stick man in the rain, the animals, always aware of her hand holding him safe, knuckles curled against his navel.

When he'd finished, she said, "You go up first."

He shook his head. "I'll help you into the ropes. I'll hold on to you as high as I can reach."

"No. I want to look a little longer. This is something I'll never forget." She smiled at him. "Thank you." But her attention was not on him, it was on the cliff face. "Now, go."

"You'll be all right?"

She nodded, no longer really aware of him, hugging herself against the wind and looking at the petroglyphs.

He wrapped himself in the ropes and tugged. "Okay, Steve," he shouted, "let's go!"

Back on top, Steve Many Hands unclasped the harness. Reuben took a deep breath. He wanted to soothe his crotch with his fingers, but the semicircle of eyes watched— students, geologists, the Earth Watch people, the two Indian boys. Now also the marshal and the guy in the cowboy hat leaning against a tree. Reuben thought he'd seen him somewhere before.

"Okay," the geologist said, "I'm next."

Reuben turned to Jim Cochran. "You going down?"

"I wouldn't miss it."

"Give her a few minutes."

Over there beside Steve Many Hands, Tina watched. Reuben looked away. The crows watched from the top of the tree, probably wondering why these creatures didn't just lift up their wings and fly. As if to show them how, one crow fluttered up from the top limb of the piñon tree, then landed again on one foot.

"Wow!" It was Jim, the geologist, out of sight now over the edge.

"You be careful!" his wife called down.

The marshal said in Reuben's ear, "Now, where was it, exactly, you were attacked?"

Reuben jumped, startled.

"Was it about here?"

Tom Hurleigh was smiling, but it wasn't a friendly smile. "No. Over there," Reuben said. "Come on, I'll show you."

He walked ahead of the marshal to the spot where the masked figure had risen above the canyon wall. "It was about here." He stopped and looked around. "Yeah. I was trying to find the spot where I'd seen the reflections from down below." He led the way to the edge of the cliff. Off to his right he could see a series of ledges, one the ledge of the picture rock. "It was right about here. I'd climbed down to that ledge, and to the one below it. There was nothing there."

They were coming up, Jim Cochran first. Bobby Ybarra got him out of the harness and dropped it back over for Freya. The geologist hugged his wife excitedly and called over to Reuben, "You know that bulge? The one that blocked the trail?"

The melted vanilla icing. He'd thought it was as far as he could go. "Yeah?"

Steve Many Hands hauled on the rope. They were bringing Freya up. Her face was flushed and excited when she appeared over the edge.

Jade danced around like a kid who had to go to the bathroom. "Oh, please, let us go down!"

"You know what that bulge is?" Jim Cochran said. They were getting Freya out of the harness. "It's seepage from an ancient hot spring in the cliff. It's the hardened mineral content." He turned to his wife. "It's travertine!"

Freya rubbed a rope burn on her arm.

Clarity said, "You couldn't get me in that harness for a million dollars."

Jade said, "I'd go down in a minute if they'd let me."

The Earth Watch widower from Calgary asked, "Can you date that seepage?"

The geologist nodded. "Should be easy. A film of it has covered some of the glyphs, though you can plainly see them through it. That means you've got as definite a time frame for that rock art as you could ever hope to find." He was smiling, his face slick-skinned in the morning sun.

Freya asked, "Are you sure?"

Jim Cochran nodded. "Once we date that bulge of vanilla icing, it'll fix the time when your prehistory artists stopped working on that cliff face." He turned to the students. "The seepage had shut off easy access to their picture gallery."

Freya nodded. "And they could no longer get to it!"

"But I got to it," Reuben said.

"At the risk of life and limb. Why would they bother? They'd just find another rock face."

"How long would it take seepage like that to form and harden?" Carmack McIntyre asked.

"We'll be able to tell that, too, in the lab. Maybe no longer than, say, twenty years."

Smiling, Freya hugged herself. She turned and wandered over to the trees. To be alone with it, Reuben thought. He felt Tina's eyes on him, but he wouldn't look at her.

The marshal said, "I've always heard artists have lively imaginations." Hurleigh was playing with him.

"You saw the mask, Marshal."

The marshal shoved his hands in his belt. "You say you didn't see anything, but you were the only one up here the morning the old man died."

Reuben frowned. No, Freya was there, too. He turned and looked at her over there where Sonny Concha and Horse Rios were trying to negotiate a trip down the face of the cliff. She raised her voice. "No, I said! I don't want to hear of any of you trying to go over this cliff. It's strictly forbidden, understand?"

Willy was knocking the piton loose while the Indian-looking cowboy watched from under the brim of his big hat. Then when Horse Rios turned menacingly toward him, the cowboy uncrossed his arms and faded back into the piñons. Reuben wondered what that was about. Watching him go, Reuben knew where he'd seen him before, but it barely registered. He was sure now the marshal suspecte*
him.

18

Crossing the pueblo plaza, John caught a fly ball and tossed it back to the pitcher.

"Hey, John, play ball!"

"Not now, man."

They clustered around him, hanging on his arms.

"Got any chewing gum, Hooper John?"

"C'mon, leggo of me." He shook them off, but they followed him. One of the boys swaggered behind him, imitating his walk. John picked up a rock and chunked it at him and the kid dodged, shrieking with laughter.

"Hey, man, Eliseo, he's gone to the clinic!"

"Whadaya . . . ! ?" John broke into a run. He rounded the adobe corner and skidded to a halt. Up ahead Cruz Domingue squatted in the sand in front of the old man's door. The head honcho himself. John whipped his gun from his holster and pointed it. *Pow.* But it was only his finger and an explosive whisper. He hiked his belt and started walking. His shadow in the cowboy hat stretched out in front of him, much taller than he was.

Cruz looked sideways up, watching him come. "Hello, John. How you been?"

"Good. I been fine." The old man's dead, John thought. Went and checked out on me. So come on, give it to me. I can take it. You can let me have it straight.

He squatted beside the governor.

"The old man's gone to the clinic. They're giving out shots today."

The air went out of John like somebody'd hit him in the stomach. He swallowed and swiped at his mouth. Finally he said, "He's been real sick. Won't eat. Won't talk. Just lays there and looks at you." In the sand in front of them the shadow of the roofline boxed them in and he could no longer see himself. "Sometimes he'll sort of, you know, laugh like he's got a secret. But he won't say what he's laughing at. Sometimes he'll disappear for half a day and won't say where he's been." He moved forward till his hat broke out of the shadow box and jutted into the sunny yard. The round shadow of his hat made his head about two yards wide, like one of those golden rings around the heads of saints.

"He's old," Cruz Domingue said. "Can't eat. Got no teeth to chew with."

"He's got teeth. He just won't keep them in," John said. "The women bring him soup and stuff, but he won't look at it." So if Cruz hadn't come about the old man, what was he doing here?

"Where you been, John?"

Here it comes. Everybody asking questions: Where you been? Where you going? What you doing? He looked away. Clouds were building over the eastern mountains. "Up the mesa," he said.

"What you doing up there?"

"Nothin'. It's a free country, ain't it?" How come you to ask?

Cruz said, "Ever hear of somebody name Jeremiah Hoop?"

John jumped, he couldn't help it. Then for a minute he

couldn't get his breath, like when Isaiah came at him with his belt.

"No!" he said. "No, I never in my life heard of nobody by that name!" Even to John that sounded excessive.

"Reason I ask," Cruz said softly, "Hoop is a lot like Hooper. You see what I mean."

"Yeah," John said eagerly. "Like a coincident."

After a moment, Cruz said, "You ever been in Arkansas, John?"

"No!" Shaking his head. "I never in my life been anywheres near the state of Arkansas. Cross my heart." He crossed his heart. Slow down, he told himself. Keep cool. They got nothing on you.

Then where'd Cruz come up with the name Jeremiah Hoop?

What do you care? He can't prove nothing.

You don't know that. They got ways. Ways and means. They got computers.

"Funny kind of a thing, how the old man come to bring you here," Cruz Domingue said.

"He loves me like a son! He said so hisself!"

But for a moment he'd confused the old man with his friend of the snowy robes and soothing voice.

Cruz nodded. "That could be. He had a son."

"Yeah, he told me. But he died."

Cruz nodded. "Truck turned over on the canyon road from Taos. Rolled in the river and he was drowned. That's when Eliseo got to drinking."

"He don't drink no more. Honest." But it wasn't true. John kept them in booze. It made them both feel better.

Cruz's hand fell on his shoulder. He sighed and stood up and gave his belt a hitch. "Okay, John. You'll tell me if this Jeremiah Hoop was to come around."

John squinted up at Cruz. "Whaddaya mean? Why would he come around? I don't know nobody by that name."

The governor's eyes were stern and sad. He knew, and John knew he knew. Sun still shining, off in the distance thunder rumbled.

"If you ever want to talk about anything—just shoot the bull man to man, know what I mean, John?—come on by my office."

Why would he want to do that? "Yeah, sure," he said.

Cruz Domingue said softly, looking down at him, "See, John, the thing is, we not gonna get the land back from the Feds till all these questions get cleared up."

"What things you talking about?" John rose slowly on the balls of his feet.

Cruz hiked his head back toward the mesa. "All that mischief been going on up there."

"Not get the land back? How come! Why not! That's not fair!"

"You're right, John. I agree. But the marshal, he tells me that's the way it's got to be."

Cruz turned and walked off down the broad dirt plaza between the houses, everything the color of adobe but the sky. The wind blew a candy wrapper after him, small and playful, mocking his heels. John wanted to run after him, too, grab his arm, spin him around, argue. But he watched him go, tall in his boots, his shadow following. And standing there all alone, the ball game over and the kids gone home, Hooper John knew what he had to do.

19

I've been remiss, Tina wrote. She was sitting on a rock outside her tent, catching up in her journal. She'd written plenty in her head, she just hadn't managed to get it down. There was too much going on. For one thing, she was in bad with Reuben.

But why was that? Because that creep Willy was sneaking at dawn back to his own bed and she let him kiss her, she didn't know why, and Reuben saw it and . . .

Up across the meadow in front of one of the lean-tos, he was right this minute talking with the marshal and somebody . . . It was her old high school friend Tito Gonzales, now of the Santa Fe PD. In the lengthening twilight, Tom Hurleigh stood with his head bent, apparently talking to Tito, Reuben listening with his hands on his hips. Tito had on new-looking jeans and a plaid shirt, but she suspected he was here in his official capacity.

The Tsorigis down by the pond must be driving tent stakes deeper because of the rising wind. You could hear the ring of steel and the whinnying of ponies unloading from pickups and horse trailers for tomorrow's rabbit hunt, and men shouting to one another, probably stringing a makeshift corral for the remuda. Thunder rumbled in the distance.

In the granny glasses she used as little as possible, she squinted at the sky, still bright overhead but darkening over the treetops to the east, then bent to the pad on her knees, chewed on her stub of pencil, and wrote: *Reuben acts like some protective big brother. Big Brother is watching me.*

She wanted to explain, but where to start? She'd better go back to the beginning. She felt compelled to get it right, but it felt like some kind of self-justification, though she hadn't done anything, had she? *I hadn't been able to sleep and it was just before dawn and I heard these voices. The reason I let him kiss me . . .* Her pencil poised motionless, she went back over it in her head, but it didn't make any sense. She closed the journal over her pencil and set it down on the grass beside her. She hugged her knees in their faded jeans, watching the crush at the kitchen *sombra*, people in their ponchos, everybody in a hurry for it had begun to drizzle.

Then the rain came in earnest and they were running for the lean-tos, sagging paper plates in hand, bare knees pumping out of all that waterproof nylon—orange, red, green, yellow. They were shouting and laughing. Out there it was raining, while here under the tree it was still dry. Then came the first loud clap of thunder followed by lightning. She watched Tito and the marshal get back in the marshal's vehicle. Then she gathered up her things and crawled in her tent.

Later, after dark, while the others crowded for warmth around the stone fireplaces in the lean-tos and the downpour beat on her tent fly, by the light of her Coleman lantern she tried again.

A funny thing, mealtimes Freya Markus usually flops at the first table she comes to and makes conversation with whoever. I admire that. I think it's her way of including everybody, avoiding cliques and hierarchies, which in a situation like this could easily form. But at lunch today . . .

She'd flopped down at the already crowded table where Tina sat with Jade and Pilar and Beano and some of the graduate students. And Clarity. The students liked to get Clarity going, and she'd been obligingly holding forth.

Tina sighed and put down her pen. Writing wore her out. Freya had dropped down at the head of the table, and though she'd never done more than tolerate Clarity, today she was listening. Any other time, she'd have been polite, smiling, her eyes wandering, ready to leap at the first opportunity to escape. God, was she taking Clarity seriously? She must be desperate.

Why?

Because there was something she had to know before they lost the dig to the Tsorigi? Or because Steve Many Hands had just made a real find? Down on the promontory pointing toward the valley, he'd flopped down in the shade of a piñon and peeled an orange. When he dug a little pit with his pocket knife to bury the rind, the soil had turned oily and black and come out in chunks. At first he'd thought it was wet, but when he smeared it on his hand, and sniffed and tasted, he got excited and called Freya over.

Just as she got there, along came Clarity, who, with barely a glance, said, "Oh, yeah, here's where we had the platform—you know, to smoke buffalo and bear and deer hides. We'd put them on the platform and cure them over a charcoal fire." And off she went while Freya knelt, fingering the black soil, sniffing, tasting, then looking up, astonished, at Clarity's back retreating off the mesa top.

The lantern was low on fuel. She turned it off and sat huddled with her arms around her knees. The rain had lessened. She unzipped her window flap and watched the light show going on in the heavens. It was spectacular. A dozen flashes of lightning fractured the sky at once. She'd seen it before, but never from a tent. It felt a little threatening.

And it was cold. She turned on her lantern again but kept it low. It warmed the tent. She stowed her glasses in their case and lay back on her pillow. After a while, the lightning streaks were farther apart and the thunder faded down the side of the world. She listened to the rain, gentle now.

Her pillow was soft, actually a pile of unfolded clothes. So okay, she was a slob. She liked having her things around her. Not like Reuben—a place for everything and everything in its place.

How could Reuben think she . . . ? But she wouldn't think of Reuben, she'd think of something else. She drifted in the hypnagogic state, hearing Jade pass by outside, her voice running on. "Yeah, he came down after supper. I was showing these pictures I just got from home. See, this is my dog, this is my sister Tracey, this is the person I was living with at the time, this is my niece I think she looks like me . . ."

Somebody scratched at her tent flap.

"Tina?" It was Reuben.

The lantern flickered. She sat up and rubbed her eyes and turned the fuel up a notch.

"Come on in." Should she play it cool, act like nothing had happened?

He tunneled in headfirst and sat back on his heels and looked at her. His shorts were muddy, there were twigs in his beard and a leaf in his hair. She reached out and took the leaf and twirled it by the stem in her fingers. "What's the matter?"

"It's the marshal. He thinks I did it. He as much as told me. He thinks I killed Rap Singleton." His voice rose with the idiocy of it.

"Oh, come on, Reuben."

"It's true. He implied I've been seeing things—the naked runner, the guy in the mask. God, does he think I'm some kind of homicidal maniac? And he said I was the only one on the mesa that night."

She frowned. "You told him you heard Rap cry out when he fell, right?"

"Yeah, but Freya must have heard it, too."

"Freya?"

"She said it must have been a bobcat."

"Freya on the mesa at dawn? What was she doing there?"

"Beats me."

The lantern flared and died. It had run out of fuel. She turned it off and the mantle glowed for a minute in the dark. Should she tell him about Freya and the maharani, what she had overheard? She would like to get his opinion. But of course the maharani's her mother, she told herself. "Look, Reuben, the other morning . . ."

"Tito Gonzales was here," he said. He sank back beside her with his head on the pile of clothes. "He told me not to leave the canyon. He said they'd be back in the morning and they expect to find me here. I think they're planning to take me in."

"No, shh," she whispered. "I'm sure you're wrong."

"I don't think so. Tina . . ."

"What?"

"Could they put me in jail? Your know, pending a hearing or something?"

"Don't be silly."

"I couldn't take that. And it would kill my mother."

"You're cold," she said. "You're shivering." She unzipped the sleeping bag and stretched it over them both.

He seemed then to be holding his breath. He let it out like a sigh. She was relieved they were together. She settled down close to him to share the warmth of the sleeping bag. "Don't worry. It'll be all right."

He wasn't so sure. The thing about being named Reuben Rubin—his dear old dad's joke of an idea, he must have been drunk—the thing about his name was, when somebody called to you, like the marshal earlier, you couldn't tell whether it was Reuben, and friendly, or Rubin, and sort of harsh.

"Look, kid," he said huskily, "I'm thinking of getting the hell out of here." You heard all kinds of things about jail. The idea of heading for the mountains and living off the land was no longer a fantasy. In his desperation it had become a real option.

"What do you mean?" She was almost asleep.

He felt her close, dozing against his arm. He stole it out from under her and put it around her. "You know, go into hiding till they find the real killer."

That woke her up. "Nonsense. If you run, that'll convince Tom Hurleigh you're guilty. He'll quit looking for the murderer and go looking for *you*."

He hadn't thought of that.

She pulled the sleeping bag up to her chin. "Go to sleep."

How could he sleep? He listened to the trees' syncopated dripping on the tent. He lay rigid beside her, and once he cupped her cheek with his hand, gently, and smoothed her hair.

She almost woke, thinking how sweet, but then she drifted deeper while he lay wide-awake, planning. Before the marshal got back he would eat a big breakfast and lift as much food as he could carry from the utility trailer. Then he'd mosey down the road with his backpack toward the path to the mesa. When nobody was looking, he'd veer off and head for the mountain, find a cave, or maybe one of the old cliff dwellings back where nobody ever went. He'd be a latter-day mountain man. His beard would grow down his chest. When his food ran out he would live on piñon nuts and birds and small animals.

He quelled a wave of anxiety and told himself he was ready for a change.

20

The marshal woke up feeling in his bones this was the day. He didn't know why. But he ate his Post Toasties and left Santa Fe early. The air was fresh after the storm. The sun was warm. The morning light turned the tree trunks bronze, and the woods were full of jabbering piñon jays. No place like New Mexico. Damn, the state had everything—mountains, deserts, sun and snow.

And tourists.

Well, why not? Tourists were just people from someplace else.

He'd seen Joe's parents, a decent-looking couple from Salt Lake, the night before, talked to them when they came out of the hospital chapel. They wanted to put Joe in an ambulance and take him to the hospital at home, but the doctors wouldn't release a patient in a coma. Poor kid, looked like he might not make it. Should he tell Freya Markus that? Driving past the cutoff to the mesa top, he saw the rear end of her Jeep Cherokee climbing through the trees.

He sighed. Maybe wait and see what happened.

Suddenly the washed-clean morning was overlaid with an alternate reality. Most of the time he lived in the real world. His job. Transmission going. But then it slipped and he was in that other place calling, Wait! don't leave me!

Would his wife be there to meet him at the end of the tunnel, or had she moved on already beyond where he'd ever catch up with her?

Ridiculous, he told himself. Dead was dead. You saw it all the time on the shoulder of the road. It was rot, decay, and unspeakable horrors you bury too deep to look at.

Without a conscious decision, he backed and turned and found himself climbing slowly behind the Jeep Cherokee.

What was she like, anyway, Freya Markus?

Loved the out-of-doors, great cook, liked the smell of pipe smoke, hated frills and dancing and eating out.

He must be getting senile. A woman like that, Ph.D. doctor, university professor . . .

The gears ground into low.

He pictured her in the living room with his wife. They just sat there. Maybeth couldn't think of anything to say, and Freya didn't say anything to Maybeth. They just sat there uneasily in the chintzed-up chairs looking at one another. He found it unnerving.

He rummaged his pipe out of his pocket and yanked the steering wheel to keep the vehicle on the twisting road. He engaged the four-wheel drive.

There it was, the Cherokee. Driving with one hand, he adjusted the rearview mirror and ran his fingers over his cropped hair, touched the scar on his temple, scowled at his chapped lips.

He slowed and almost stopped, but then passed her vehicle parked in back of the house trailer and drove to the end of the road. It didn't take him far. He pulled up and stopped and sat with the door open. Now what?

He got out and slammed the door and headed across the mesa toward the fall site on the cliff. The trail climbed a little and turned from sand to stone. Why was he walking on his toes? If he made a little noise, who would hear?

He emerged from the trees and the view spread out before him. After all these years it still took his breath. She was standing there with her back to him, right at the edge of the cliff, frowning down at something. He was shaken.

She would think he'd followed her. Well, in a way he had, hadn't he? What was she looking at?

He cleared his throat to announce his presence.

Startled, she turned, looking annoyed and guilty. Guilty of what? He nodded and walked up beside her. She was almost as tall as he was. Maybeth had been a little thing. He saw she'd been looking down at the Indian encampment.

"They're getting ready for their to-do." He nodded at the camp down there around the lake. His pipe had gone out. He was glad of a chance to stoop and strike a kitchen match on a rock and draw deeply till he got it going. "You're up mighty early."

"I like to get up here before the students." She sounded like she was defending herself.

Things were busy around the pond—women shaking out blankets and sleeping bags after the night, breakfast fires going, kids running around, old men squatting on their heels talking, young men racing up and down the road on their ponies. The scene made the marshal feel lonely. He turned and looked at her and cast around for something else to say. "You always up here this time of morning?" Maybeth always woke with the birds. And apparently Rap Singleton had, too.

She turned and looked at him with those startling eyes. "I have to get back to the ruin," she said.

Nodding, blowing out his match and slinging it over the edge, he watched her turn and hurry off down the trail. Then he squatted, smoking, looking down on the Indians around the lake. He envied them. They were like a big family, gossiping, cooking, the men always talking together. The whole tribe took part in the dances. It had been years since he'd danced. Over by the pond some of the men were knocking together a platform out of two-by-fours and one-inch lumber.

Squatting there, at first all he saw was an Indian camp around the pond. But after a time with his thoughts elsewhere, he took the pipe out of his mouth and felt his muscles tense. He got slowly to his feet and cursed silently.

Great God Almighty. How many times had he stood on this spot? But it had always been to peruse the site itself for what it could tell him about the murder, or to look down to where Rap Singleton had landed. It was only now, with his mind free and wandering, that he saw what was right out in the open, there for anybody to see. His breath caught in his throat. He knew he was looking at Rap Singleton's "big picture."

His pipe went out as he pointed with his finger, counting. There were four of the damn things. He whispered "Crimunetly," the old-fashioned epithet he'd used around the house so as not to scandalize his wife.

And looking down at these four dead giveaways, instantly he knew what was missing from the RV, so obvious he'd never have thought of it.

He got up and ran toward his vehicle. He had to get down there before the Indians unwittingly destroyed his discovery. He must have been blind. How in God's name had he missed seeing the obvious? He knew now what Rap Singleton had been doing up here on top of the mesa that fatal morning.

21

John rose early to prepare himself. He would surrender in full regalia, like a warrior. He wasn't sure if that was Indian or samurai, but it didn't matter. It was the spirit of the thing that mattered. He was glad it was the time of Naposunshare. They would all be there to witness his heroic deed. On rabbit hunt day he would save the tribe, give them back their land by immolating himself. He wasn't sure what "immolating" meant, but he liked the sound of it and he thought it designated an unselfish act.

And that was as it should be. A hero thought not what his people could do for him, but what he could do for his people.

He would ride up boldly and surrender, with pride and dignity, and the marshal would meet him like General Miles met Geronimo. Excitement shortened his breath.

With skunk pelts clasping his ankles and turtle shells rattling at his knees, wearing the ancient breechclout he'd found in his secret place, with his hair undone and flowing around his shoulders and his face streaked with paint, black smears under his eyes and turkey feathers in his hair, bareback Hooper John approached the canyon. Some of the Indian youths were racing up and down the road, eager for the hunt. Another cluster jostled each other over by the remuda, pointing, giggling at the crazy painted gringo approaching on the Appaloosa.

John averted his eyes and looked straight ahead. He was pleased to see the marshal there by the pond with Cruz Domingue. They were squatting beside a pile of rocks, the marshal with a rusty tobacco can in one hand and a piece of paper in the other. The two of them frowned over whatever was on the paper. Then Cruz stood up and pointed—there, there, and there—and some of the men around him nodded and trotted off along the shore of the lake. Something was going on, but nothing, John told himself, to what was about to happen.

The marshal put the paper in the tobacco can, and the can in his hip pocket. He watched Hooper John approach. He stood up and smiled, and that annoyed John as it was not in the script. He slowed his pony to a walk and moved toward the marshal at a stately gait. A breeze rippled the lake, and the grass on its margin sparkled in the sun from last night's rain. An old squaw straightened with a frying pan in her hand and looked at him.

He reined in his pony. "Hou," he said solemnly.

"Hou," the marshal answered.

John was aware of the young horsemen following him off the road. They pulled up behind him and sat listening, pointing, snickering. One was Horse Rios.

He waited till he had all their attention, then said without so much as raising his voice, just as he'd planned it, "I have come to surrender."

"Giving yourself up, eh?" the marshal said, still smiling, glancing at Cruz. But Cruz wasn't smiling, he was squatting there looking at the sandy ground like something embarrassed him or made him sad.

John took by its head the stone club he'd found in the cave and drew it from the string of his breechclout. Holding it by the hilt, he offered it to the marshal.

The marshal grinned. He stepped forward and took it. John didn't like that grin. He didn't like the way the marshal was playing his part, so he didn't answer. He grasped the hilt of his hunting knife.

The marshal watched. "You're surrendering your weapons to me, is that it?"

"That's right." John straightened his back and made sure his voice carried. "I'm giving myself up for the sake of my people!"

Behind the marshal, Cruz lifted his head and looked at John. Cruz wasn't smiling.

"Your people, huh?" The marshal glanced back at Cruz, but Cruz didn't look at him. "And just what are you giving yourself up *for*?" the marshal asked.

"I'm your man. I hereby before God and these witnesses—" he looked around "—confess to what all I done."

The marshal nodded, his smile fading. "You're confessing . . . ?"

"To what all's been going on around here."

"I see." The marshal nodded slowly.

"So you can take me prisoner and return to my people their hereditary lands." He'd spent most of the night choosing his words, rehearsing silently while the old man slept. He looked up at the sky, incredibly blue, telling himself it was a good day to die, though dying was far from anything he had in mind.

He drew a deep breath. "It was me set the fire. I'm the one let loose all of them snakes." It was quiet but for the youths' ponies snorting and shuffling behind him. He felt proud and excited. He saw the scene like in Technicolor on a big screen, his mounted self in costume at the center.

"I see," the marshal said, serious now, moving closer, reaching out to grasp the Appaloosa's reins. John lifted his leg over the horse's head, preparing to slide down the way he liked, with his back to the horse.

"I see," the marshal said again. "You're confessing to the murder of Rap Singleton. You shoved him over the cliff."

John's motion stopped. This wasn't in the script. He stared down at the marshal.

"Whadaya mean?" He swung his leg back over the horse's head till he sat astride again. "I never kilt nobody." He yanked his reins, but the marshal held on. The pony jerked its head up. John jabbed with his heels and the pony reared straight up on its hind legs. John almost slid off the crupper, but he grabbed the mane and clung. Leaning low over the pony's neck, he forced him back down.

The marshal lurched, trying to retrieve the reins, but John wheeled the pony around. Wide-eyed, the pony screamed. John yelled, "I never in my life kilt nobody!" He sawed on the bit in the pony's mouth, backing him toward the road.

Nothing was going according to plan. He grasped the handle of his knife. The sheath dropped to the ground, and that confused him—it was nicely tooled, he'd done it himself and didn't want to lose it—but he leaned off his pony's back and jabbed as the marshal lunged, slashing his flannel shirt under the armpit.

"Get away! Get back! I ain't confessing to no murder! I don't know what you're talkin' about!"

"Now calm down, son. Hand me that knife." The marshal was reaching again, trying to move closer.

Behind John, the Indian youths on their ponies were closing in. Then he saw, coming abreast down the road from the meadow, some of the women students, heading for the path to the mesa top. They slowed in the road to see what was going on. John's laugh sounded hysterical even to him. He lashed his pony with the end of the reins, galloped past the Indian boys and, swooping, grabbed the woman nearest. He almost fell off his horse, with her screaming and kicking and tearing at him, him bareback and nothing to hang on to but the pony's mane. But hugging the pony with his legs, he pulled her over in front of him, her long hair streaming around his naked chest, her mouth open like she would scream, but she didn't make a sound. Arms clamped around her, knife at her throat, John yelled at the marshal, "Keep back!" And to the mounted Indian youths, "Keep away or I'll . . ." He made a slashing motion with the knife at her throat.

The marshal stopped in his tracks and put out an arm like holding the others back, the way John had once seen a quail mother do her little ones before crossing a road. The Indian boys held in their horses.

With the knife at her throat, his hostage grew very still. Then, one hand holding the hunting knife, with the other John swung the pony's head around. In that moment all he could hear was the ponies' hoofs, scuffling as the boys reined them tightly. Then while they watched, he flew past the marshal's four-by, galloped beyond the rabbit hunters, and swung into the arroyo, losing speed in the heavy sand.

"We got him," Horse Rios yelled. They all knew, even the marshal, there was no way out of that box canyon.

Just then, with his pack on his back, Reuben swung down the road. He heard them yelling something about a hostage. He stopped and turned, and while helplessly everybody watched, high up in the narrow hot-spring canyon the rump of John's doubly burdened pony disappeared into the tamarisks.

Reuben looked around. "Tina," he whispered, more to himself than to anybody else. He thought he saw all the other women, but he didn't see Tina. "Where's Tina?" he yelled.

Nobody answered. Whooping and hollering, beating their horses' rumps with the ends of their reins, the Indian youths galloped into the arroyo—this was better than a rabbit hunt—and the marshal ran to his four-by and made an urgent call on his field telephone.

"Where's Tina!" Reuben shouted again, and heard behind him an Indian woman whisper, "The one with the long hair, he took her with him."

The marshal cranked into four-wheel drive and plowed across the road into the deep sand. When he left his vehicle and caught up with the young Indians, they were bent low off their mounts, looking for hoofprints. One young Indian—it was Horse Rios—dismounted and led his horse, reading sign.

Then ambling toward them from the end of the little box canyon came the Appaloosa, nibbling at coarse grasses and trailing its reins. It stopped at the hot spring, but only sniffed and twitched its nose at the water. One of the young Indians dismounted and caught the pony and brought it like an offering to the marshal, who, not knowing what to do with it, tied it to a *piñon* branch. Then he and the Indian boys made their way on foot up the steep box canyon, searching amid fallen boulders and rabbit brush. But John and his hostage had disappeared.

Reuben ran up the arroyo after the marshal and the rabbit hunters. Witnessing their bewilderment, he lifted his eyes from the baffled search party to the ledge where he'd seen the flashes and where the apparition had risen miraculously up the face of the cliff.

He turned and hurried down the arroyo. When he came to the horse the marshal had tied to the piñon tree, he slowed and eyed it, started to go on, then stopped. He dropped his backpack and moved closer.

"Nice horsey."

The horse looked asleep with its head down and one foreleg resting daintily on the tip of the hoof. He reached tentatively for the reins.

"Nice horsey."

He untied the reins from the piñon limb. The horse swiveled an ear toward him and opened its eyes, then allowed itself to be led over to a knee-high boulder. Reuben wished for a saddle. He'd once as a child ridden a pony in a ring at Coney Island, but the pony was wearing a saddle with a security knob you could hang on to.

"Nice horsey, good horsey."

He climbed onto the boulder and tried to get a leg over, but the horse had already started off. He fell across its back as it ambled down the canyon.

"Whoa, horsey! Where you going?"

The horse stopped to nibble grass, and that let him get a leg over. He fiddled with the reins, got one in each fist.

"Giddy-up."

The horse jerked up its head and broke into an easy trot down the arroyo. Reuben almost slid off, but hanging on by the mane he emerged onto the road. That was better. He might get the hang of it. What did you do with the reins? They were for steering, he knew that much. He pulled the left one out to the side. The horse slowed and its head snaked around.

Okay, that wasn't it. He eased up on the rein and it fell on the horse's neck and the horse turned away from it.

That was it. Nothing to it. Like a shot they were on the mesa path and climbing at a smooth little running walk. He thought he knew where to find John and his hostage, though he'd no idea how they'd got there. And he meant to rescue Tina before the marshal and his ragtag posse scared the fugitive into some rash act.

He kicked the horse because he felt like kicking something, and the Appaloosa leaped atop the mesa, stretched out, and ran along the trail beside the drop-off. Leaning low and clinging to the mane, Reuben held on for dear life. Up ahead, the crows flew out of the dead piñon. How did you get a horse to stop? Now he remembered: You pulled back on the reins.

But he'd lost the reins a while back. They were bouncing along in the sand. He tried to reach them and fell off with a thud on his shoulder and rolled onto his back and lay there. The pony stopped abruptly of its own accord and looked down at him and, after a moment, nudged his cheek solicitously with its muzzle. And Reuben muttered, "Hold on, Tina, I'm coming. If that goddam son of a bitch so much as lays a hand on you, I'll tear him limb from limb, so help me God."

22

"Jesus loves you."

"Shut up! Keep away from me! Git back over yonder like I told you and stay there!"

She retreated to the pit in the floor and crouched, but she wasn't cowering. She didn't act like she was scared of him, and that was unnerving.

John watched her another minute to make sure she didn't move again, and then chewing on his stub of pencil, he bent over the scrap of paper on his knee. He began to print in big block letters. He had no idea how he would get this message to the marshal. The only thing he'd come up with so far was to fold it into a paper airplane and skim it off the ledge and let it waft down to the canyon below.

"If only you realized you're a child of God," she said, "you wouldn't behave like such an asshole."

He spun around and jabbed at her with the knife, but he didn't even come close. She looked from the knife to him like they were both made of the same piece of shit, and that made him madder than he already was.

"Hush up," he said. "Just shut your mouth."

And silently to his friend of the white robes: Please. Make her shut up.

What he wanted to do was look at her, get up his nerve and touch her, and here she was, spouting all that crap like Isaiah Hoop. He'd never seen her up close before. She was more beautiful even than he'd thought, and that preyed on him, eating away at his resolve.

The old man's kerosene lantern threw eerie shadows around the cave. Big and black, they loomed overhead. It wasn't like the same place now that he had company, though this particular company was exactly what he had longed for.

Isaiah Hoop's sermon on the sin of cupidity echoed inside his head: The only thang worse than not agittin' what you want is gittin' it. If it's a woman, give'r up. If it's cards, tear 'em in two and th'ow 'em out the back door. If it's riches, toss 'em in the hat my boy is passin' this very minute and offer um up to *Chesus*!

Never even learned to talk right, for all the time he spent listening to his competition on the radio. That was mostly when they were traveling in the old Ford truck lopsided on its springs from the camper Isaiah had built himself out of old barn timber and painted with Bible scenes—Noah's ark with polecats and possums and little raccoons scrambling up the gangplank, Jesus taking out after the moneylenders with a rawhide whip, the whole town out on a sunny afternoon stoning Mary Magdalene.

He tried to listen for sounds outside the cave, but the redhead wouldn't leave him alone. "Do you intend to rape me?" she demanded.

Christ, the way she talked! "Don't *say* stuff like that."

"If you come one step closer, I'll scream."

He hadn't come anywhere near her. "You better not aggravate me," he said, "if you know what's good for you."

Though he still hadn't moved, she drew back against the wall and her shadow shrank, which he found gratifying. "If I scream, they'll find this cave and capture you. They'll put you *under* the jail."

That unnerved him. He'd already been in jail, and what they did to him there was not something he let himself dwell upon. "Hush up. Quit running your mouth."

"The Constitution of the United States guarantees me freedom of speech."

The stuff she came up with. He jabbed the knife again in her direction to show her what was what, then went to listen again at the front of the cave while she examined everything around her.

"Heavens above!" she whispered. "What have we here!"

That was better, he liked that. He was perfectly willing to talk if she was nice. "Nothing much," he said, feeling boastful, a little proud. "Few old rock clubs, them *metates* over there . . ." —impress her some with the words he knew. "I found this loincloth I got on, and some little bitty old dried-up corn on the cobs . . ."

She pursed her mouth like whistling without a sound. He wished she wouldn't do that. It struck him as unwomanly.

"Hand me that lantern."

Now she was ordering him around. He picked up the lantern and handed it over.

"My goodness!" She was examining the scratchings that covered the walls. Folks had to have something to do on rainy days, he figured. One looked to him about like tick-tack-toe.

"Would you look at that!"

"What?" He kept the hunting knife in his hand. He saw the figure she was looking at and turned quickly away.

"What's that woman doing?"

"That ain't no woman." His face was burning.

"Oh, sure, men always interpret everything in their own terms. If that thing's a penis, where's the scrotum?"

"Cheez!" He clapped his free hand over his ear. "Hush up. Don't talk like that!"

"Are you a prude or something?"

"What do you know! You don't know nothing!"

"I may be a born-again Christian, but I'm also a scientist. Scientists use exact terms."

He didn't know what to say to that, so he didn't say anything.

Now she looked at him sweetly. "I can help you, if you'll let me."

"I don't need no help!"

"Oh, I see." She was prissy again. "You're perfectly sane, I guess, running around in your miniskirt, kidnapping people from public roads with your face painted worse than a whore's."

"Yeah, I guess you know all about whores," he said scornfully.

"What's that supposed to mean?"

He was torn. He wanted to confront her with what he'd seen down at the hot springs, but he didn't want to admit he'd been watching her. So he said lamely, "I never kidnapped *people*. I've just got *you*—" he was beginning to wish he hadn't "—and you're not kidnapped, you're a hostage." Then he repeated words familiar from the television news. "You are being held hostage." Was that official enough for her?

"Oh, I see. We're into the finer distinctions. What's your name?"

He became grim and secretive. Ought he to tell her? "John," he said, though strictly speaking that wasn't the truth.

She lowered her voice seductively. "Are you saved?"

"Why don't you shut up?" Of all the females in the world, he had to pick this one. "I don't want nonna that talk!"

He doubted the cave spirits wanted it either. A small gust of wind hit the lantern wick, and the black shapes of bats on the ceiling trembled like leaves. Where had that come from? The hair rose on his arms. "Shhh!"

"Why are you shushing me?"

"Hush!" He thought he'd heard something. Maybe a sound from down below in the box canyon where he'd left the horse. Maybe they'd found his secret way up the canyon wall. It was up against the cliff, behind a stand of tamarisks and hidden by the soft, silky green foliage. A kind of shaft. If you sucked in your breath and weren't scared of getting wedged in, you could shimmy up it a little way by pressing your back against one side and pushing with your feet against the other. You came out behind a boulder you could step up on, and from there find easy footholds out. She'd almost got stuck. She was broader in the beam than he was. He'd had to give her a shove from behind when she needed it.

Not an inch of that little canyon but he knew it by heart. Until the diggers arrived, he'd thought of it as his, which was verified when, high up its wall, he'd found the cave. But it was hard for him to imagine anything belonging to him, so he'd tried to make it his own by putting his foot down on every inch of it—a task sufficiently herculean to render him worthy if he ever managed its accomplishment. That's what he'd been doing when he heard the voice behind the tamarisks. *Wooo,* it said, and *yooo.* And he knew it was calling him, beckoning, wanting to show him something. So with a quickening in his breast, he'd brushed through the silky green and there it was—the slitlike opening to the shaft in the rock.

The memory fortified him. The spirits were on his side. They'd led him here to their secret place, hadn't they? They'd taken him in.

The sound outside came again. He knelt and pushed aside the rabbit brush at the cave entrance. Nothing out there that he could see.

"You can't hide in here indefinitely, you know."

He whirled around. She'd moved up close behind him. "Get back! I never said you could move!"

"After a while you'd need food and water."

"I got plenty of food and water. I got jerky and cornmeal and Baby Ruth bars. I been storing things up for some time."

She laughed scornfully, disbelievingly. Then she got that stern look around the mouth. "I'd advise you to repent now.

The Second Coming's just around the corner. You better tell
God you *believe*."

"I don't believe in nothing. Except I mean to build myself up till I can run nekkit in the snow like the old ones,
and make myself strong. I'll be more of an Indian than
these latter-day boys'll ever be."

"Wow, you really are crazy." She moved away from him
and her shadow shrank again. She stood with the lantern in
the middle of the cave, holding it up, looking at the wall
paintings. "What's this?" she said. "Looks like a man
standing out in the rain."

That's what it looked like to him, too, this stick man
standing outside and the rain pelting down. The artist had
carved each individual drop. Rain just about filled that part
of the wall, coming down all over the stick man's head and
all around him.

The lantern light disturbed the bat colony hanging from
the ceiling. One of the bats swooped down and disappeared
in the shadows. She crouched and put her hands over her
head and moaned. "Dear Jesus, get me out of here."

Good. She was scared of something.

She asked suddenly, peering out at him over her arm,
"Did you see a movie called *The Collector*?"

This was more like it. He was crazy about the movies.
He used to always sneak in whenever he had the chance, or
if he could steal enough from Isaiah's collection plate.

"I never seen that one," he said. "What was it about?"

"It was about a crazy guy that kidnapped this red-headed
girl and locked her away in a basement and fed her and en-
tertained her."

"How come he done that?"

"He was in love with her."

"Well, I ain't in love with you!"

She got up and moved over to sit on one of the low
walls rising from the floor. "This must have been a storage
cyst," she said softly, touching the wall she sat on, then
wiping the dust on the thigh of her jeans. "I bet we could
excavate floors beneath floors."

"So go on, what happened?"

"What happened to what?"

"The guy and the girl he locked up." The idea was interesting.

She looked around, then up at the bats and shivered, and shifty-eyed said, "The British Army stormed the place and shot it up with assault weapons and rescued the girl."

He didn't think she was telling the truth, something about the way she avoided looking at him. "So what happened to the guy?"

"He got wasted. It showed his body all riddled with bullets. It was awful." She shuddered. "Not like something human, more like something animals had been at. I couldn't look at it."

He laughed. "So how come you know what it looked like?" He reached out and grabbed her by that long red hair and touched the knifepoint under her chin, forcing her to look at him.

She clamped her eyes shut. "Get your hands off me!"

He let go. "They never kilt that guy!"

"Yes they did. They blew him away."

"No they didn't. They never even found him. He was too smart for them."

"You said you never saw the movie!"

He laughed in triumph. "I fooled you! I never saw it! I never even heard of it!"

He had showed her who was smart and who wasn't. All keyed up, he said, "We'll be nice and comfy here. Nobody gonna find us. Nobody got the least idea this cave is even here. We're gunna get along just fine. We're gunna get to know each other real good."

Restless, excited, he was moving around again. She bent over with her face in her hands and wept. Shocked, he stopped and looked at her, at first averting his eyes, then letting them rest on her breasts underneath the T-shirt. He took hold of her chin and made her look at him. "What's your name, anyways?"

"Margaret Shippers," she whispered. "They call me Beano."

He didn't care for Beano. "Margrit," he said, and tried it again, "Margrit." He was close to her, and it didn't scare him a bit. He was the one in charge. He smiled. "How you doing, Margrit? Let's hear you call me John." He put out a hand to touch her, but she knocked it away. That was all right. He could bide his time. He leaned closer.

"Don't you know Jesus loves you?" she pleaded.

He sprang back, hot all over with rage. "I don't have to listen to that crap."

"You may not know it, but you already belong to Him."

"I don't belong to nobody!" His voice broke. He sounded like he'd sounded when his voice began to change and Isaiah took his white robes and white wing-tipped shoes away from him and burned them in disgust.

She saw the fear in his face and came closer, repeating, "Jesus loves you!" The cave walls bounced it back at him.

Sobbing, he lunged and got her by the throat. Struggling to press her down with the weight of his body, he let go of the knife to get a better hold. He didn't see her grope for it with her fingers and, even while she choked and her eyes started bulging, pull it closer till she could get hold of the hilt.

23

When Reuben could get his breath, he left the horse grazing and moved to the edge of the cliff and looked around. Place was deserted except for the crows.

He stood up and crouched, cautious, arms out for balance. Then he skidded down the slope to the first ledge and stopped. He edged forward and peered over the lip. Nothing down there either.

No place to hide on that narrow ledge totally visible to the eye. But the masked guy couldn't have materialized out of thin air. He had to come from somewhere. The notch in the opposite canyon wall, thin as a knife, framed a picture of pastures and cattle to the west. What if he had a house up here? Or maybe just a cabin to come to and get away from it all. A log cabin. He could build it himself out of stuff off the land.

He peered over the edge again, baffled. He'd been so sure. He started down the aspen pole to the lower ledge. On top of the cliff, the horse was chomping grass. You could hear his big teeth grind. Already he had a soft spot for that horse.

It was eerie, standing there alone on the lower ledge, knowing they were near when there was no way on earth they could be. Nothing but a stony ledge with a few clumps of rabbit grass up against the cliff. But plainly he heard voices. And something else—not voices, a kind of whomp and a grunt, followed by a cry and scrambling feet.

A bloody hand fumbled the rabbit brush aside, opening up a hole in the cliff, and a vaguely familiar figure in a moth-eaten breechclout fell out of it with a scared look on his face, seeing Reuben and reaching to him for help. Out of the hole after him scrambled Beano Shippers, murder in her eye and a bloody knife in her hand. Where had she come from? Where was Tina?

Before Beano could bring down the knife, Reuben sprang and grabbed her hand. Christ, she was strong as an ox.

"Let go of me! Bastard was going to . . . !"

"I never!" the make-believe Indian shouted. He got to his knees, grabbed the aspen pole with his one good hand, and went up it swift as a monkey.

Reuben looked unbelieving at his own fingers. He sat down hard, staring at the blood, while John disappeared over the lip with an angry Shippers right behind him.

Rocking back and forth, growing rapidly nauseous at the sight of blood, it took him some time to realize the blood on his fingers wasn't his. When he got hold of himself be leaned over and picked up a piece of paper the wind was trying to launch off the edge of the cliff.

What was he doing? Cleaning up litter? It looked like one of the paper airplanes he'd sailed over his sixth grade teacher's head. He wiped at his bloody fingers with it and stuffed it in his pocket. He grasped the aspen pole and made it up to the first ledge, and from there to the mesa top. Beano Shippers was disappearing fast down the trail toward the dig, and back in the trees with the crows, the guy in the breechclout peered out from his hiding place in the piñons. Then looking somehow pitiful in that ragged piece of fur, he grabbed the reins of the grazing pony and swung aboard. Reuben started after him, but something sharp caught him on the forehead, and his assailant pitched across the mesa toward the steep north slope.

When he opened his eyes, all he saw was red. He was sure the rock had hit him in the eye and it was the stuff of his eye oozing down his face. But when he swiped at it, it was only blood from where the rock had hit him on the forehead.

24

Freya's laugh was short and breathless with excitement. "They're Platonists," she said, pointing to the bats hanging undisturbed from the ceiling. "They know we're immaterial." She circled, looking around her. "My God," she breathed, "what wonderful cave art."

But something told Tina this place was not meant to be disturbed. She watched Caspar circle warily with his lower lip stuck out like he didn't believe this, it wasn't real, it was a stage set for the gullible unwary.

"Look!" Proprietary now, Beano Shippers held the lantern higher, pleased that she'd led Freya to such a find but keeping a wary eye on the bats.

Caspar said disparagingly, "Yeah, you see that in the petroglyphs around here—stars with faces."

"Look at this little guy," Beano said. "Looks like he's standing out in the rain."

Freya Markus moved close to the wall and touched lightly with her fingertips one of the incised raindrops falling on the vulnerable little figure. Then she turned and circled the cave. "That's a worktable." She walked over to the huge, raised stone off to one side of the big cave room. "Look at these." She bent and picked something up off the floor.

"What is it?" Beano whispered reverently.

"Flint chips. Here's where they worked their points." Then she asked herself, "What kind of points?" She bent and ran her fingers over the stone floor. "They're large. Not arrowpoints. They're spearpoints."

"Doesn't mean a thing," Caspar said. "Somebody's made off with the arrowpoints because they were better-worked."

"Maybe." She nodded. "But if there are no arrowpoints here, it could mean this cave is as early as I think it is."

Beano held the lantern higher as Freya approached the dip in the floor. "This is a child's bed," she said. She touched the brittle willow sticks that had once been supple springs. "It was covered with a rabbit skin robe. Look. Dried bits of it still cling to the willow. And this is a storage bin." She moved to the rectangular enclosure at one end of the room, reached in, and picked up a small dried ear of corn. She took the lantern from Beano and moved up close to the painted walls. She stopped before the squatting figure. "You again. It's the same as the petroglyph on the cliff face." She dropped to her knees. "What's this?" It looked like an opening to a niche at floor level.

Tina dropped to her knees and felt around, then peered inside. It was not a niche but a tunnel. She described it to Freya. "It's very shallowly arced and the ceiling falls from the apex inward, like drapery. The floor dips down from the entry. The end of it's walled off."

"What do you mean?"

"It's been sealed off with rocks and mortar."

The dip in the floor hid the top of the mortared wall. She could only see the bottom. "The plasterer left the mortar bulging as it dried." She was puzzled. Usually when a woman plastered a niche, she smoothed the plaster to keep people from finding her hiding place.

"Maybe she was in a hurry," Beano said.

"Maybe the men did it," Caspar said. "They wouldn't go in for the niceties."

"Oh, sure," Beano said. "They'd be into more important things—like killing off the animals and each other."

Tina said, "Working in that space had to be difficult."

Freya said bitterly, "Wouldn't you know. We've found all this when we're about to be run off the dig." Then she was all business. "There's not much time. Beano, go get the trowels. And we'll need the cameras. Caspar, go with her. Bring plenty of film. Where's Reuben? Now where can he have got to?"

25

This part of the Indian village was deserted, but it was where the trail of disturbed pine needles down the north side of the mesa had finally dumped him. Maybe the place was deserted because of Naposunshare. Maybe this morning they were all camped out around the pond.

Visitors were not welcome in this part of the pueblo. At the other end of the plaza, an old woman rolled away the flat rock from her oven door and peered inside. He'd lost his quarry. So what did he do now? The old woman rose up flushed from the heat of her oven.

He crossed the plaza. "Baking bread this morning?" he said inanely.

She looked him over. Her long hair, cut into square bangs on her forehead, hung in a braid down her back.

She nodded yes and bent to roll the rock back in place and close up the *horno* again. She looked around the deserted plaza and back at him as much as to say, What's an Anglo doing here?

"I'm looking for a friend," he said. "I think he just got home. He was on his horse."

She pointed disdainfully with her chin. "Over there."

The chin pointed across the way, but at which house?

"You been out here before?" she asked.

He shook his head. "I've been busy. My job."

She nodded approvingly. "You got you a job?"

"I'm a painter."

"My grandson, he makes things and sells them on the plaza in Santa Fe."

"So he's an artist, too."

She raised her eyebrows doubtfully.

He was looking around the wide, empty area. "Which house?"

"That one by the alley, over there." She pointed with her chin again.

"Thanks." He started off with his hands in his pockets.

"You still here when the bread comes out, I let you have a loaf."

He was surprised. "Thanks a lot. I'd appreciate that. Can I buy it?" Nothing like Indian bread to dip in chili. He could taste it, hot and bland, soaking up the flavors.

She shrugged, turning away.

He stood outside the door of the house beside the alley. It was cracked open. He held the door so it wouldn't squeak on its hinges, and stuck his head in the dark interior. The blankets on a *banco* across the room were disturbed, like somebody had slept there.

When his eyes became accustomed to the dimness, there he was, the *chulo* he was looking for. Still wearing only the breechclout and moccasins, he had his back turned standing over another *banco*, this one made up with an Indian blanket stretched tight across it. The only light in the room came from the door cracked open and one high window on the south wall. It was a poor room, only the *bancos* and a couple of chairs at a homemade cottonwood table in the center. The ceiling went up and up, so if there was any smoke it'd rise out of the way.

You could smell the burning piñon. A fire on a warm day like this? He felt the heat of the room escaping around him out the door.

His quarry was rummaging in a niche in the wall over the *banco*, taking something down, fingering it, mumbling like he might be praying, but then Reuben heard plainly, "I know I ain't talked to you for some time. I ain't been wanting to bother you none. I ain't even sure if you're there anymore, or if you're listening."

Reuben looked around. Nobody else in the room. Was

this guy crazy? The irregular breechclout hung in places to his knees, an old moth-eaten thing with holes in it. Maybe an ancient deerskin. He brought a little spiral notebook out of the niche and held it up in front of him along with a ring of keys. It looked like he was going through some personal ritual.

Reuben watched him fumble at something hanging from a thong around his neck, something small, a few inches square, in a leather case that he raised up, too, like an offering, and Reuben got a good look at it.

"If you're here, if you're listening, I wisht you'd give me a sign," he said.

Reuben was across the room in three strides of his dirty Nikes, grabbing him, locking his arms against his chest. "That's Rap Singleton's Brunton compass, buddy-boy!"

John, startled, tried to see over his shoulder. "They're mine!" he shouted. "I found them! Finders keepers!"

For a moment he struggled. Reuben put him at about sixteen or seventeen. He wouldn't weigh much, but he was strong. Then his body went suddenly limp. Reuben spun him around and threw him down on the *banco*. The boy drew his feet up under him, crossed his legs, and sat slumped against the wall, sniveling, his nose running. He looked pretty harmless.

"What do you mean, you *found* them?" Reuben leaned menacingly over him.

"Up on the mesa. At the edge of the cliff. I spent that whole night in the cave." He said it defiantly, bragging. "And I was on my way home. I come on thisere little book and thisere other thing." Fingering the compass reverently like an object of worship.

It was Rap's compass, all right, the leather case old and scarred. That's what had struck him as familiar. That's what he'd seen around the apparition's neck, along with the *paho*, when he rose up off the cliff. Reuben snatched it away.

John said eagerly, "Open it up, why don'tcha. Pull on that little copper thingamajig."

Reuben opened the compass.

"Wha'd I tell you! Lookit the little mirror! Go on, look at it!"

It could have been reflections from this mirror he'd seen from the hot spring. Maybe this mirror and not a gun at all had occasioned his treacherous climb up the canyon wall. "How'd you disappear up that canyon," he asked, "taking Shippers with you?"

"Cheezus, I wisht I never!"

Then John told him about the chimney in the rock behind the tamarisks, and how you climbed it, bracing your feet against the opposite wall and inching up. He told it like they were conspirators, like he was sharing valuable secrets with a friend.

"You're not an Indian," Reuben said scornfully, leaning over him, inspecting him closely. "So how come you're got up like that?"

John looked affronted and told him he aspired to *become* an Indian. It wasn't easy, he said. It was plenty hard. "You got to learn to stand the cold in winter, and run nekkit like the animals. I been practicing at night, running nekkit like that." Eager now, like he was sharing secrets he'd longed to share with somebody. He sagged again against the wall. "But now it's summertime, so it's easy."

"You run naked at night?"

"Yeah. Sure." He looked up at Reuben hopefully.

Pelawi. Bird Boy. The owl flew down the road, and this boy, naked, ran back up it toward the canyon. Reuben was disappointed. He'd liked the mystery better. "The animals have fur," he said, "and they grow it thicker in winter. They don't go naked."

The boy leaned forward and said eagerly, "Yeah, but Eliseo, he told me the old ones, they—"

At that moment, an aged hand, trembling, took hold of the door and shoved it open. The boy stopped talking and watched. An old man came in all wrapped up like an Arab in a pink and white cotton blanket. He began to cough, a hollow rattling sound. He glanced at them without interest, eyes sunken into deep recesses. He crossed and dropped heavily on the unmade *banco*.

The boy watched anxiously. "I reckon you're sick again," he said with mingled scorn and anxiety.

The old man sat there a minute, then slowly drew up his legs, lay back, and rolled over with his back to them.

The boy crossed the room and bent over him. "Why'd you come home? You know good an' well they tolja to stay over there and take your medicine."

The old man didn't say anything. The boy put his hand on the old man's forehead. "Burnin' up with fever. You make me sick!" He hung over the *banco*, bracing himself with his hand on the adobe wall, his other fist balled up, threatening, in the old man's face.

But the old man didn't see it. His eyes were closed.

"Won't do nothin' for yourself! Won't let nobody hep you none! You want to go ahead and die? Is that it?" His voice broke.

The old man reached around and drew the thin blanket around his shoulders and over his head.

The boy's eyes filled with tears of frustration. He dropped to his knees on the floor beside the *banco* and put his forehead against the old man's flank. He had the bunch of keys in his hand, fingering them. "Well, go on, go ahead then, die!" he sobbed. "See if I care!"

Embarrassed to witness this private scene, Reuben hung his head and put his hands in his pockets and found the paper airplane. He fished it out and smoothed its folds. Something was written on it. He leaned toward the light from the door and read:

I dump thet passel of snakes an I set thet fire but I never kilt nobody no never. But it ain't to late to git stardit so don't nobody come after me.

He stuffed the crumpled note back in his pocket and looked up at the dark *vigas*, overcome with confusion. He'd caught the guy red-handed, hadn't he? That would get him,

Reuben, off the hook with the marshal. Trouble was, he thought he believed this kid's note on the paper airplane. So now what? He looked at the boy kneeling there, hand covered with dried blood from where Beano had grazed him with the knife, fingering his ring of keys like they were beads and mumbling again what sounded like angry prayers. Slowly Reuben focused on the ring of keys. Then he lunged and grabbed them out of the supplicant's hand.

John looked up at him, startled, the paint on his face smeared by his angry tears.

"Where'd you get these?" There were two rings, the small one snapped onto a larger one, D-shaped and shiny.

"Just some old keys. I ain't done nothin'! I ain't stole 'em, if that's what you think!"

At that moment the door opened and flooded the room with a lot more light. Cruz Domingue stepped inside and looked at them. He spoke sadly over his shoulder to somebody behind him. "Here he is. That's him. I 'spect this is your escapee Jeremiah Hoop."

The boy in the moth-eaten breechclout sprang up with his back to the wall, cornered.

26

"Careful, Tina Martinez," Freya said. "Don't touch anything if you can help it."

Kneeling at the entrance to the tunnel, Tina felt the dead weight of responsibility. Steve Many Hands stripped off his sweatshirt and handed it to her. She pulled it over her head. It came down below her knees. She fell onto her stomach, and even through the sweatshirt the stone of the tunnel floor was cold.

They had with difficulty opened a small hole in the sealed wall, Jade doing the chipping as she was the smallest. But she had suddenly panicked and had to be pulled out, sweating profusely, her hair wet and clinging to her face. "Claustrophobia," she whispered.

So Tina had been elected to slither through the tunnel and see what lay beyond. She shoved the lantern carefully before her. The falling-rising level of the tunnel floor made progress difficult. That wasn't the way your body was meant to bend. She wormed her way forward. It was, she fancied, like the birth canal, like returning to the womb. She tried to look inside the hole Jade had opened in the sealed wall. But all she could see was part of the stone floor overlaid with a thin sprinkling of sand that had been there undisturbed back through the reaches of time. She'd heard of floors in caves suddenly falling away to untold depths. She'd visited Carlsbad as a child, and the memory still terrified her. She was grateful the lantern had not disclosed a yawning pit.

Why hadn't they thought to bring a flashlight? With a flashlight she could maybe see inside without going in. No telling how big the room was. Freya said it was probably a burial crypt. The draping rock walls pressed down on her.

"Okay, here goes," she muttered, shoving the lantern before her. "Steve? Are you there?"

"I'm right behind you."

"Hold on to me, will you?"

"Sure, babe. I got you. Awright?"

His fingers closed around her ankle. He must have entered the tunnel a little way.

"Okay?" Freya said impatiently.

Tina took a deep breath. "Yes, right. I'm going in."

Holding her breath, pushing with her elbows, she stuck her head inside and instantly felt cut off from the world. At first all she could see was light pooling on the floor. The cave room smelled musty and dry.

She wriggled forward, first her shoulders, then, holding her breath, her hips. Nothing blocked her. She was all the way in except for the foot Steve had hold of. Maybe she could sit up if she wanted to. But she lay there on her stomach with her head up.

"I'm right here, babe," Steve said, but his voice on the other side of the wall seemed far away.

Freya whispered, "What's in there? What do you see?"

"Okay," she said. She made herself lift the lantern. It was hard to breathe on her stomach like that. "Against the wall to my left—it looks like a flat-topped stone slab." A giant *metate*? No. It wasn't dished in the middle and it was way too big. "It's not a *metate*." Great. So what else was it not?

Had it been chiseled? She inched closer. There were no chip marks that she could see. She propped herself on her elbows and raised the light higher. "On top of it . . ."

"Yes, what is it?"

She couldn't tell. Moving closer, she inadvertently jerked her foot free of Steve's hand. She lowered her head and swallowed.

"You okay, babe?"

She peered back under her arm at the tunnel where his disembodied hand groped around, searching, out of reach.

"I'm okay," she whispered, then cleared her throat and repeated, "I'm okay."

"You want me in there?"

She badly wanted it, but she doubted Steve could get his shoulders through.

"No!" Freya said. "I want as little disturbed in there as possible."

Tina felt the roof of the niche bearing down. Overwhelmed by a sudden terror, she dropped her cheek to the floor and gasped, then closed her mouth. It was so dry, she couldn't swallow. She broke into a sweat that felt cold and slimy on her skin.

"What's going on?" Freya asked from far, far away.

Hold your horses. Give me a minute. Let me breathe. She curled her legs close to her chest. She cleared her throat. "There's something on top of the slab. It's like on an altar."

"What?" Freya asked. And when she didn't answer right away, "What is it?"

"It's all wrapped up."

"Wrapped up in what?"

Whatever the wrapping was, it had retained some of its color. "It looks like—*feathers*?" A cloth made of feathers?

Out in the big cave chamber they exclaimed excitedly— arguing, guessing, consulting. Tina maneuvered onto her elbows and found herself facing the pictograph of a single figure on the wall, the colors clear and bright as the day the artist had painted them. The figure was squatting, its legs out squarely to each side and ending in little stick feet. Something emerged beneath the crotch. Whatever it was, it was two-pronged.

She caught her breath. It was little stick legs bent at the knee, little stick feet turned out to the side like the feet of the figure itself. It was a woman giving birth to a baby feet-first. It was a breech birth! She raised the lantern higher. Giving birth out in the rain. Little chipped-in raindrops fell all around the mother figure.

"What are you doing in there?" Freya called, her voice sounding hollow out in the big cave chamber.

Tina fell onto her belly and rested with her cheek on the floor close to the sealing stones Jade had left in place because Freya wanted as little disturbed as possible. Funny. Unlike the outside wall, inside the plaster was smooth over the sealing rocks. She saw it clearly, but something was the matter with it. She shoved the lantern closer.

Freya was asking urgently about the object on the altar stone.

"It's all wrapped up," she repeated absently, examining the finished plaster, "about the size of . . . a big loaf of bread." She frowned at the plaster. The ocher plaster had little black flecks in it, and other flecks that caught the lantern light and sparkled. Mica. And there were fingerprints.

She thought of the plasterer—a woman dead these hundreds of years, yet there were her fingerprints.

"What's going on in there?" It was Steve, just outside, for she had stopped talking. Something nibbled at her consciousness, compelling her to see ... what? She frowned. Then a peculiar sensation took her attention away from the prints in the plaster. She tried shrugging it off because it was impossible here, wasn't it, that feeling you get when you know you're being watched?

She heard her grandmother's voice, *Wherever you put down your foot, wherever you breathe the air, at that place your spirit trace remains.*

The breath went out of her. Afraid to turn, she stared at the fingerprints on the wall as impossible knowledge slowly dawned. She knew why the plaster outside the entry had been left unfinished. How had she missed it for even a minute?

Because the answer was inconceivable.

She stiffened. She knew she had to turn around, but she couldn't move. There was a presence in here beside her own.

Granddaughter.

Those outside the entry tunnel might have been worlds away. A cry rose in her throat only to be blocked by her heart, which was lodged there and pounding. Then she relinquished to a part of herself much older than she was, its age incalculable.

Do not be afraid.

Steve said, "What's the matter, babe?" She heard his words, but the language was strange, while another language, one she had never known, spoke to her total comprehension. Time was unraveling. She was alive in a recurrent dream she'd had as a child: she was in her mother's house discovering doors she hadn't known, that opened to larger rooms than the ones they lived in, and the floor fell away to unknown levels where people called to her by her Indian name. *Kupta.* Corn Tassels Dancing.

Granddaughter.

Questions bombarded her from the other side of the wall: Can you hear me? What are you doing? What have you found in there?

But to answer other voices, she had no need of words: I'm here. I'm back. I've come home.

She rose to her knees. The hair on top of her head brushed the ceiling. No longer from fear but with a sense of ceremony, she turned.

They confronted each other across space that was narrow, time that was long. She felt herself smile. She didn't hear herself scream, or see Steve's hands groping as far as he could reach inside the tunnel and, as she scrambled backward in terror, grasping her ankles to pull her out.

Back in the big cave room she opened her eyes and gulped air. She had been holding her breath like a swimmer underwater. She was lying on her back, panting, trembling, clutching Steve's T-shirt, aware of Caspar's eyes magnified behind his glasses and of Polly Quint staring down. Faces bent over her.

"What's wrong? What happened? My God," Freya said, "you're cold as death." Freya had her hand and was stroking it.

"It's just claustrophobia," Caspar said.

Caught up by tremor after tremor, for some time Tina couldn't speak.

"Stand back, everybody," Steve said. "Let her get some air."

Breathing easier now, finally she gasped, "There's . . . Oh, God, Freya, there's somebody in there."

27

Reuben huddled in the back of the marshal's four-by next to the spare tire, weighing his options while the marshal broke the speed limit all the way into Santa Fe. So far, so good. Santa Fe was where he wanted to go.

There'd been no time to get an ambulance out to the pueblo for the old man, so with the help of the nurse from the clinic, they'd loaded him into the marshal's vehicle and laid him wrapped up in blankets on the backseat, the boy kneeling on the floor and holding him. Cruz Domingue sat up front with the marshal till, outside his office, he jumped out and got into his own pickup. He was following them in.

They were slowed once by a state highway patrolman, but Tom Hurleigh signaled and the patrol car passed them, turned on its siren and, flashing its bank of roof lights, led them all the way down St. Francis to St. Michael's Drive and the hospital.

The marshal had the Brunton compass and the red notebook sealed in his Ziploc lunch bag, but Reuben had held on to the ring of keys. As the old man was downloaded onto a stretcher, he brandished the keys again in the marshal's face. "Look, Marshal, do you know what this is?"

But the marshal brushed him aside. "Don't press your luck, Ruby."

Reuben followed him, shaking the key ring at him, trying to explain while attendants in green scrubs wheeled the old man into the ER. John's nose was running and he kept swiping at his eyes and smearing his war paint. Barefoot, with his paint-streaked torso and moth-eaten loincloth, he was a fantastic sight in the sterile waiting room. An old man in a faded work shirt waiting in one of the chairs looked away embarrassed. The receiving nurse watched from her cubicle with a smile.

"Marshal, just listen to me a minute," Reuben said.

The marshal scowled.

"The kid found this where he found the notebook and the compass." He shook the ring of keys in the marshal's face.

The marshal turned away annoyed. "Okay, Cruz," he said, "I'll leave you here with the old man, but I'm taking the kid down and booking him for murder one."

"No, look," John sobbed, "Lemme stay. He's dying, I tell you."

Cruz said, "How 'bout it, Tom? I'll vouch for him."

The marshal said, "You know I can't do that."

Reuben gave up on the marshal and looked around to get his bearings. Where was Joe? He hadn't a clue. The hospital was a big, odd-shaped building on several levels. He backed toward the door.

But once outside he didn't know which way to turn. He rounded the side of the building where a white ambulance was backing up to a ramp. There stood Joe's parents, holding on to each other and watching two male nurses—one plump and white, one thin and black—wheeling out a stretcher.

Bob Jurney hailed him. "Nice of you to stop by. You almost missed us. We're leaving in a few minutes."

"Leaving?" Reuben looked around. The hospital hall was empty except for a doctor walking toward them with a clipboard.

"We're taking him to a toxicologist at UNM Hospital in Albuquerque," Jean Jurney said. The wind on the hospital hill whipped her short brown hair.

"Great!" Reuben said. "That's a great idea!"

"We hope they can do something for him," Bob Jurney said. Graying at the temples, going soft like a desk-bound former athlete, he stepped over to the stretcher and looked down at Joe lying so quietly. The black attendant was checking the IV hanging from its wheeled contraption.

"How is he?" Reuben asked.

The mother looked away. She was crying. The father said, "No change."

Reuben wished he'd kept his mouth shut. All he could see of Joe was the top of his head, his thick dark hair.

"I was going to ride in the ambulance with him, and Mother was going to drive our car," Bob Jurney said. "But Willy offered to make the trip down with his buddy—" Bob Jurney gently touched Joe's arm "—so the two of us can drive down together. We'll follow behind."

"Where is Willy? Is he here?" Reuben scanned the parking lot. It was another bland, innocent day, perfectly clear, the sky blue and the mountains purple in the distance.

"He should have been here by now."

But Willy was nowhere in sight. The gurney was loaded. The white attendant emerged from the ambulance. Joe lay perfectly still. The IV bottle dangled over him, trailing its umbilical to his arm.

The doctor with the clipboard—young and balding— emerged from the hospital. While he spoke to the parents, Reuben circled the vehicle. The driver waited by the open door. The ambulance was ready to leave. Still no Willy.

The doctor shook hands with Joe's father. His mother moved over to the ambulance. She reached up and smoothed Joe's hair, then started to climb in.

Just then the little red Japanese pickup spun up the drive and swerved into a parking space. Willy leapt out and ran toward them. "Sorry, folks." He eyed Reuben.

"Think your equipment will be safe in the canyon, son?" Joe's father asked with a smile.

"Yeah." Willy was sweating. He wiped his face with the bottom of his T-shirt, exposing a bronze, muscled chest. "I moved it down to the lower meadow. The dig people will keep an eye on everything till I get back. Is my truck all right parked there?" he asked the doctor anxiously. "I wouldn't want it towed or anything."

"I'll mention it to the parking lot attendant," the doctor said.

At that moment a flight of fighter planes from the air force base in Albuquerque thundered overhead. They all looked up, squinting into the sun. And inside the ambulance Joe moaned.

They all heard it. The doctor leapt up beside him and hiked one of his eyelids and took Joe's wrist in his fingers.

Bob Jurney whispered hopefully, "Is he coming around?!"

"Joe, honey," his mother said. Joe lapsed back into silence and she turned anxiously to the doctor. "It's a good sign, isn't it?"

The doctor hovered over Joe another minute, but then shook his head. "They'll sometimes move or make a sound. Doesn't necessarily mean . . ."

"Willy, you ride down in the car with Bob. I'm not leaving Joe," Jean Jurney said.

"Come on, honey—all that way on that little bench?"

Later, Reuben tried to put it together in some kind of logical sequence, but it all happened too fast—Joe opening his eyes and trying to lift his head; Tom Hurleigh emerging alone from the ER and crossing to his four-by, one long, skinny boot already inside, then seeing them, hesitating, stepping back out and ambling toward them; the ambulance driver surreptitiously dropping his cigarette and stepping on it, getting in the cab, ready to take off. He would always be able to summon up Willy's face when, startled, pausing as he was about to get in the ambulance, his pale eyes darkening, he saw the keys brandished at him in Reuben's hand.

"Where the hell'd you get one of my carabiners?"

"I didn't know it was yours," Reuben said, concealing his excitement.

"You know damn well it's mine. Look at it, you'll find my initials. They're scratched on all my equipment."

Willy glanced aside as the ambulance doors started to close, and Reuben grabbed him by the front of his sweatshirt and did something he'd wanted to do ever since that foggy dawn in the meadow when he'd come upon him with Tina.

Reeling backward, Willy clutched his bloody nose. Somebody shouted. Reuben surged over Willy, and they fell struggling to the tarmac.

The marshal said, "What the deuce?" and pulled Reuben off, pinning his arms behind him. Reuben struggled. "Goddammit, Marshal, let go! You don't know . . ."

Then Joe started talking. The doctor leapt back into the ambulance. Jean Jurney jumped in beside him. "Joe! It's your mother!"

And the scene froze to that single frame—Joe's voice muttering, Willy frozen there, Jean Jurney saying, "He heard my voice!" and the doctor: "We never know what brings them around."

Then Joe cried out Willy's name.

And sudden movement as Willy, startled, his face mottling, turned and fled toward his little red pickup.

Reuben kicked backward as hard as he could. His heel landed sharply on the marshal's shin, the marshal yelled and let him go, and he was halfway across the parking lot before the little red pickup started, backed, and sped toward St. Michael's Drive. The lot attendant stepped outside the gatehouse to stop it, but when the pickup failed to slow down, startled, he stepped out of the way and let it pass.

"You stupid bastard, let me go!" But Reuben was pinned again in the marshal's grip. While they watched, another small red pickup gave chase, and then another identical small red pickup.

The marshal exploded, "What the hell!"

When all three red pickups converged at the exit to St. Michael's Drive, you couldn't be sure anymore which one was Willy's.

Watching the chase, the ambulance driver said, "Hospital security. They patrol in those little red pickups. They'll get that guy, speeding like that on the premises."

The marshal yanked Reuben's arms. "What the hell's going on here, Ruby?"

"If you'll let go of me I'll tell you."

"This better be good," the marshal said.

One of the pickups turned and headed back up the hospital drive, giving up the chase.

Reuben said, "Looks like he's getting away."

Tom Hurleigh headed for the radio in his vehicle. "I better get some roadblocks set up, find out what the hell this is all about."

"Wait, Marshal," Reuben said. "Willy's not sure we know why he ran off like that."

"He's right, I don't."

"Yeah, but I do, Marshal. You needn't bother with the roadblocks. I know where he's headed."

Behind them Joe was becoming articulate while his father and the doctor looked on and his mother smoothed his hair.

The marshal stood there undecided. Then he said, "Okay. Get in. Let's go."

28

They had crawled out one by one through the rabbit hole onto the sunny ledge, but Tina couldn't stop trembling. She crouched against the warm face of the cliff. It radiated heat but she couldn't get warm. Every few minutes she was caught up in rigors. Only Steve Many Hands seemed to notice. He laid his hand on her arm.

"How'll you move her?" Jim Cochran wanted to know.

"Don't ask," Freya said.

"You'll have to tell the tribe she's here," Steve said softly.

"Don't you dare!" Freya shot at him.

Their voices floated over Tina's head. Bess Cochran said, "It's very unusual to find a mummy aboveground. It must be the dry air, and sealed up that way." She turned to Tina. "Would you say she's well preserved?"

"She has long hair," Tina whispered. "She's sitting there against the wall." She had to get Cruz up here.

"We can't get her out without opening up the rest of the sealed wall," Freya said.

Bess Cochran said, "You have to get all your pictures first."

Freya blew out her breath, moving wisps of hair that had fallen over her forehead. "IknowIknowIknow." She circled with her head down. "I have to go easy. I must have a plan—step *one*, step *two*, step *three* . . ." She stopped and looked at Tina. "This could be it." Her voice had that calm of utter excitement. "This could be what I've needed."

Needed for what?

"We can date the body," Freya said, "and that means we can date the occupation of this cave."

Tina asked herself where were her loyalties now. And she knew indisputably that the choice had been posed the minute Cruz put her on the dig. Another rigor shook her. She pulled Steve's sweatshirt closer and crossed her arms over her knees.

As she sat there rocking, hugging her knees, Steve's hand hardened on her arm. She shook it off. He wasn't Pueblo, he was Plains. But he looked steadily at her, trying to tell her something.

"When they removed King Tut, they took him out in his sarcophagus," Caspar said.

Freya's shadow tossed its head—What's Tut to me or me to Tut? Laughter rose in Tina's throat. "And the thing on the altar?" Freya grasped her shoulders and shook. "Wake up. Pay attention."

"On a big rock slab," Tina muttered.

"How big can it be if it had to go through that narrow tunnel?" Freya's shadow hung over her. "Wrapped in some

kind of cloth—that sounds like a burial. A child, probably.
So there are *two* mummies in there. I was right. It's a burial
cyst."

"No."

"No *what*?"

"The rock slab was there already. You can see where it
broke off and dropped from the ceiling."

"Oh, *where* is that girl with the flashlight?" Freya had
sent Beano Shippers to bring one from the dig trailer. "How
would you estimate the dimensions of the room?"

The room sprang to life before Tina could stop it. She
shook her head. She was trembling again.

"How could they ever dig out a room like that?" Freya
marveled. "How could they get all the debris out through
that little tunnel?"

"It's probably a natural cave in the basalt layer," Jim
Cochran said, "a bubble that formed in the volcanic flow."

"Damn, where's my cameraman when I need him most?"

Freya's shadow paced away and Tina was glad for the
sun again. If she didn't look at them, she could keep them
at a distance, relegated to nothing more than alien visitors
at this place.

Freya's shadow fell over her again. "Reuben's not here.
You'll have to get back in there with a camera."

Not on your life. I'm not going back.

It wasn't just that she was afraid. It was the *presence*
she'd felt. It was definitely friendly. In some way it had laid
claim to her.

Was she willing to be claimed?

Say something. Distract them. Buy a little time. Steve
was looking at her. Now she looked back.

"There's something else," she said softly, glad for the
sun, the air, the view down-canyon of the encampment by
the pond. "The room, the way it was sealed . . ."

"Yes, well?"

She looked up, squinting in the light, and met Freya's
pale eyes. She heard it like her own echo, flying away even
as her mind tried to grasp it. "It was sealed from inside."

Freya looked at her uncomprehendingly.

Tina said, "There's this big basket that held the wet mortar. It's still lined with it, dry and cracked and grayish. You can see her finger swipes where she dug it out. And even a few leftover stones in a little pile."

She heard Freya gasp.

Tina said, "Her fingerprints are all over the plaster inside there, clear as day. They could almost be fresh."

Freya stared down at her with those coyote eyes, at first seeing her, then boring through her like a laser while the mind behind them worked.

"Are you saying . . . ?"

"She sealed herself up in there to die."

Freya opened her mouth, but nothing came of it. Then she mouthed it, soundless, and repeated it out loud. "*My God.* Then it was suicide."

Something had come home, something had fallen in place like the last lost piece of a puzzle. Tina saw it in Freya's eyes.

"Go get the cameras, Caspar!" she cried, and to Tina, "You'll have to go back in while there's still . . ." She looked down at the Indian camp where the dances would soon begin.

It started before she knew it, then of its own volition her head kept on shaking. "No," Tina said. "I'm not going back. Send Shippers."

Freya laughed. Shippers was a big girl.

"So okay," Tina said, "Steve can take pictures through the opening."

"No way," Freya said. "I've got to have close-ups of everything. And if we had to remove all of the seal to get a larger person in there, the fingerprints might be lost."

You could hear Caspar loping off down the trail. Beano Shippers appeared on the upper ledge, then she climbed backwards down the aspen pole with the big square flashlight in one hand.

Tina looked down at the pond. The young men on horseback were moving out, and lined up behind them, the pickup trucks, everybody on their way down to the river flats for the rabbit hunt. A little red Japanese pickup appeared over the rise, hurtling toward the canyon. Willy, back from visiting Joe in the hospital. "All right," Tina said softly. "I'll go back in."

Freya squeezed her shoulder. "That's my girl!"

Was she, Freya's girl?

Once in the bubble in the cliff, she would be rid of them, she'd have time to think. Once in there, she could pray that Cruz would come and keep them from moving the old woman, the *kwiyo*.

29

The marshal's foot was heavy on the gas. These past few days he had learned every twist of the road by heart. Something in him quickened at each approach to the canyon. It quickened now, but he could not admit to himself that what drew him had little to do with chasing a quarry.

They crossed the river into the open lands of Santa Ynez Pueblo. At the cutoff to the canyon, out in the sage young Indian men waited in a circle on their ponies for the signal.

The marshal cursed under his breath. The narrow two-lane blacktop was gorged with pickups from the Indian camp. They crowded the shoulder of the road, spilling over into the road itself. People lined the barbed wire fence and sat on hoods and fenders, little kids on top of the truck cabs. He had to slow to a crawl.

A rifle cracked and the horsemen fell over the necks of their ponies, whipping them to a frenzy. The slings in their hands began to whirl.

No point in tootling his horn. All attention was glued on the field. He had to stop. "Look at that," he said with a mixture of awe and exasperation.

Reuben was looking. The riders whooped and hollered, leaning half off their flying mounts, the stone-loaded slings twirling in their hands.

"Listen and you can pick it up," the marshal said. "That whirring noise."

But Reuben heard only the hoofbeats drumming the hard-packed ground. He thought if he got out and stood there, he would feel it quake. The circle, bigger in diameter than a football field, rapidly collapsed toward the center where dust rose and bellowed as men and horses clashed like a cavalry battle. Yelps and shouts rose out of the dust.

Hunters began to emerge triumphant, a man here, another there, standing in their stirrups, twisting in their saddles, holding jackrabbit carcasses aloft by the ears, thrusting them this way and that, showing them off. The rabbits swung heavily, like they had stones in their bellies.

Reuben had never seen anything like it. "Wow," he breathed.

Shaking his head, the marshal nosed his vehicle off the crowded blacktop and into the bar ditch, crawling so close to the fence that he almost scratched his paint. "They've been doing that for centuries," he said. "Before the Spanish brought the horse, I bet they did it on foot." He was finally able to pull back onto the blacktop.

They rode in silence as the road began to climb. Reuben could still see it—the thundering horses, the dust, the rabbits hanging. He still heard the shouts.

The marshal reached out and picked up the carabiner and held it in front of him on the steering wheel, frowning, fingering it.

"It's for rock climbing. You attach it to the harness," Reuben said. "It clips in place, see? And there's his initials." He pointed. "He's scratched them on everything he owns."

The D ring was shaped something like a brass knuckles. The marshal said, "Okay, so the kid says he found it . . ."

"Right where he found the notebook and the compass."

The marshal tried putting it all together—the morning, the mesa top, the cliff, Rap Singleton squatting there for the big picture. "But what's the motive?"

Reuben shrugged. "Something to do with the diamond Rap found?" The road began to flatten out. Farther along, there was nobody around the pond but a few kids and old people. Everybody had gone to the rabbit hunt.

"I don't know, Reuben," the marshal said. Okay, so what if he did have a beard? Artists were supposed to have beards. "Who would kill for a diamond?" He shook his head.

"Maybe he thought there were a lot of them. Maybe he thought he'd find a diamond mine or something."

The marshal snorted. "Shoot, around here you'd be more likely to find gold." He was thinking of all the lines and figures on the back of Rap's bank statement. He was pretty sure he and Cruz Domingue had discovered the same numbers and figures on the paper inside the rusty tobacco can. He'd spied four rock cairns from the mesa top—one piled up around the spigot from the well the BLM engineers had sunk for the use of campers, another standing like a buttress against the curb of the concrete sluice emptying the pond's overflow, the other two on the banks of the pond, completing the corners of a square, or, seen from the mesa top, the apexes of a diamond. The tobacco can had been buried in the one by the well.

"Where you find diamonds, could that be an indication of something else—like maybe some valuable mineral?" Reuben asked. "Uranium? Something like that?" But before the marshal could answer, he burst out, "Now I remember why he said he was going into Santa Fe that day. He said he was going to the courthouse!"

"Why the hell didn't you tell me that?"

"I almost had it the day we searched his camper, but I

lost it." Because of the beaver diving outside. "It got away from me. Why do people go to the courthouse?"

The marshal grunted. "You don't if you can help it." But then he added, "You go to pay your taxes or make a court date or to register a claim." His vehicle slowed of its own accord as they approached the cutoff to the mesa top.

"No," Reuben said. "Keep going. Go on up the canyon."

30

Tina fell facedown on the rising floor of the tunnel. There wasn't enough air. She was sweating from anxiety. She closed her eyes. *Be calm.* She made herself breathe slowly, deeply. She thought she'd heard somewhere that this was the way to deal with hyperventilation, but maybe she'd made it up.

She didn't move because she was afraid to touch the walls—they were too close—or the roof, too low over her head. She imagined daylight, the meadow, the stream. Her heart slowed. Finally she breathed normally. She slithered forward. The room at the end of the tunnel was better than this narrow space.

She didn't want to look at the mummy against the wall, so she put that off. What had it meant to that long dead woman sitting there—this room, the swaddled thing on its altar, the petroglyph of the breech birth in the rain? Why had she sealed herself in here to die? For grief, Tina thought, grief for a dead baby all wrapped up on the altar stone.

She took the film out of the camera and shoved it down in her jeans pocket, then aimed at the ceiling and pressed the button. When the flash went off she shut her eyes. Out there in the cave, all they would see was the flash of light. That would satisfy Freya for a while. Meanwhile, she was committing the room and everything in it not to film, but to memory.

The camera was a little automatic Fuji, Reuben's favorite. It had a built-in flash and a zoom for close-ups. Everything in here was close-up. There were thirty-six exposures on the roll she'd just removed from the camera, and on two more rolls in her pocket. That made over a hundred frames. Freya had said take at least three from every angle. If she took her time, letting them see the flash at reasonable intervals, she could stall for quite a while. Freya would think she was getting what she wanted.

You've become duplicitous, she told herself as she clamped her eyes shut and clicked the flash again. She sent a silent message to Cruz: *Please come.*

She examined the fingerprints in the plaster, the prints in the dried, cracked mud in the basket, the basket itself. It was about two feet tall, very well made, the weave so tight it had once held water. Designs in black circled it— serpents, it looked like, or lightning. She closed her eyes and hit the flash button again.

She examined the little pile of stones left over after the room had been sealed. They had not been chiseled or shaped in any way, so far as she could tell. Just stones still there on the floor beside the basket, exactly where the woman behind her had dumped them centuries ago and then not needed these few to complete her enterprise.

She clicked the flash again. That was three. She had to keep count because Freya out there would be counting, too. She moved up close to the pictograph. The baby's feet emerging from the womb had once been stained red, though the stain had flaked off. To represent blood, she thought.

The woman giving birth was a different matter. The head was turned up, in agony or to catch the falling rain. You couldn't see her face. Her stick arms were akimbo, hands on her thighs, the fingers drawn like long triangles, three to a hand. Her legs were squared out and bent at the knee, ending in feet that were toeless slabs. A line below her waist might have been the string that had held a loincloth. Her breasts were spirals drawn on her chest.

Except for this drawing, the walls of the niche were bare. The pictograph was immediately above the bundle on its altar. She clicked the flash. Four.

The altar stone rested squarely on the floor with the feather-wrapped object on top of it. She clicked the flash—five—and prayed again: *Cruz, please come.*

What was it all about? What was the significance of the rain? The altar seemed to be to the woman giving birth. Giving birth out in the rain? Why hadn't she gone inside? She clicked the flash on the empty camera again. Six.

"That's right," Freya called. "Take your time. Get as many frames as you need."

She hit the button again and in the flash saw her for an instant against the wall, that long hair. She'd heard that after you die your hair keeps growing.

She pressed the flash button again. Seven.

She steeled herself and moved closer and for the first time really looked. The mummy's cape was made of feathers. It was fur and feathers, thousands of feathers, some now only feather spines, covering her torso like gossamer, the colors hardly faded in the dry desert air.

Tina sat slowly back on her heels. That cape meant days and months of toil—snaring the birds, plucking their finery, all that weaving. The blue feathers of piñon jays. The yellow and red of western tanagers. And green. Good lord, the green of parrots. That was from Mexico. This woman was no ordinary citizen, she was a personage. She must have been a medicine woman of some kind.

She hit the flash several times in quick succession, then sat very still and listened. How long had she been hearing the drums? No telling, but they'd been there for some time, as if the reverberations came to her through the rock, a rhythm she'd learned as a child to take for granted like her pulse.

She looked at her watch. Rabbit hunt in the morning, dancing in the afternoon. But the rabbit hunt had got off to a late start when Shippers was kidnapped. But it had to be over now because the drums were beating, which meant the dance had started. It could go on for hours. She'd seen it happen. And then the ceremony.

"What are you doing in there?" Freya was impatient. *Hurry, Cruz.* But Cruz would be on the platform with the dignitaries. "Tina, do you hear me?"

To placate Freya, she hit the flash. She hit it again and again at shorter intervals. Finally she moved very close to the mummy. She expected to be overwhelmed by horror at the dead woman sitting there against the wall, but she wasn't. Instead, she felt a curious tenderness. The head was bent ever so slightly on the chest, and the long black hair threaded with gray pulled forward over the emaciated frame. She steeled herself and looked at the face. The eyes were closed, the lids sunken. The woman was like a cedar carving. She had become a statue of herself.

I won't betray you to them, Grandmother. She set off the flash.

"Is that roll finished?" Freya called. "I thought I counted thirty-six."

Tina said, "I'm reloading."

Liar.

"Toss me the roll you've finished. Caspar can start developing."

She couldn't think of an objection. "Okay. Hang on." She took one of the unexposed rolls from her pocket, wrapped it in her handkerchief, and tossed it out through the tunnel. *Hurry, Cruz.* But she knew better than to expect Cruz any time soon.

"Got it!" You could hear the excitement in Freya's voice.

Tina bit her lip. She heard Freya entrusting the film to Caspar with instructions to run down to the big trailer and develop it right away. How long would that take? Tina wasn't sure. She sat cross-legged in front of the feathered personage. *I can't hold them off much longer,* she told her. *Tell me what to do.* She hit the flash again. *Please, Cruz, come.*

31

Heading back to the pueblo, John sat on the edge of the seat in Cruz Domingue's pickup, bracing himself with a hand on the dash and looking straight ahead. He was holding himself in. Had to, or he'd bawl. He hated that about himself—that when he was really mad some part of his inner workings betrayed him and he bawled like a baby.

Old Eliseo had bought it. He'd gone and died in the emergency room and not one thing you could do about it. John swiped at his nose with his naked arm. He wished he had on his jeans, not these moth-eaten old Indian things from the cave. He would never make it now. It had all come to nothing, all his training, all his dreams of belonging to something better than Isaiah Hoop.

Before they came and stuck things in his mouth, in his arms, while the tiny pencils wrote on what looked like little TV screens beside the bed, old Eliseo had opened his eyes and looked at John. He had actually chuckled. "What's this mean? What's that mean?" Teasing. John didn't care. He could tease all he liked if he'd just keep on living.

"Let's try and keep him quiet," the nurse had said, sticking her head in and vanishing.

He'd felt Cruz behind him, against the striped curtain of the cubicle, keeping out of the way like he knew Eliseo was dying.

"Come on, old man," John said, shaking Eliseo's arm, thin as a stick, no flesh on it, no muscle left. What was wrong with him anyway? At the clinic they said old age.

Old age, shoot. John once met a gringo in a pizza parlor in Moab, Utah, who told him there were ways you could live forever. Not forever maybe, but a whole lot longer than nowadays. He told John about some people over a hundred years old. They lived in Bulgaria or some such place. They lived on yogurt, stuff like that. This young guy said he himself planned on living to a hundred fifty. Said he would tell John how to go about it, but vanished while John was visiting the Men's.

When the old man opened his eyes and chuckled and said, "What's this mean? What's that mean?" teasing, mimicking him, John wished he'd tracked that fellow down.

Sweet, mean old man. He'd gone to his happy hunting grounds, leaving John unfinished. Maybe he'd keep an eye on John from up there somewhere. Likely he'd chuckle down and shake his head.

Eliseo was different from John's white-robed friend. He was more human-like. He teased, and though John hated being teased, he knew the old man did it because secretly he liked him. He'd told him lots of things, hadn't he? He'd sung him secret songs, one of them a moonlight song that was meant for courtship. Said one day John might need that one. And laughed. But even if he laughed and teased and shook his head, they bunked together, didn't they?

Where was he now?

On ice in the hospital morgue. Cruz had to sign a paper.

But that wasn't what John meant. He meant where had he gone to when he passed away on the emergency room table. He hadn't gone to Isaiah's hell. John didn't believe in it. Shoot, nobody knew anything about it except the dead, and they weren't talking, so you might as well believe what you wanted to. John wanted to believe in lush pastures full of daisies and spotted cows. He liked cows. They had great eyelashes, and there was something peaceful about them. So, okay, pastures and daisies and cows with long eyelashes. What else? Ice cream—black walnut, John's favorite—because in that place it was always warm.

Maybe Eliseo would come back and haunt him. John was afraid of ghosts, but not if it was the old man's. Sitting up on the edge of the seat, nose close to the windshield, not looking at Cruz Domingue, he clenched his fists. Just when he'd thought he was settled down with a place to live. Now where would he lay his head?

"You found those things that morning on top of the mesa, right?" Cruz said.

John swiped at his nose. Why go over it again? Wouldn't anybody ever in this life believe him? Let somebody accuse him of something, he couldn't help it, he acted guilty. He knew this about himself, but he couldn't seem to do anything about it. Best just keep his mouth shut or they'd send him up for murder.

They were on Indian land now. What were all those pickups doing? Oh, yeah, the rabbit hunt. Looked like it was over, he'd missed it, but everybody was still milling around, just hanging out. That was the thing about the Indians, they were always together. Maybe they were skinning the rabbits, he couldn't tell. Probably have rabbit stew for supper up yonder around the pond.

"And you just picked them up because nobody was around?"

"Yeah," John said. "They were just lying there."

Cruz nodded. "You found the notebook . . ."

"And the thing in the leather case."

"The Brunton compass. They're used by prospectors and surveyors, miners, geologists, people like that."

"Yeah. And the big key ring I put on my belt." All of a sudden he was bereft of everything that mattered—the old man, all of his private stuff.

"How come when you heard a man had been murdered, you didn't come forward and turn them in?"

Christ, why hadn't somebody told him the old guy'd been knocked off? The morning he found those things at the edge of the cliff, he hadn't even known anybody had fallen over. He hadn't heard anything. Just running along home, he'd come up on those things lying there.

"I didn't know nobody'd got kilt," he said gruffly. "I just thought finders keepers."

Cruz nodded, looking straight ahead at the road.

"But I reckon you don't believe me."

The Tsorigi governor didn't say anything for maybe half a mile. Then he said, "I expect I do believe you, son. I don't believe you'd kill anybody for a few trinkets, and you never even knew he'd found a diamond."

"A diamond!" That's what it said on the last page of the notebook: Diamonds. He could see it written big on the page.

In the rearview mirror mounted on his door, Cruz watched a silver stretch limousine turn off the highway and follow him in toward the canyon. "See that?" he said.

John looked over his shoulder.

"That's the governor's limousine," Cruz said.

"They gonna give the land back?"

"If the senator's with him, that'll be the sign."

As they slowed, nearing the pond, you could hear the drums. Then see the people up ahead, already dancing. Cruz nosed in beside the other pickups pointed toward the lake. In the clearing circled by onlookers, the dancers bobbed and turned, all women, barefoot, in heavy black wool dresses halfway down their legs and pinned up over one shoulder, the other shoulder bare. Dancing stately, like balancing whatever it was they had on top of their heads. It was squat and black and pointy at top, looked something like a beanbag. Eyes down, the women bobbed stately in time with the drums, middle-aged women, old women, mothers, grandmothers, not pretty young squaws.

"I didn't know it was just women," John said, disgusted.

They got out on opposite sides of the pickup and walked closer. John wanted to watch the dancers, but he kept his eye out for the young braves. They'd chased him up the box canyon, and they might come after him again.

The drums stopped, then started up again, slower. As the

dance rhythm changed, young male dancers appeared over the high bank of the dam. They were dressed in the hides of animals, animal heads pulled over their own heads so you couldn't see their faces, deer heads, mountain lions, buffalo, bear. "Hot damn, lookit that," John said. All hunched over, they walked on all fours, their forelegs nothing but sticks of wood.

"Stay here," Cruz said.

"I ain't going nowhere."

"They're going to want you to hang around for questioning."

The animals pranced around the dancers, lunging at them, running away like asking to be chased, like kids pulling stunts, anything to get their mamas' attention. But the women just danced and danced, stately, like dignitaries from some august realm. Wouldn't even look at the young men in animal hides. No, the young men were just gnats or something, nuisances. The women just went on dancing like something important that nobody knew about but them depended on them dancing.

"Can I stay in the old man's rooms till I'm, you know, ready to hit the road?" John asked.

Cruz shook his head no.

Okay, that's it, John thought. I knew it.

Cruz said, "You'll stay with us." *Us.* That was Cruz and his wife and his grown daughter Jessie. Cruz said he didn't think his wife would mind. They had plenty of room, and the marshal had after all turned John over to his safekeeping.

John was so pleased he couldn't speak, but he shrugged like he didn't care one way or another. To stay even, he wanted to give something back. "I got something to show you," he said. "Something up the cliff I bet you'll find inneresting."

Cruz eyed him suspiciously. "Sure," he said, "okay. Soon as the program's over."

John watched him walk over to meet the stretch limo with tinted glass nosing in between two tall fir trees. The driver got out and went around to open the doors. The first thing John saw emerge was a nyloned knee, then a white hand with a lacy handkerchief. Then out stepped the white-haired wife of the governor of the state, smiling, tugging at her skirt. Cruz took her hand. Then out came the governor of New Mexico himself.

John watched the limo anxiously. Then jutting out of the limousine came a thin gray-clad knee. And sure enough, it was the solemn young senator in a gray business suit with a silver and blue striped tie. Cruz looked all swollen with pleasure as he led them toward the platform and handed them up.

They took their seats on the folding chairs among the big men from the pueblo—the *caciques* and war chiefs—all dressed up in their Pendleton blankets. The governor's wife looked right at home in a bright red suit with a purple flower pinned on her shoulder, but the senator and the governor looked drab in their business suits next to the old men in reds and royal blues and purples, their long hair braided with colored strips of felt and hung forward over their shoulders, ending in tufts of feathers.

When he moved toward the platform for a better view of the goings-on, John saw Horse watching. The young Indian sidled toward him with his hands in his pockets. John backed away. Horse came on, joined by some others, smirking at John with their hands in their pockets.

He backed away toward the road up the canyon, but they moseyed after him. John turned and ran, thankful for all his midnight training. He was headed for the arroyo and the secret chimney in the cliff, but glancing up at the ledge he cursed. There were people up there. He ran on up the canyon road. He had to get off it and find someplace to hide. He could hear them pounding after him.

The road turned where the stream crossed under the stone bridge. He ran onto the bridge and leaped over the parapet into the water. Water left no tracks they could follow. He ran up the shallow stream to a patch of scrub oak, then left it, making for the granite outcropping up there over the road.

When panting he gained the top, he could see the road in both directions, and also see the meadow. And something else. Below him, in the cleft where a big rock face had long ago dropped off the front of the cliff to make a hidden alley, there in the brush was the little red Japanese pickup that belonged to the outsiders.

Crawling down the road from the campground came the marshal's four-by with the bearded guy driving and the marshal walking alongside. The marshal's hand hung down, and in the hand was a .38. The gun startled John. It looked like they were looking for somebody. Looking for who? For him? He slithered back from the edge but kept the road in sight. Horse and the others pounded toward the bend, on a collision course with the marshal's four-by.

The vehicles stopped. The marshal conferred with the driver, this Reuben guy. The Pueblo boys stopped on the stone bridge over the stream. They must have figured he'd left the road because they didn't see him up ahead. They were looked down at the water, then up the stream.

Then the marshal came down and conferred with Horse. Horse shook his head and looked up toward the meadow, saying something, maybe saying they'd lost John, he'd left the road and was somewhere in the cliffs above. John felt sorry for himself. Why was everybody after him?

The marshal kept talking. Asking questions, it looked like. The rabbit hunters clustered around the vehicle. Just then John heard something behind him. He turned. But it was just nerves, nothing there. He looked down at the red pickup hidden in the cleft. The truck bed was packed full of stuff—mountain bike, sleeping bag, rolled-up tent, all of that climbing equipment, diving stuff. Why was the truck hidden like that? Somebody scared his things would get stolen?

Not a bad idea. But John couldn't think of a way to go about it. He looked covetously at all that expensive sports equipment, and Isaiah Hoop whispered in his ear, *Forget it. Put it outa yore mind. Th'ow it away.*

Again he thought he heard something. He turned, and there was Willy behind him, crouching in the brush. John felt a moment of pleasure. They were both hiding. Maybe he had a coconspirator. He opened his mouth to whisper something, but Willy, his face mottled red, sprang at him with a hunting knife. John's first reaction was hurt and disappointment that somebody else would want to hurt him. He sidestepped, avoiding the knife, and shoved Willy away from him as hard as he could.

It was over in an instant, and all in silence. Willy hovered a moment on the edge, looking startled, his arms going like windmills as he tried to get his balance. Then he went over. John scrambled to the edge and looked down. Reuben leapt out of the marshal's four-by and peered up at Willy sprawled out on his back in the tops of the scrub oak that had punctured him here and there but also broke his fall. The marshal walked over and together they reached up and lifted him down and set him on his feet. He stood there unsteady, trying to look defiant, bleeding all over himself from scratches and a gash on the side of his head.

Then Horse spied John on the outcropping. But with the marshal there, John thought it was safe to come on down. Eyeing Horse and the others, he passed them and walked over to the marshal. He pointed to the cleft and told the marshal about the little red pickup.

Willy looked at him with hatred, then looked at the ground.

The marshal asked Willy, "How come you to give us such a chase? What were you running from?" But Willy looked sullenly at the toes of his hiking boots.

Down below, around the pond, the drums and the chanting had stopped. You could hear Cruz's voice over the makeshift loudspeaker introducing first the governor of the state, then the senator who'd come all the way from Washington.

"Got your truck all packed up, looks like you were getting ready to leave out of here in a hurry," the marshal said.

Some of Horse's buddies were over there pawing through the equipment in the truck bed, but though Willy watched with hatred, it looked to John like he had made up his mind to keep his mouth shut.

32

Tina hit the flash. If she were actually shooting, she thought she'd be close to the end of the second roll. She'd lost count. She heard running footsteps. Caspar returning. Out in the cave a whispered conference.

Someone walked over to the mouth of the tunnel.

"Okay, Tina," Freya said, "what the devil do you think you're doing?"

Tina put her face to her knees and laid down the camera.

"Explain your reason for this treason." Freya waited. "How could you do this to me?"

Tina backed against the wall, out of sight from the tunnel, and huddled inside Steve's sweatshirt.

"Divided loyalties," Freya whispered, not to her, to whoever was still out there. "I'm going in."

"I doubt you can," somebody—maybe Bess Cochran—whispered. "It's pretty low and narrow."

Scuffling, sliding, then, "Christ, I can't do this." Tina pictured Freya wedged in the tunnel. She felt the urge to laugh.

Then it was quiet out there. Finally a large hand, fingers outstretched, stole around the mouth of the entry, reached one of the stones piled there, and fingered it carefully all over. Fascinated, Tina watched the disembodied hand feel its way around. She turned off the flashlight. The dark was sudden and total. She closed her eyes to shut it out.

"Tina, listen to me."

How could she not?

"I've been aware from the first day why they wanted you on the dig."

She had to keep quiet, say nothing. Otherwise she'd be lost in a bog of justification.

"But I think you trust me. Don't you?" A pause. "Okay, look, I'm not out to do you or your people any harm. Just—please take the pictures."

If she did, would they keep their hands off? Would they be satisfied with photographs? *Cruz, where are you? Cruz!*

"Okay, listen," Freya said. "What I'm after is nothing like points or potsherds. Do you hear me? It's something far more valuable." She raised her voice. "You guys go on outside. Wait for me on the ledge. No need for everybody to be in here. Let me know what's going on down at the pond."

Tina didn't hear the others leave the cave, but she soon heard them out on the ledge talking, and distantly, down-canyon, still the sound of drums.

"Okay, Tina, I'll lay it out for you," Freya said. "Look, it's just a theory. I'm looking for evidence to support it. I believe in every culture, at the beginning, back when people were hunters and gatherers—and back somewhere we all have hunters and gatherers for ancestors—back then, in all cultures, I think men and women were equals. Equals in power because they were equals in physical strength—height, weight, stature, everything.

"So what happened? When and how did men—in every culture, all over the world—take over? Why did women lose out?"

Tina's head came up off her knees.

"I'll tell you why. When they were hunters and gatherers, women had their babies on the move and nursed them for several years. They had to. The infants couldn't eat the nuts

and roots and seeds and small animals the tribe lived on."
She paused. "Are you following what I'm saying?"

But Tina kept quiet.

"Okay," Freya said, and after a moment continued. "And
as long as the women ran alongside the men, and nursed
the babies, they didn't get pregnant. Running long miles
and nursing provided them with a natural birth control. You
probably know that nowadays women athletes who run
long miles daily have trouble getting pregnant. Anyway,
back then women had plenty of time between births to re-
coup their strength."

In the dark, Tina was listening.

"And as long as women were not the weaker sex, they
were equal to the men. So what happened? When people
settled into communities and began to grow crops and do-
mesticate animals, the babies no longer nursed. They were
fed animal milk. The men still hunted far and wide, keeping up their physical prowess, but somebody had to stay
home and mind the kids. So okay, but that left the women
free for other things, like cooking and basket weaving.
Great, right?"

Tina was thinking about it.

"Not great," Freya said. "Without their natural birth control operating, women got pregnant every year. They no
longer had time between births to retrench and regain their
strength. One pregnancy after another, and they lost ground
physically. They no longer hunted alongside the men, no
longer ran mile after mile, day after day. Over time they
lost muscle, height, stature. They became the weaker sex."

Freya waited, but Tina kept silent. She heard Freya sigh.
"So where does that leave us?"

In the silence the drums beat one last emphatic boom-
boom-boom. The dance was over. Then a voice over the
makeshift speaker system. Tina thought it was Cruz.

Freya was asking, "So what am I doing here at this site
on the mesa? Down in Mexico and Central America, where
I've done most of my work, the people went through this
phase much earlier. I came here in hopes the Anasazi would

afford some evidence of that transition." She paused, then, "Okay, where do you think the kivas originated, Tina?"

Tina frowned. Kivas belonged to the men. Women were barred from entering except on special occasions or to bring food.

Freya said, "It originated from the pit house. The house was the woman's, right?"

Still is, Tina thought. The Tsorigi and other Pueblo tribes were still matrilocal. The houses belonged to the women. A man lived in his mother's house till he took a wife. Then he lived in his mother-in-law's.

"Men must have felt like second-class citizens, like women today," Freya said.

There in the dark, Tina nodded.

"And the earth, according to tribal legend, is what?"

Tina whispered, *"The mother."*

Freya said, "The earth is the mother, and what is *sipapu*, the place of emergence?"

Tina had begun to suspect.

"It is the place of emergence from the womb of Mother Earth. *Sipapu* is clearly a female symbol. But where do we find *sipapu*? It's a hole in the floor of the men's house, the kiva."

Tina nodded.

"Men couldn't give birth. They hadn't that primal power. Early on, they didn't even know they had anything to do with making babies. That was the female mystery. A mystery so great I daresay it overwhelmed the men, made them feel small because it was the woman who had the power of life itself." Freya stopped. "Are you listening?"

Tina said softly, "I'm listening."

"Good girl. Okay, to gain power men had to appropriate this power for themselves. And making it theirs, they made it grandiose, which suggests the power it had over their imaginations. No longer was it women who gave birth, it was Mother Earth. People didn't just emerge from the wombs of women. No. *Sipapu* was the place of emergence of the whole tribe into this world. By mythologizing, symbolizing the mother and the womb, and putting *sipapu* in the kiva, which was originally the pit house of women that the men had taken over, men became the priests of the mysteries that had belonged to the women. The pit house became the men's kiva. The mother was no longer woman but the earth womb itself. And the vagina, the place of emergence, was *sipapu*, a hole in the dirt floor of the men's house."

It made all kinds of sense. Tina turned and looked at the mummy against the wall. *Is that the way it was, Grandmother?*

"Men no longer emerged from the womb of woman," Freya said. "They emerged from the center of Mother Earth, not through the birth canal, but from the sacred *sipapu*. They turned the whole thing around. They turned it upside down and wrong side out. They made the myth the reality, and the reality no more than a small, human thing. Do you see what I'm talking about, Tina?"

Tina saw.

"Once men took over the mystery of life, women became nothing more than supporting cast."

Tina slid the flashlight switch forward and flooded the niche with light. She heard Freya gasp. "God. There she is. I can see a little bit of her."

Tina looked at the woman against the wall still wrapped in her ceremonial cape. What could the *kwiyo* tell Freya of all this? Tina had no idea. Where was her uncle?

She bit her lip. Here she was, waiting for *the man* to tell her what to do.

She heard Freya shift a little out in the tunnel and say "Ruth Benedict recorded a saying from a West Coast tribe: we're given a cup of clay, and from it we drink a life. What'll you do with your cupful, Tina?"

Tina couldn't answer.

"I need those photographs," Freya said. "You have to ask yourself, right now, my girl, this minute: What are you first? An Indian? Or a woman?"

33

It was like déjà vu, Willy lying there at the foot of the cliff. It struck Reuben as some kind of freak retribution, if you believed in such.

After they'd lifted him off the scrub oak all scratched and punctured and set him on his feet, and after Tom Hurleigh had told him he was being held for questioning, the marshal asked Horse, "What're you fellows doing here? Why aren't you at the ceremonies?"

Another vehicle ground up the rise. They turned and watched it come, a Santa Fe patrol car.

Horse cast around for an answer. One of the Indian boys said, "We was just playing with him," nodding at John. "We was just going to strip off them old Indian things and see was he white underneath."

John said indignantly, "They're always pestering me!"

While a voice came over the speaker system down below, the police car pulled up and stopped. Lieutenant Tito Gonzales of the Santa Fe PD stepped out of the passenger side.

The marshal told Willy, "Stay right here. You're not going anywhere." Willy didn't look at anybody. The marshal shook hands with the lieutenant.

"I just took a statement from the youngster at the hospital," the lieutenant said. "He's sitting up and eating a meal."

Reuben looked at Willy. Willy never even looked up. "What's the story?" the marshal asked.

"Says his pal killed the old guy. Way he found out, this Willy character took off his hiking boot to shake out the sand, and the old man's diamond fell out of the little knife pocket."

They all turned and looked at Willy's boot. There it was, on the side of the high-top hiking boot, a little snap pocket. The marshal strode over and undid the snap and stuck in his finger and fished around while Willy just stood there. The marshal dragged out the diamond. It was opaque, milky white, like the glass tumbled by water that Reuben had found as a kid on Jones Beach. The Indian boys jostled each other to get a look. The lieutenant touched it lightly with his finger.

"I've been looking for this," Tom Hurleigh said.

Willy made a sound and everybody turned and looked at him, but he didn't say anything.

"So anyway, this kid Joe," the lieutenant went on, "he says they come up here to camp out during spring break from the School of Mines in Socorro, and they found this—" he fished a paper out of his pocket "—this 'tektite,' he called it, and they got pretty excited."

"That right, Willy?" the marshal asked, but Willy wasn't talking. He was looking down at the road with his lower lip caught between his teeth.

"Anyway," the lieutenant said, "a tektite could mean a meteor fell around here somewhere. They're pretty valuable. The kid says people have made millions selling meteors or parts of meteors. They thought maybe this one fell where years later you BLM guys built the dam and made the pond, because that's where they found the tektite. Said it was lying just below the pond, in the sluice, dropped there by the spring runoff. Said the pond looked like a natural depression to them, and that would fit their ideas."

Willy looked up at the lieutenant with hatred in his eyes. The lieutenant chuckled. "Makes you about half-mad, dudn' it, boy. So the two of you took the thing back to the School of Mines and tested it in the lab to make sure what it was. Right?"

Everybody looked at Willy, but Willy kept his mouth shut.

The lieutenant shrugged. "So they came back here as soon as school let out. All the sporting goods was just to hide their real purpose, which was to scuba dive and find the meteor."

The marshal gave a long, low whistle, looking at the diamond on his palm. Reuben saw Willy cut his eyes and look, too, then look away. Horse moved up and peered at it, and jostled elbows with John, who also peered at it.

"What's a diamond got to do with a meteor?" the marshal asked.

The retired rancher from Calgary materialized at the outer edge of the little crowd in the middle of the canyon road. The boys parted to let him through. "Diamonds," he said, "have been found at sites where meteorites have landed. To produce diamonds, the impact has to generate great heat and pressure."

The marshal was eyeing him with a smile, but the man from Calgary didn't look at him.

"Under high temperature and pressure," he said, "a scientist at GE has made artificial diamonds from peanut butter."

"No kidding," the lieutenant said. "Peanut butter!"

"The South African diamond fields," Carmack McIntyre said, "are shaped like funnels with the mouth pointing up. They're called diamond pipes, or diatremes. Like Shiprock, they've been thought to be the necks of extinct volcanos."

The little man's eyes looked wet, like they always did. How did he know all this?

"But they may be, instead, the sites of some very large meteor impacts."

"Are you saying," the marshal said, "that Rap Singleton found this diamond around here because the foot of the canyon is the site of a meteor impact?"

McIntyre nodded. "Very likely."

"Yeah," the lieutenant said. "The kid at the hospital said Willy knew as soon as he saw the diamond that the old guy was on to something."

The night of the seminar, Reuben thought.

"And when he was in his cups he told these boys he was going into the courthouse in Santa Fe the next morning to file a claim."

The marshal nodded. "We found his rock cairns around the lake, and in one of them, his coordinates. In a tobacco can." He chuckled. "That's where the prospectors put them in the old days."

"He was about to claim the land where the boys expected to find a meteor," Carmack McIntyre said.

"Yeah," the lieutenant said. "So Willy here followed him up the mesa that morning and shoved him over. You let the other kid think the old man just had an accident, didn't you, Willy, till the diamond fell out of your boot. Kid at the hospital threatened to go to you, Marshal. That's why he's in the hospital. Right, Willy?"

Reuben was remembering their fight the morning Rap's body was found.

"So you poisoned the whole kit and caboodle to get Joe out of the way," the marshal said.

"Yeah," said the lieutenant. "He took an extra big helping of potato salad for himself, then gave most of it to his buddy, who said he could eat a whole tub of potato salad by himself, as Willy knew, didn't you, Willy."

Willy's face was mottling red and white.

"He'd planned on going to Albuquerque in the ambulance with Joe. The poison had failed, so you meant to try more drastic measures, didn't you, boy. But when Joe started coming around, you ran."

Then the lieutenant read Willy his rights. When he was through he motioned to his driver, and the driver got out and handcuffed Willy and put a hand on his head and shoved him down into the backseat of the squad car. Reuben watched. He'd never liked Willy, but he never thought he'd turn out to be a killer.

"Beats me why he didn't keep on running," the marshal said. "How'd you know he'd come back here, fella?"

Reuben looked in the open door of the squad car at Willy's knees in his chinos and his handcuffed hands in his lap, young-looking hands, with squared-off nails. "I knew he wouldn't abandon his equipment."

The lieutenant got in the patrol car. It rolled slowly across the stone bridge. Willy's head through the rear window looked small against the seat back.

"I want to talk to you," the marshal said sternly to Carmack McIntyre, taking the small man by the elbow.

But McIntyre shook off the marshal's hand. "I know what you want. I've known for some time you were on to me."

"Where'd you put it?"

"How did you know it was me?"

"The way your right boot's worn at the heel." The rancher flushed as they all looked down at his built-up shoe. "It matches the footprint you left in Singleton's RV. Okay, where'd you put it?"

McIntyre smiled sadly. "I threw it in the stream."

Reuben wondered what they were talking about. As if the marshal had read his mind, he turned and said, "He's the guy broke into Rap Singleton's RV. I knew what he'd taken soon as I saw those rock cairns."

"I'll show you," McIntyre said with a sigh.

The marshal turned and hiked purposefully up the road, and the rest of them followed. Reuben had wanted to see the Indian dances, but he tagged along, curious, aware of Hooper John close by his side and matching his stride.

They lined up outside Rap's camper where the stream widened to a beaver pond. One of the Indian boys started to shed his boots, but Reuben said, "No, wait, let me." He stripped down to his shorts while the marshal told him what he'd be looking for.

He waded in. In the middle of the pond, in front of the beaver lodge, he did a shallow surface dive. Underwater everything was clear, the silted bottom, roots sticking out of the bank. He swam closer to the lodge. He thought he could see where the beaver had made his underwater door, where he would dive in and come up on the dry island inside his house.

He'd stirred up the silt and the water was getting cloudy. But there, at what had to be the entrance to the lodge, on the sandy bottom of the stream rested one fist-size rock. As he ran out of breath, he seized it and surfaced gulping air. He raised it over his head.

"That's it," Carmack McIntyre said.

Reuben trudged up out of the water in his sagging Jockey shorts and handed the rock to Tom Hurleigh.

Carmack McIntyre took it from the marshal's hand, turned it over, and pointed to a clearly etched hole about half an inch deep in the rock. "There's where the old man found his diamond. His metal detector picked out this meteor fragment. It's full of nickel and iron. That must have been puzzling. But I guess when he saw the diamond lodged in it, he was so excited he forgot about that."

"Well, I'll be damned," the marshal said. "When I saw the four rock cairns around the lake, I thought he'd marked out a mining claim." The marshal fingered the hole, so clear and precise it might have been made with an electric drill.

Carmack McIntyre said, "That's probably what Singleton had in mind. He must have thought he'd found a diamond deposit. He didn't know it was the rock itself that was valuable. He just kept it as a paperweight."

The marshal said, "You saw it the day we searched the camper?"

Nodding, the little man touched the rock reverently. "It looks like a pallasite."

"What the devil's a pallasite?" the marshal asked.

"It's the most valuable of all meteorites. It's a rare stony-iron."

"So why the hell did you throw it away?"

"It was my way—clumsy, I'm afraid—of trying to save it for future generations, protect it from all those who want it for their own selfish reasons. I believe they carry profound messages about the universe that we are neither, by virtue of our consciousness nor our technology, as yet able to decode. They should be left untouched till we can decipher what they have to tell us."

"Yeah." The marshal was nodding, eyeing the man from Calgary with a look somewhere between suspicion and respect. He took the diamond out of his pocket and fitted it into the hole. The fit was perfect. "So this is the meteor."

The retired rancher nodded. "Or part of it."

34

Dozing in the dark of the cave, Tina dreamed again of her mother's house. She walked through a door she hadn't known was there, and descended steps to levels she had never visited. Then Cruz's voice outside in the cave and her head came up. She sat up wanting to wash her face. It felt puffy and creased. How long had she been in here?

"I tolja," an eager voice was saying. "Looka here. Lookit that."

Freya said, "It's a very early dwelling cave."

Cruz didn't say anything.

"Was the senator here for the dances?" Freya asked. Cruz must have nodded because Freya sounded defeated. "So be it then."

Tina's joy was not unmitigated. They had got their land back, but now Freya might lose the dig.

"It's a remarkable find," Freya said. She was talking about the big cave chamber.

Cruz mumbled something. She couldn't understand what he said. Then her scalp crawled and the hair on her arms stirred. The presence again. *Speak to me, Grandmother,* she prayed, mouthing it in the dark.

But there was no answer. She turned on the flashlight and winced at the brightness. Out in the cave, male voices muttered together—the geologist, Caspar, one that sounded like a boy's: "Hit's somethin', ain't it! I'm the one found it. I been coming here for some time."

And Caspar said, "I'll get a paper out of this."

The geologist said, "It's a layer of basalt on top of . . ."

They were all claiming the cave. Without knowing she'd made a decision, Tina reached for the camera.

When Reuben crawled through the rabbit hole into the cave, he was instantly aware of weird flashes in the semi-dark. John in his motheaten finery was pointing to the wall paintings, talking to Caspar, but Cruz, head bent, was listening to Freya.

"It's all right," he said finally. "I met with the *caciques*. They say for now go ahead. But whatever you find belongs to us. We must know all about it before we allow you to remove it from this place. You finish. Then we'll see." He was watching the weird intermittent flashes coming from close to the floor where there seemed to be a hole in the wall.

"All right, then," Freya said, nodding, taking the best offer she was apt to get. "We've discovered a niche." She looked like she'd prefer not to tell him that.

Cruz nodded as if letting that settle so he could read its meaning. Finally he said, "What's in there?" looking down at the hole where the flashes continued.

Freya described a basket and an altar and the pictograph. She hesitated. "And there's a mummy, apparently a woman."

Cruz looked startled. "A *kwiyo*?!"

"Yes," she said. "In a feather and fur robe, probably a shaman. And there's a second mummy." She was intent on his face.

"Two people?"

She nodded. "She sealed herself up in there, probably with her stillborn child. It looks like a suicide."

Cruz wiped his mouth, then grasped his lips and pulled at them thoughtfully.

"What is a *kwiyo*?" Bess Cochran whispered to Steve Many Hands.

"A wise old woman," he said, "a medicine woman, a shaman."

"I want to bring them out," Freya said.

Cruz shook his head. "No. You mustn't disturb the dead."

"It's very important. It may be the only way we can date this cave dwelling."

Cruz turned away. He walked over to the wall paintings and looked up at them, John eagerly watching his face, Reuben watching them all. Cruz walked to the storage cyst and stared into it. He looked up at Freya. Finally he nodded. "You can bring out the baby," he said. "Then later we put it back." Freya gave a shallow nod, as if grateful for small favors.

Ordinarily, Reuben knew, she would have taken more time, more care. But more time could not be counted on. She knelt at the mouth of the tunnel. "Tina!"

The flashes stopped.

"Are you listening? We're going to remove the child. I want you to take the baby from the altar stone. Be very careful. I want you to bring it out."

Silence from inside the niche.

Cruz bent to the tunnel entrance. "Do as she says, daughter."

The flashlight's beam moved. They waited. Nothing.

"What's the matter?" Freya asked, impatient as always.

Tina said something they couldn't understand.

"Speak up! We can't hear you."

"I can't move it."

Freya snapped, "Why not?"

"It's too heavy."

"What do you mean?"

"It can't be a baby."

Freya raised her face and closed her eyes.

Reuben knelt on the floor. "Tina?"

"Is that you, Reuben?"

"Can you kneel in there?"

A silence, then, "Yes, but just."

"Okay, bend your knees and get your arms around it."
He waited.

"Yeah, okay," she said.

"Now, don't lift it with your arms. Hold it tightly against
you and straighten your knees." He waited. "Have you got
it?"

"I've got it, but I don't know if I can move with it. It's
very heavy."

"Okay, turn slowly toward the tunnel and let it down on
the floor at the tunnel mouth." He could hear her moving.
"Have you put it down?"

Silence, then "Yes" came to them on a great exhalation.

He looked at Freya. "I'm going in."

Down on his stomach, he peered into the tunnel. At the
end of it he could see the bundle on the floor. How heavy
could it be? Would he be able to lift it lying on his stomach? It was clear his shoulders couldn't make it through the
opening at the other end. What about Steve? Steve wouldn't
make it either.

He propelled himself forward, dragging himself by his
elbows. The tunnel dipped, then narrowed toward the other
end as the ceiling lowered. When he was finally able to
reach out, he could just touch the thing, whatever it was.

"Can you roll it toward me, Tina?" He stretched out his
arms with his hands palm-up.

"I'm afraid it'll crush your hands."

"No it won't. Let's try it. Just get your hands under it
and turn it gently."

She was right, it was heavy. His cheek dropped down on
the tunnel floor. He swallowed. Then, using his hands as a
sled, he began to back. The stone floor tore at the skin on
his knuckles. He got the bundle to the middle of the tunnel,
where the ceiling was higher, and tried to lift it. His arms
ached and trembled as the muscles strained. He couldn't do

it. He slid his hands out from under it and backed clear of the tunnel.

Steve said, "Let me try. Maybe I can grab it by both ends."

"Be careful," Freya said.

The others had come over to stand watching. Steve let himself down and slithered out of sight up to his hips. "I've got it," he said. "I think I can lift it a little off the floor."

Then they heard grunting and thrashing. Steve's Adidas wriggled sideways. More grunting. He slithered backwards and emerged. "Okay," he said, "now I can reach in and pick it up."

They stood in a circle looking down at it. John held the lantern close. Through colored feathers frayed from the passage they could see what it was.

"Oh my," Bess Cochran whispered.

"Well, I'll be," her husband said. "It must be . . ."

"She sealed herself up in there to die *with the meteorite*?" Bess Cochran said.

Freya was nodding, nodding, her eyes alight in the lantern's glow.

Cruz said, "What is that thing?"

"It's holy," a voice said behind them. John lifted the lantern, and Carmack McIntyre emerged from the gloom. "Nininger found one in an ancient ruin in Central Arizona. All sealed up in a stone cyst, walled over and covered with rocks like the burial of a child. The burial was a thousand years old. The Navajos covered their own Black Iron, *Pish le gin e gin*, with rocks to hide it from the white man. At Casas Grandes in Mexico they found the grave of a meteorite in a big room, wrapped in a feather cloth like this."

Jim Cochran scoffed, "What are you telling us, man?"

Carmack McIntyre said, "Native Americans regard them as sacred, and the ground under them is sacred, too. Can't you see that's why the pond down there has always been their sacred dance ground? Because that's where the meteor struck."

Freya said, "A Hopi legend tells of a god descending

from heaven in a rain of fire and disappearing beneath the desert floor."

Jim Cochran said, "That story's about the Berringer Crater in Arizona. It fell twenty-two thousand years ago. There weren't any people around."

Standing there tall, looking down at the meteor wrapped in feathers and fur, Freya murmured, "There's evidence— disputed, of course—that people were in this area twenty-eight thousand years ago."

"Do you believe it?" Bess Cochran asked.

Freya didn't answer.

Carmack McIntyre said, "And there's one associated with a woman, the crone god, who placed it as a boundary marker in the desert between tribes to the north and the Aztecs to the south."

The flashes from the niche had stopped. Tina came slithering backwards out of the tunnel. Reuben reached down and gave her a hand. Wobbling, she tried to stand. He put an arm around her and steadied her. She dug in the front pouch of the outsize sweatshirt she was wearing and handed something to Freya—yellow, cylindrical, a roll of film?—which Freya grabbed and stowed quickly in her own pocket.

Cruz watched but said nothing. Tina laid a hand on his arm. "There's a *kwiyo* in there, uncle," she said.

"Sounds like you're implying," Jim Cochran said to the Canadian, "that these things have some kind of other-worldly significance."

Carmack McIntyre said with a secret smile, "We don't know, do we."

Reuben told Freya, "We found a meteor fragment. It came from Rap's trailer. Rap found it with his metal detector. The diamond was stuck in it."

Bess Cochran said, "What we have are probably two parts of the same meteor. The rest is probably still buried under the pond."

"Who owns a meteor once it's found?" Steve Many Hands asked.

"They're owned by whoever owns the land," the Canadian said. "The finding place."

Cruz nodded and cleared his throat. They waited for him to say something, but he only stood there, looking down at the "baby" wrapped in its winding sheet.

35

Okay, he thought he had it now.

Alone on top of the cliff at the site where Rap had fallen, Reuben went over the way it must have happened—Rap squatting at the edge of the cliff, checking his coordinates with his Brunton compass, in a hurry to get to the courthouse before Naposunshare so even if they got the land back, the tribe would have to honor his claim.

Reuben saw it all in that pale gray dawn he'd awakened to after chasing the owl and seeing Pelawi: Willy sneaking up behind Rap with the carabiner on his fist, hitting Rap over the head and stunning him, Rap struggling with Willy as he went down, dropping his notebook and Brunton compass, Willy fishing in the old man's jacket for the diamond, then putting a foot in Rap's back and shoving him over. Again he heard Rap's death cry.

Dropping the carabiner beside the compass and the notebook, Willy would have drawn his hunting knife and cut off a piñon branch to brush out his footprints. He had brushed them out all the way to the tree line when here came John, singing his Indian chant on his way home after the night in the cave. Hiding in the trees, Willy probably watched John stop, pick up the notebook and the compass, and then the carabiner. That must have got to him. His carabiner!

But so what? Let it go. If they ever found those items, wouldn't it identify the Indian kid as the murderer?

Hiding there in the piñons, Willy must have been pleased at what he'd gotten away with.

The maharani was leaving but in no hurry to go. The same sleek Jaguar had come for her. It waited patiently outside, the driver hidden by the tinted windows, while inside Freya's trailer, draped in her strange costume, she gathered up her things.

Tina spoke softly. "Maharani?"

The old woman looked at her and emitted that low rumbling sound that was her laugh. "Yes, I've heard that's what they call me."

"It's apt enough," Freya said from the kitchen area where she was filling a thermos with black coffee for her friend's travels.

"What is it, child?"

"Your flask," Tina said shyly, handing over the silver flask.

"Ah, yes, thank you."

Though Tina wanted to ask them what all this meant, that took more nerve than she could muster. But she'd made her choice, she'd taken the photographs, she deserved something in return.

The maharani spoke as if she knew Tina's mind. "So what do you make of it, Freya darling? Tell me your tale before I go."

"The car's waiting," Freya said with what sounded to Tina like annoyance.

"Let it wait." The old woman stood at the window looking out at the meadow. "So beautiful," she murmured, "the trees."

Freya said with a grim little smile, "In a former life she was a druid."

Tina smiled back. "We could ask Clarity."

Freya laughed.

"Get on with it," the maharani said. "What have you made of all this? I know you've come up with some out-landish tale. I want to know what it is before I read it in some popular journal where you'll stir up a fuss." The old woman put up her chin. "Out with it."

"All right." Freya paused, glancing around the little space as if looking for words that weren't to be found in the couch cushions or the pale wood paneling. "We start from what we know. Centuries ago these people used to stop here for a few days each year in their seasonal round that probably stretched several hundred miles. The cave gave them shelter. It was a good place. There was game in the mountains and water in the arroyo. So when they chose to settle into a permanent village, they settled here. First they lived in the cave, where they began building storage cysts, painting pictographs. It was here that they witnessed the miraculous fall from the heavens. It was awesome, frightening. It made a horrendous sound, shedding sparks of fire that lit up the landscape as it shot through the night at terrific speed. The impact shook the earth and the shock waves reverberated.

"They drew it on the cliffs," she said lightly. "That's not rain falling down on those figures in the petroglyphs, it's sparks from the meteor raining down over the landscape. And sometime that night a woman suffered a breech birth. I should have seen at once what the figure was. I saw it on the picture wall, but I was too excited when I realized the face might be a calendar to notice what the figure was doing. And it was there on the wall of the cave, too, but I still didn't see."

The maharani turned from the window and looked at Freya.

"Don't you see, Solveig? All the legends and myths sur-rounding prophets confer on them just such a magical birth, usually marked by something unheard-of in the heavens—like a brilliant star where there's been no star before. And the birth itself is always unusual—say, a baby born to a virgin." She smiled. "Even Zoroaster was supposed to be born of a virgin, and nature was said to have rejoiced, though I'm not sure how. But here, the marvelous birth was a child born feet-first, and the heavens marked the birth with the fireworks of a meteor fall."

"I see," the maharani said, smiling. "You've put it all together, haven't you. Maybe you should write a novel."

Freya ignored her. "The birth, the meteor fall, filled the people with awe. They immortalized it in petroglyphs. They retrieved a part of the meteor that fell that night. It was the sign from the Great Spirit, and they attributed to it enormous powers. They found rocks they'd never seen before, and they carried them in their medicine pouches or buried them in the corners of their rooms."

"Do you mean," Tina said, "the *kwiyo* in the niche is the woman who gave birth that night?"

The maharani, looking at Freya, shook her head. "No, child." She chuckled. "She means the *kwiyo* herself was the baby born that night."

"Yes," Freya said, "it's always the religious leader who enters the world under mysterious signs. In this case, upside down, feet-first, already prepared to walk."

The maharani's eyebrows went up. "Perhaps on water."

Tina looked from her to Freya, who was smiling. "Right," she said. "Her finery of feathers and fur identifies her as a shaman."

Tina said, "But why did she seal herself up like that to die?"

"I think she chose to die rather than give up the stone from heaven," Freya said. "I think it was the time of the transition of power, when the men built the kivas, and rather than let them take it, she wrapped it for burial and hid it on an altar in a cave. Rather than give it up, knowing her time was ending, she buried herself with 'the babe' that was the sign from heaven of her powers."

"How could she do it?" Tina whispered. "How could she just seal herself in, sit down, and die?"

Freya shrugged. "She probably took a plant poison.

There's plenty of it around—that yarrowlike stalk along the stream I warned all of you to leave alone, that's hemlock. That way she wouldn't have to wait to starve or run out of oxygen in there."

"But if the meteor was the god-symbol, why didn't the men find her and dig it out?"

"Perhaps," Freya said, "it was the shock of the meteor's impact that broke off the front of the cave roof and brought it crashing down, effectively sealing it up. That would have been a sign, too, that it was *her* place, put off limits to ordinary mortals by an act of heaven. I suspect the men would have been afraid to enter, and she knew it."

Over by the window, still looking out, the maharani chuckled softly. Freya fell down in a chair and slouched, pouting, with her legs sprawled in front of her. "Go ahead, laugh, Solveig. I think I am right."

The old woman nodded. "You may be right." She moved toward the door. "But even if they allow you to bring her out, you will never prove it."

Freya didn't rise to see her out, just looked at her from under dark brows.

"Good-bye, my dear," the old woman said. "You are incorrigible."

Tina leapt to open the door. The maharani paused long enough in parting to lay her hand gently along Tina's cheek, murmuring, "Lovely, lovely." Then she tsked and said, "Ah, youth. Let it not be wasted on you, child."

Tina watched while the driver got out and opened the door of the silver Jaguar and stood aside. The old woman nodded without looking at him, then turned back to look at the trailer. Would Freya rise and go to the window and wave? No. She sat there sprawled, into herself, thinking. So Tina waved vigorously enough for them both.

She saw Reuben out there in the meadow grass, looking strange, wandering in circles like he was drunk. He let the Jaguar purr past him without a look. Tina glanced back, but Freya was lost in thought. Perhaps it was grief at the old woman's leaving.

Whatever it was, Tina felt like an intruder. She closed the door quietly behind her and walked up the meadow to where Reuben meandered, looking up at the cliffs.

"What are you doing?" she asked, approaching him carefully.

"I'm not going back!" he said, as if that surprised him.

"Going back where?"

"I can paint it now."

"Paint what?"

"Because now I *see* it. Not out there—" he flung out an arm and she followed its arc, which took in the meadow, the canyon, the cliffs, and the sky "—but in *here*—" he struck his chest with the heel of his fist "—not overlaid with *ideas*, for Chrissake, but as it *is*. Because now I've lived in it."

She wanted to laugh, but she restrained herself. Reuben was given to declaiming. He focused his eyes upon her and said in his normal voice, "Maybe I'll go back now and then to see my mother."

She bit her lip to contain herself. "What's happened?" She meant, What's happened to you? But that seemed like prying when he was in this exalted mood.

"I have seen the beaver," he said, "that sleek head with the sun on it, the wake fanning out like a flight of geese."

He flopped down on the grass with his legs crossed in front of him, supporting himself on his elbows. "Then suddenly he dived and disappeared, and the pond was quiet again like it'd never happened."

She dropped down and sat cross-legged beside him. They squinted in the sunlight, not looking at each other, while up on the road on their way to the mesa top the Earth Watch women waved good-bye to the maharani and waited for the sleek car to pass.